QUINTANA MCCONNELL

when tides meet

Gilded Horizon
Books

https://gildedhorizonbooks.com

Cover Creation by Paula Saavedra

Beneath Whiskey Waves

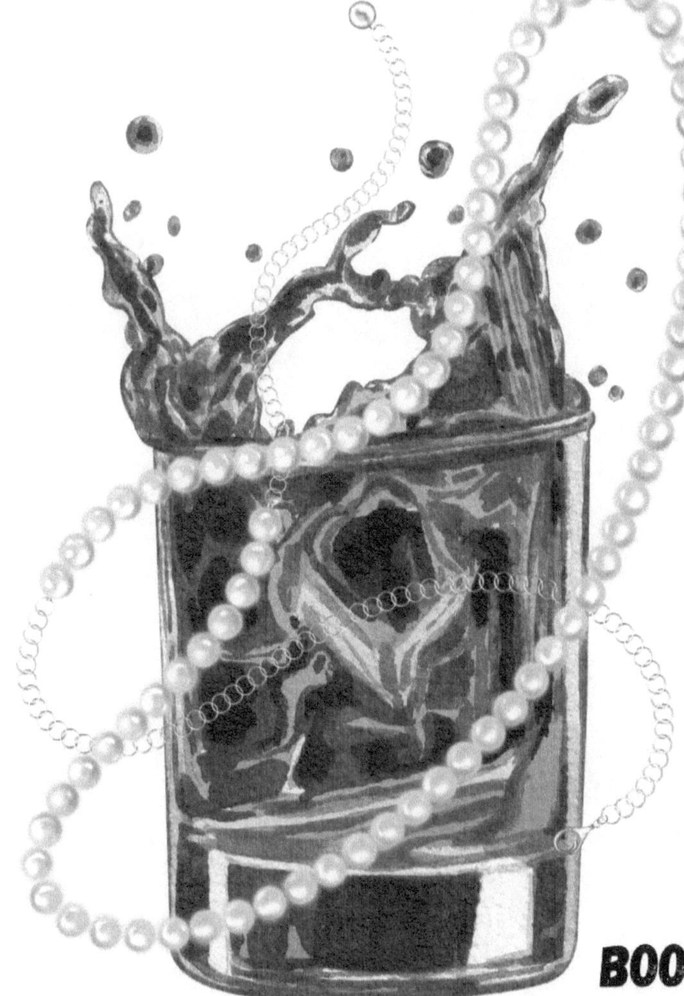

BOOK ONE

To all the challenges of the past, for leading me to discover the depths of my own resilience. And to those who have struggled to believe in love—

this is for you, a thousand times over.

I think you have to

live through what

love is not

before you can truly

appreciate what

love is.

Dante Paladino

Maris

Her Birkenstock-clad foot tapped the paver beneath it. She scribbled furiously in her well-used notebook, her bottom lip caught between her teeth. Things had been hectic lately, but Maris made it a point to forget all of that when she was writing.

She heard the waves lapping on the shore from where she sat at Salty Sands Café. With the rhythmic sound offering familiar comfort, she collected her thoughts, her grip on the pen tightening. The ocean had always been her solace, her place of calm in an ever-changing world. Sitting at the breezy table, her folders and journals were stacked neatly. The organization created a sense of order amidst her unruly thoughts.

She had, after all, moved up here from Carlsbad to find motivation and embrace her creativity. Aspiring writers in California found abundant inspiration in the bohemian artistic atmosphere and rugged coastline. Or at least that's what she'd told her parents when they'd all but begged her to continue living at home. But Maris had become restless working as a server in a high-end restaurant on State Street and longed for a life of her own. She had been the last of the Oakwood girls under her mom and dad's roof and thought that, at twenty-eight years old, it was about time she changed that.

Despite a depleted bank account thirteen weeks into the new year, Maris's independent journey ended forty-five minutes from her origin. She'd fallen in love with the sights and sounds of the area in the six months that followed. Now, it was September, and whatever Californians consider fall was in the air. The temperature was seventy-six degrees instead of eighty.

Maris smirked as she thought of the unique subtleties she had learned to pick up on from an early age by living in this controversial state. She remembered how her mom and dad had quibbled over little things like taxes and gas prices as she and her sisters, Alex and Jemma, were growing up. Illuminating her olive skin as she reminisced, the warm, golden light peeked through the opaque umbrella, making her appear radiant from within.

For a moment, she was lost in the world of her past. Conversations hummed around her and the tension in her shoulders melted away. For just an instant, all was almost completely still.

Hearing the buzz of her phone, she was abruptly returned to reality. It was an email from her client requesting urgent updates for an article she hadn't even started yet. A fresh wave of tension washed over her, as she realized she'd have to juggle this with the procrastinated task of wedding preparations. Liza, her childhood friend, was getting married at a beautiful, oceanfront, boutique-style hotel. Maris had been looking forward to the event for months. Not only would it be a chance to reunite with old friends, but it would also be an opportunity to forget about the stressors she had and just enjoy the festivities.

She and Liza had been next door neighbors in third grade and had bonded over a shared love of fairy tales and afternoons spent having tea parties in Liza's treehouse. Although, their families didn't stay in the same neighborhood for long, their friendship had survived the highs and lows of adolescence and adulthood.

"Miss, would you care for a coffee refill?"

Maris pulled away from her introspection and realized that the handsome server with a wide grin was expecting a response. With a heavy sigh, she kindly refused the refill. Unfortunately, few things come free, and, with her dwindling amount of freelance work, she knew that she needed to save more and spend less.

Note to self, she thought, *don't eat out so much.*

However, a twinge of remorse came over her as she thought about how much she'd shelled out for the stylish cuffed, wide-legged jeans she was wearing and the button-down knit vest she had paired with them. In moments of stress, Bloomingdales was a friend to her melancholy, but certainly not to her credit card.

With the last bite of her croissant, she began to gather her belongings.

Organic lattes and Negroni-filled cocktail hours were tasty, but not very budget-friendly. Her more responsible paycheck management in the past meant those outings were strictly celebratory. But when work had picked up during her first couple of months in Orange County, she'd slacked off on making immediate deposits. Things were trending downward again, and she considered whether she would ever find the right balance between recreation and total abstinence.

It saddened her to leave the casual, European charm and easy-going climate of the cafe behind as she moved on with her day. The atmospheric patio there had a way of making her comfortable, even amidst internal struggles. Stepping into the sunlit street, she felt a pang of regret, her mood clouded by the abrupt shift in surroundings. However, as she neared the beach, the smell of freshly ground coffee beans faded, and the sight of the blue-green water reminded her why she'd chosen this place.

Before she could feel sand between her toes, Maris's love for the ocean had begun. Her mom and dad had always made it a priority to spend their family time near the sea. Since her stroller days, Maris's parents introduced her to the magic of coastal life. As a small child, she would race toward the crashing waves with no fear and splash in the frothy surf. The ocean was her playground, her haven. She was utterly consumed by the ocean's rhythms, a connection so profound her family wondered if she was of this world.

As a child in Carlsbad, she spent countless hours collecting shells, building sandcastles, and learning to surf. Early mornings and sun-soaked afternoons at Terramar Beach had taught her resilience. High tide brought softer, slower waves, while low tide created faster, steeper ones. Conditions changed by the day, even by the hour, and many times she was knocked off her board, tumbling her into the breakers and leaving her breathless. Determined, she got back up each time to ride the next wave.

Some days Maris felt as free as the ocean breeze. Like the little girl that once nurtured mermaid fantasies. Other times she felt like she was floundering in a sea of hypotheticals, caught in the unpredictable tides of adulthood.

That strength and persistence she had as a child, though, carried into her adult life, becoming a cornerstone of who she was today. Maris had faced her fair share of challenges, from navigating the pressure to attain excellence at school to dealing with the heartbreak of her first love. She always overcame the obstacles. The adaptability and expectation of change that applied when she was surfing were two things that seemed to apply in every other aspect of life as well. Yet, the anticipation of new challenges threatened to disrupt the cozy life she'd carved out for herself here in Laguna Beach.

Liza's wedding resurfaced in Maris's thoughts. She was excited and nervous. Her adaptability would come in handy over the weekend. She had learned to navigate social situations with ease, a skill that would be valuable as she mingled with old friends and met new people. Thinking of the guest list Liza shared, her mind wandered. One name stood out: Colton Vance. Maris had never met him, but Liza had alluded to him a few times in their conversations. He was a successful entrepreneur and a close friend of the groom. From what Liza had said, he was not only attractive and intelligent, but also fiercely loyal.

Maris felt compelled to speculate about this intriguing stranger. She wondered what he would be like and if their paths might cross at the wedding. Perhaps he was among the mysterious, carefree groomsmen she'd heard whispers of. Who was Colton

Vance, really? And why did the mere mention of his name stir something deep within her?

A message from Liza appeared, coincidentally, as if her phone read her mind.

Hey Maris! Can't wait to see you this weekend. Make sure to get plenty of rest. It's going to be a blast!

Her friend's enthusiasm amused her, renewing her excitement. With the wedding only days away, she saw it as a pivotal moment in her friendship with Liza.

She checked her watch. It read shortly after 10 A.M. and Driftwood Shelves would have just opened. It was a quaint, independent bookstore with an enchanting façade and a cozy interior. The staff was friendly and knowledgeable, local art was on display, and, best of all, the bookcases were overflowing with titles of all genres. This was a favorite hideout for Maris, where she could lose herself in books. Whether it was to do research for a freelance project, as was her purpose today, or to explore new worlds of fiction, the bookshop was a cherished gem.

Her current assignment was to write a series of articles on sustainable living by the coast. Many Laguna Beach businesses and residents championed eco-friendly practices and environmentally conscious tourism. Maris thought that investigating the topic from the angle of how the community worked together to protect their natural environment would render her first article an easy, yet contemporary read.

As she crossed the threshold of the bookstore, she heard the familiar ding of the doorbell, and the smell of aged paper greeted her like an old friend. Chrissy, the store owner, directed a dazzling smile at Maris. Her large round framed glasses and petite stature made her even more approachable, and Maris acknowledged her with a shy wave.

"Good morning! Back again so soon?", Chrissy teased. An ever-present twinkle was in her eye.

"I just can't stay away from this place. What can I say?" replied Maris. "I'm working on an article about sustainable coastal life and thought I'd start my research here. You always have the best selection."

Leaning against the counter, Chrissy nodded. "Sounds cool. You know we've got a bunch of books on that stuff. I can show you where they are and recommend a few local authors who are big on sustainability."

Maris beamed. "That would be great! Thanks!"

Overlooking the ocean from the store's front, Chrissy pointed to a homey table near the expansive bay window.

"Why don't you set up over there? I'll grab those books and bring them over."

"You're the best," Maris remarked, as she took her laptop out of its case and pulled numerous pens and pads from her tote. At that time of day, only a few customers were present, and the silence, broken only by whispers or the shuffling of papers, created the perfect setting. She savored the scene and reminded herself to jot down some notes on the mood for one of her future novels.

Returning with a stack of books a few minutes later, Chrissy leaned in and whispered, "Hey, there's a carpenter from South Carolina who's been making sustainable furniture for a new business in town. His name's Colton Vance. Ever heard of him?"

Hearing Colton's name, Maris felt her heart skip a beat.

"Actually, yes. He's on the guest list for a wedding I'm attending this weekend."

Chrissy didn't seem fazed. "Small world, huh? Colton's been shipping his pieces to Laguna Beach. He's been working on some impressive designs. Might be a great interview for your article." With that, she headed back to the counter, leaving Maris to work.

Maris contemplated how Chrissy, a spunky, forty-something, Ohio-native, ended up on the West Coast, unmarried and owning a bookshop. Despite the job seeming decent, she felt certain that it would involve many lonely nights. The most spirited people often had the most skeletons in their closet, and she wondered if Chrissy was one of them.

Maris shook off her curiosity about Chrissy's past and, with it, thoughts of Colton Vance. She attempted to concentrate on the task at hand. She opened the first book and found it to be filled with practical guidance and actionable tips for integrating sustainability into everyday life. As she read, the pages revealed captivating details on composting, water conservation, and renewable energy. To ensure meticulous annotation, she carefully highlighted each key point after jotting it down.

While working, she switched between Chrissy's books and online stories about impactful Laguna Beach locals. There was a surfer who had started an organization to clean up the beaches, a chef who sourced only organic, locally grown ingredients for his restaurant, and a family that had transformed their home into a snuggly, eco-friendly sanctuary.

The more she read, the quicker the hours passed and soon Maris found the clock inching towards two in the afternoon. It was high time she saved her work and closed the laptop. She was satisfied with completing a significant part of her assignment, and with deepening her connection to the city she loved.

Before her departure, a few alerts on her phone notified her of events she missed while engrossed in Chrissy's study materials. Among these were a few social media item updates. There were several likes on her most recent photo. Maris liked to think the aesthetic of her literary-centric feed was expressive and photojournalistic, conveying the emotions behind the stories she shared.

Compulsively, she checked her follower count. 4,629 followers. The bookstagram algorithm was increasingly difficult to manage lately, and each interaction with your content mattered. Maris was diligent in scheduling consistent reels and carousels to keep her followers updated on what she was reading. Even simple "day in the life" videos usually attracted some attention within the book community.

Two hundred twenty-four people had double-tapped her candid capture of best-selling local author, Samuel Blake, surrounded by piles of books and journals. Enveloped in his work, he intently gazed at the pages before him, clutching a steaming cup of coffee.

The post was popular, beginning discussions about Blake's recent thriller, "My Sinister Bloodline." Moments like these reminded her why she enjoyed sharing her literary adventures with the world. One day, she might share her own published manuscripts with those same book lovers. The thought filled her with glee.

She hoisted her packed bag onto her shoulder and proceeded to the counter to pay for her purchases and bid Chrissy farewell. "Thanks again for all your help today. I made great progress."

Chrissy looked up from her conversation with another customer and gave a thumbs up. "See you next time, Maris!"

As she stepped outside, although she had straightened it that morning, the sea breeze turned her long blonde hair into tousled, windswept waves. She took a deep breath, feeling beholden to Laguna Beach for the flood of imagination it provided. She was inspired. There was a considerable distance to go to reach her goals, but she was ready to face whatever came her way.

With her work for the day done, Maris headed back to her bungalow to prepare for the upcoming weekend and settled into her routine. She organized her notes, tidied up her space, and laid out an outfit for the wedding. Because the celebration offered a chance to explore new experiences and build relationships, making a good impression was crucial.

Maris had chosen a stunning, midnight blue satin dress with delicate lace detailing along the off-the-shoulder neckline. The color complemented her complexion, and the silhouette had looked better trying it on before the mirror than it did on the mannequin at the boutique. Because of this outfit, Maris, who lacked confidence earlier, found herself feeling more assertive.

Standing in front of the glass, she reflected on how her cornflower blue eyes had always been a source of fascination. Their unique and striking color had often drawn attention. She saw them as a symbol of her distinct personality and strength. Her irises, with their captivating hue, mirrored her embrace of her one-of-a-kind self and the beauty of her individuality.

With her attire chosen and anticipating the weekend's events growing, Maris slipped her sandals back on and headed outside to watch the day come to a close. Evening had approached without her knowing it. The low-hanging sun cast a golden glow across the sky. Because the air was clear, the sunset was undoubtedly going to be breathtaking. She had a weakness for SoCal sunsets, and, as she gazed before her at the burnt orange, dusty pinks, and muted yellows, her thoughts lingered on the possibility of meeting Colton.

As the last rays of sunlight dipped below the horizon, Maris couldn't shake the feeling that something—or someone—was about to disrupt the fragile peace she enjoyed. It seemed as if this time in her life was pushing her toward the brink of something new. A breakthrough into the unknown. Maybe that was exactly what she needed.

Even as she drifted to sleep that night, the sense of impending change lingered, weaving its way into restless dreams that left her feeling unsettled throughout her slumber.

The next morning, Maris woke to the distinctive sound of calls from the seagull family that had taken up residence on her roof, accompanied by faint bicycle bells in the distance. Laguna Beach on a vibrant Friday morning was full of sights and sounds to keep the senses alive. She groaned and rolled over in her queen-sized bed, taking the blankets with her and shoving her head under the pillow. She had tossed and turned all night, fielding nightmares about her inadequacy as a writer. Her emotional exhaustion was overwhelming. A massive amount of coffee was required to get through the day, despite her promise of frugality previously.

Without opening her eyes, she reached toward the rattan nightstand and groped for her phone. Frantically, Maris emerged from under her linen duvet, nearly knocking over the Himalayan salt lamp. She thankfully noticed no harm had been done, then snatched her cellphone from next to the essential oil diffuser, whose blinking red light warned that it was empty.

Ignoring its noiseless insistence, she glanced at the 6.9-inch screen that sometimes seemed to hold her very existence.

As the device lit up, she saw the notifications: three missed calls from her sisters. Breathing deeply, she calmed herself. Maris suspected they had likely called only to check in, but she felt a pang of guilt that she hadn't been better about keeping in touch, and the sight of the missed connections was just a tangible reminder. She didn't want to avoid them—she merely lacked the energy to explain her anxious thoughts over the phone right now.

Besides the unanswered calls, a surge of work-related uneasiness washed over her. Chrissy's suggestion from yesterday about interviewing Colton had stuck with her, intertwining with her own insecurities. What if she was unable to secure the interview? What if her article failed to meet her client's expectations? The weight of her professional reputation seemed to press down on her, adding to the significant burden she already had.

After Maris locked it, the phone screen turned black. She made a mental note to email her sisters later with an update. Sadness set in when she thought of the fact that neither of them was going to make it to Liza's wedding this weekend. Alex was only two years older than her, but she was almost eight months pregnant with baby number three. The pregnancy had been complicated, and the doctors advised Alex against unnecessary travel. Since Alex's husband had gotten a job in Chicago last year, they were about 2,000 miles too far away to render the trip convenient.

Jemma was a story of her own. Maris was five years older than she was, and they differed in almost every way. With a lack of self-discipline and a carefree attitude, she lived without commitment. Living her best life in Maui, Jemma, a social media influencer, enjoyed her freedom. Brands paid her to promote their products, from swimwear and environmentally friendly sunscreen to travel gear and unique island experiences. She had cultivated a substantial following, and every photo she posted showed her tanned and cheerful. Her excuse for not attending the wedding was that she couldn't get out of work. Maris rolled her eyes. She loved each of her sisters. It was just that Jemma seemed to get away with behaving irresponsibly, whereas Maris always made the logical choice.

Shaking her head, she released the contemplations about her siblings and decided to reframe her morning. The idea of a run was appealing, provided it finished near her favorite coffee place. So, pulling on her go-to Lululemon shorts and matching sports bra, then adding a surf-inspired tee, Maris checked her reflection. She looked quintessentially Californian as she pulled her hair back into a loose ponytail and dabbed on some lip oil. As she retrieved her running shoes by the door and stepped out into the glorious daylight, she felt more alive and less like a zombie.

Conquering her remaining self-doubt, she headed toward Heisler Park. The refreshing air and the rhythmic pounding of her feet on the pavement, coupled with her upbeat playlist, provided a welcome sensation. But even as she jogged past the stunning coastal views, her mind traveled back to the interview with Colton. She grasped how much making this connection might mean for her career, but the potential opportunity seemed overwhelming.

Her thoughts drifted further to her former life in Carlsbad. She hadn't only left because of her writing aspirations. The real reason was more complicated—her falling out with her childhood best friend, Hendrix. They had been inseparable since kindergarten, sharing countless milestones and adventures. Maris remembered the time when she was twelve years old and almost drowned in the sea. She fell off her surfboard and a strong current caught her; panicking, the waves pulled her under. It was Hendrix who saved her. Without a second thought, he had jumped into the water, his fearless nature driving him to pull her to safety. He was an exceptional swimmer, and she recalled his boyish, determined face as he battled the ocean to reach her. That moment had solidified their bond, giving them a sense of shared invincibility.

In high school, however, things changed when he confessed his romantic feelings. Maris's emotions differed, and their friendship never recovered. Despite the tension, she came back to Carlsbad for six years after graduating college, trying to build a life in the town she had always known.

Nevertheless, it became difficult to see Hendrix around the city. The boy who had once been her confidant had changed, and not for the better. He had become distant, bitter, and prone to petty conflicts. Maris often heard rumors about his reckless behavior and poor choices, which only deepened her sorrow over the loss of their friendship. Each encounter with him was a painful reminder of what they had lost, and the awkwardness between them was almost unbearable.

With all this pulling her down, she slowed her pace and crossed the street. The building she ducked into wasn't much to look at on the outside. Its pitched roof, minimalist décor style, and earth-toned walls made sure that it blended away into the surroundings. Directly approaching the window revealed the simple white lettering, Malachi's Beach Brew. The cafe, understated and casual, served one of the best local cups of java.

As Maris lined up in front of the counter with a host of other patrons, the shop instantly soothed her nerves. Small and alluring, the establishment featured wooden communal tables, diverse indoor plants, and a soundtrack of soft indie music. A few regulars turned in her direction, and she gave a polite smile.

She was surprised to find Malachi himself manning the espresso machine. A tall, broad man with a perpetual grin, an impressive beard, and a passion for crafting the perfect cup of coffee, he was a staple in the community.

"Maris! The usual?" he asked, his expression warm and welcoming.

"Hey, Malachi. Yes, please," she replied, grateful for the familiarity.

"Rough morning?" Malachi asked as he prepared her order.

Maris chuckled. "You could say that. Just trying to shake off a restless night."

"Well, nothing a good cup of coffee can't fix," he replied with a wink.

As he handed her the steaming cup, she took a deep inhale, savoring the rich aroma. "Thanks! You're a lifesaver," she said, genuinely appreciative.

Maris brought her latte to a corner table, sat down, and looked around the café, appreciating the calm setting. She needed to clear her head and find some clarity amidst the mayhem of her mind. Itching to write in her notebook, she cursed herself for not taking the time to journal before leaving the house. She hoped that documenting her thoughts later would help to untangle the web of emotions and expectations.

She noticed a woman at the next table who seemed to be studying a set of design blueprints spread out before her. The woman had an air of effortless elegance, with her chic, clean aesthetic and perfectly styled hair. Maris couldn't resist studying her flawless demeanor.

The stranger looked up and caught her eye, offering an inquisitive smile.

"Morning," she said, her voice inviting.

"Morning," Maris replied, blushing. "Those blueprints look fascinating. Are you an architect?"

"Close. I'm an interior designer," the woman answered, extending a hand. "Eve Vasquez."

Mirroring the greeting, Maris offered her hand as well. "Nice to meet you, Ms. Vasquez. My name is Maris Oakwood. Whatever you're working on looks amazing!"

"Thank you," Eve said, her eyes lighting up. "I'm finalizing plans for a new project here in Laguna Beach. We're collaborating with a carpenter from South Carolina who specializes in sustainable furniture. His name is Colton Vance."

Maris nearly choked on her coffee at the mention of Colton.

"Colton Vance? I've heard of him. His work sounds incredible."

Eve nodded enthusiastically. "He's extremely talented and passionate about environmentally friendly design. I'm excited about this collaboration."

Maris hesitated for a moment, gathering her courage. "Actually, I'm a writer, and I'm working on an article about sustainable living. I've considered reaching out to Colton for an interview, but I've been a bit anxious about it. Do you think he'd be open to it?"

Eve's smile was reassuring. "I believe he would be very receptive to the idea, especially if it highlights the importance of keeping things green. Colton can be intense, but he's very dedicated to his work. If you'd like, I could help facilitate the introduction."

Within minutes, the women had exchanged contact information, and Eve promised to reach out to Colton that afternoon to set something up. Maris felt light-headed as she stood up to leave. Had that happened? She had networked successfully! The upcoming wedding and the potential interview with Colton still loomed ahead, but now she was a bit more relaxed. On the way back home, she was in disbelief.

When she reached her doorstep, she attained a mild sense of calm. Her jitters significantly tamped down. She huffed, short of breath in the heat. The humidity was higher today than usual. It had gone up as the hours had passed. Having unlocked the door and slid inside, she placed her coffee cup on the counter. Goosebumps prickled her skin as the air-conditioned space engulfed her. She removed her shoes and socks, noting the cold porcelain tile on her bare feet. The sun filtered through the sheer curtains, casting a warm glow over the living room.

She dashed for the bathroom, eager to wash off the sweat of her run and her intermittent anxiety. As she stood beneath the hot water's spray, complete relaxation washed over her for the first time that morning. She replayed meeting Eve in her head and excitement bubbled up inside her as she contemplated the prospective interview.

After her shower, Maris wrapped herself in a fluffy towel and headed to her bedroom. She dressed in comfortable clothes—a pair of soft leggings and an oversized sweater—before settling onto her bed with her journal. With a fresh page opened before her, she wrote down her thoughts. Her handwriting was a blend of decorative flourishes and unique letterforms. She poured out her nerves, hopes, and the lingering memories of her past with Hendrix and found peaceful solitude in relinquishing those emotions.

Once she finished journaling, Maris moved to her desk, where a plethora of books and her laptop awaited her. She spent the next hour catching up on her reading, losing herself in the words of her favorite authors and drawing inspiration for her own writing. She'd been neglecting the task most days, if she was honest. Finally, she opened her computer and typed, transforming her scattered ideas on sustainability into a more organized and logical narrative.

Maris, at long last, was ready to confront the dreaded chore she'd evaded long enough. She paused briefly over the blank email to collect her thoughts. An update was owed to her sisters, and she realized she needed to stop avoiding the conversation.

She slowly typed into the subject line: *Time to Share Everything*

Hi, Alex and Jemma,

I'm so, so sorry I missed your phone calls. What kind of sister am I?! I've meant to write to you for a while now, and I finally decided to sit down and divulge what's been going on with me, here in Laguna Beach.

First, I want to say that I really miss you both. It's been tough being away from family, especially with everything that's been happening lately. I have been struggling with a lot of anxiety over… well, all of it. It feels like I am constantly on edge, and I just wanted to let you know what's been on my mind.

Liza's upcoming wedding has me feeling excited and nervous. I can't help but worry that our relationship might change after she gets married. It's absurd, but I've been experiencing this for a while. I'm scared of losing the close bond we have. River is going to take care of her, but will I still have my gal pal to gossip with?

On top of that, I've felt stressed about an upcoming interview with Colton Vance, a sustainable furniture designer from Charleston, South Carolina. Chrissy suggested I talk to him for my freelance article, and I think it's a fantastic opportunity, but I'm so worried that it might be a colossal flop. I want to make sure I do justice to his work and my writing.

On the topic of authorship, I've had trouble mustering the motivation to complete the novel I began two years ago. The fear of not being traditionally published has been holding me back, and it's been weighing on me. I know I need to push through, but it's been hard.

I just wanted to share all this with you because I miss your support and our special sister sleepovers. Remember those? My heart overflows with thankfulness for sisters like you. I really want to hear how you're doing and catch up on everything happening in your lives.

Sending lots of love and hugs, Mar

She sent the email and activated her screensaver with a few final clicks. The day had been full of unexpected turns, but she was more at peace than she had been in ages. She folded her hands behind her head, savoring the long-awaited serenity that settled over her.

Colton

Colton leaned back in his used desk chair and pinched the bridge of his nose, anticipating a headache. With drawings and calculations spread before him, he took a deep inhale. Beside his calculator sat a pile of bills and his to-do list. Running a business, it seemed to Colton, was not for the weak.

Wood shavings littered the ground of his workshop, and the smell of freshly cut lumber filled his nostrils. Day in and day out, he worked on one new project after another—measuring, cutting, sanding, and staining. It was rare that Colton ever built the same thing twice, and he liked the innovation and creative freedom he had as a carpenter. But, some days, when it seemed like he'd never break even or make enough money to outrun his demons, it was pretty darn difficult, too.

Producing sustainable furniture solutions for a California-based company had been his focus lately. Some fancy spa was opening in Laguna Beach, and their interior designer had seen his work on one of her trips to Charleston. She said that his eco-friendly creations would enhance the natural, calming atmosphere that this high-end health retreat aimed to provide and, when she waved her checkbook in his face, it was too irresistible an opportunity to say no.

The commission was a lifeline for Colton, offering him the chance to showcase his talent on a larger stage and attract more clients who appreciated his commitment and the quality of his work. Long hours in the workshop, pushing his creativity and craftsmanship to the limit, were also a part of it.

Despite the exciting collaboration, Colton's nagging worry about meeting deadlines remained. He prided himself on his attention to detail and on perfecting his designs. Mounting pressure and the expectations of others were both increasing. As he rubbed his temples, he glanced over at a newly completed coffee table, its smooth, matte surface shining under the workshop lights.

Colton exhaled sharply. It was clear to him that a single mistake would risk damaging the entire project and his professional reputation. He still needed to prepare this final shipment for tomorrow if it was going to be delivered on time.

He pulled out his phone and sent the interior designer a brief, but reassuring, message.

Things are on track. I'll ship in the AM. Look forward to being on site this week.

Colton closed his eyes, remembering his childhood. Raised in the south, carpentry had always been his calling. His father, a stern and traditional man, had been sure to include woodworking in his boys' upbringing. He had learned it from his dad, Colton's grandad. Colton's brother, Axel, hadn't taken to the skill like his younger sibling, and, instead, spent his time on many vices he found more interesting. Colton, however, was an exception. He enjoyed the steadiness of the wood and his ability to picture the finished product before sawing.

His mother, a dedicated schoolteacher, had always encouraged his go-getter spirit. She had constantly reminded him that hard work and passion would pave the way to success. With her support in high school, Colton had taken on minor projects in the neighborhood, building everything from custom furniture to intricate cabinetry. Word of his talent spread swiftly, and soon, he was receiving orders from clients far beyond his hometown. A reputation for quality over quantity propelled his childhood aspirations into a thriving business, making him well-known.

The passage of time, however, had put a strain on the bond with Axel. Axel's choices had led him down a path of self-destruction, forcing Colton to pick up the pieces more than once. Despite Colton's efforts to support his brother, Axel often resented his success and the comparison to their father's expectations. The tension between them only grew when Axel had borrowed money from Colton, promising to turn his life around, only to disappear for weeks without a word. Their most recent confrontation had ended in a heated argument, leaving a rift that seemed insurmountable.

Colton was endlessly grateful for carpentry, since it had helped him pay his parents' medical bills when his mother fell ill last year. It had been a terrifying time for Colton and his family. His mother was diagnosed with Hodgkin's lymphoma which, while in the early stages, required expensive chemotherapy and radiation treatments. The doctors had warned them that her recovery would be a long and grueling journey, though the success rate for curing it was high.

Colton had stepped up, working long hours and taking on additional projects to ensure that the bills were paid. The weight of responsibility had been heavy, but it had also given him a renewed sense of purpose. Every plank of wood he measured, every nail he hammered, was a step towards ensuring his mother received the care she needed.

Thankfully, she began to show signs of improvement. Her strength gradually returned, and the once-persistent fatigue that had plagued her became a distant memory. Colton still remembered the day she was finally declared cancer-free—a day filled with tears of relief and gratitude.

Carpentry had not only provided a means to an end but had also become a source of solace and pride. It had been an outlet for his emotions after his wife left him. To him, her name was insignificant now, but he still saw her face every time he drove past the diner where they'd met. His ex had told him she wasn't suited to be a wife and that they had married too young to really know each other. The next thing he knew was that she was relocating to Florida, and he was signing divorce papers. Fortunately, they hadn't had children who would have been dragged through the turmoil of their separation, a small mercy in an otherwise painful chapter of his life.

Colton's phone chimed, prompting him to pull it out of his pocket as he pushed away unhappy thoughts.

A calendar reminder popped up on the screen:

Flight to California - 8:00 AM Tomorrow.

Blast! He hadn't realized he'd made such a tight schedule for himself. The next morning would be here in a matter of hours, and he was nowhere near ready to leave. He'd have to make a go of it if there was any hope of getting to relax in this century. True, going to the wedding was doubling as a work trip, but it was also a chance to step away from the workshop and find new inspiration.

He was unable to squander any more time. He let out a tired sigh, rolled up his sleeves, and started working. He still had packing to do, and a few final touches on the project required completion before morning. Despite his craving for rest, he hoped this trip would justify the rush.

His thoughts drifted to River and Liza, the couple whose wedding he was attending. Colton and River were friends since fifth grade, when they were paired together for a science fair project. Their model of the solar system had sparked a friendship that grew stronger with each passing year. Their attachment forged through countless adventures and shared challenges. River had gone on to college and Colton had taken another path, diving straight into his passion for carpentry. Despite the miles and different life choices, their bond deepened over time.

In the weeks leading up to the ceremony, Colton had dedicated himself to crafting a handmade wedding canopy inspired by the design of a huppah. River and Liza, while not Jewish themselves, were captivated by the huppah's beauty and wanted it included in their wedding. Colton desired to create something special that reflected both his skill and his gratitude for their friendship, especially in the harshest year of his life. Using carefully selected reclaimed wood intricately carved with symbols of love and unity, Colton crafted the canopy. The delivery had arrived a few days earlier, and he was delighted to hear how overjoyed River and Liza were.

In hindsight, Colton understood this project's significance to him, exceeding mere artistry. Building the huppah proved cathartic; it was a way to cope with his heartbreak and find solace in his familiar work rhythm. Each stroke of the carving tools had been a step towards healing, a reminder of the strength that came from within and the love and support he still had in his life. The structure symbolized not only River and Liza's commitment to each other but also Colton's journey through his darkest times, emerging scathed, but intact.

Eventually, pushing up from where he sat, he stretched his arms overhead, exposing his lean, muscular abs. He was drowsy, but not enough to go straight to bed. He still needed to pack his luggage, but instead of going upstairs to his loft apartment, he strode over to the liquor cabinet and took out a bottle of 15-year-old Glen Moray whiskey. It had been a long day.

As he poured himself a glass, Colton's thoughts landed, once again, on the wedding and the people he could meet there. Many years had gone by since he was able to travel partially for pleasure. River had mentioned an enthusiastic writer named Maris he'd hoped to introduce Colton to. While he had brushed off the idea of River's suggestion, he now found himself curious about what she might be like. A strange sense of anticipation about her washed over him. What was it about Maris that intrigued him? The way River had described her made her sound almost too good to be true. Was she really as captivating and genuine as he implied? And why did he feel a magnetic pull towards a woman he had never met? The questions swirled in his mind like the amber liquid in his glass, leaving him with a lingering curiosity that refused to be dismissed.

He willed the sensation to pass as he drained the tumbler. Colton placed the empty glass down and stared out the window into the night. Usually, the distant sounds of crickets and the cool breeze rustling through the trees calmed him, but tonight, the inkling coursing through his veins that the trip to California was a turning point, not just for his business but for his whole life, was almost electric. He tried to ignore it and went upstairs to pack, regardless.

The loft was a blend of industrial and rustic, and the worn fabric elements gave it a very lived-in vibe. It didn't have any outstanding features, aside from the exposed brick walls, which weren't adorned with much, considering it was a glorified bachelor pad. The ambiance of the place was warm, inviting, and almost poetic. Colton had few visitors, so, for a semi-recent divorcé, this was living large.

He got his weathered leather suitcase from the closet and put it on the bed. With methodical precision, he collected his necessities. He was unsure how kids in California dressed these days, but, edging close to thirty-eight, he wasn't too concerned with being trendy. He added his favorite work boots—shabby, but comfortable. They had seen him through countless projects and long days in the workshop. On top of some clothes, he placed a leather-bound journal. The notebook held sketches of his designs, notes on techniques he wanted to try, and even the occasional personal reflection. It was a constant companion and record of his journey.

As Colton snapped the suitcase shut and set it by the door, the sense that this trip marked a fresh beginning persisted. He wondered if it was leading to something that would change the course of his future. What lay ahead was uncharted territory and unfathomable opportunity. He knew he would need to look beyond his current circumstances if he was going to project the best outcome for himself. It was daunting, but it also raised a resolve inside of him that he hadn't felt in a while.

He sat on the edge of the bed and, once more, pulled out his phone. This time, he opened Instagram and began aimlessly scrolling. Photos of polished homes and stunning landscapes, along with pregnancy and engagement announcements from friends and community acquaintances, and the occasional motivational quote filled his feed. He paused on a few posts, double tapping to like them, but his mind was elsewhere.

Recognizing a familiar style, he suddenly stopped. It was two of his own pieces—a pair of mid-century modern, upholstered armchairs—featured on the interior design website's Instagram account, Laguna Luxe Studio. The caption praised the craftsmanship and the sustainable materials used in their creation.

A rush of pride came over him. His work's display and recognition on any platform was validating, especially with thousands of likes and shares, plus many positive comments from strangers. It was a reminder that all the long hours and hard work were worth it. He took a screenshot of the post and sent it to his mother with a simple message:

Made it, Mom.

Satisfied, Colton put his phone down and stood up with a renewed sense of purpose. After changing into some age-old sweatpants with tattered drawstrings, he turned off the lights and slipped into bed. Tomorrow would be the start of something new.

With his mind set on the changes ahead, the night passed in swift suspense, carrying him swiftly into the next day's frenzied activity.

As Colton stepped out of the gangway and into the terminal at LAX airport, he was overcome with people. Passengers, both arriving and departing, appeared limitless. The constant sound of boarding calls, flight updates, and other announcements filled the air. Dining options, restaurants, and various shops lined the expansive hallway, offering everything from fast food to gourmet meals and duty-free shopping.

Colton scanned the area for guidance to baggage claim. Walking speedily in its direction, avoiding eye contact with the sea of strangers, he appeared annoyed. But even extroverts need downtime, and Colton was way overdue for his.

Between the delays and layovers and lack of leg room, he was ready for a long, hot shower and doom scrolling on the tv guide channel. Though it didn't amount to only that either. He had gotten up every day for the last year, pretending to be without pain. Putting on a front like his heart wasn't shattered. It resulted in the kind of fatigue you couldn't sleep away.

As Colton retrieved his luggage from the carousel, a pang of nostalgia overcame him. The sight of travelers reuniting with loved ones and the familiar hum of airport activity brought back memories of happier times. He thought about the countless flights he had taken with his wife, their shared goals, and the dreams they had once nurtured together.

Now those experiences felt burdensome. The end of his marriage had left him with a void that he struggled to fill. Despite his best efforts, the pain was still raw.

With bag in hand, he made his way toward the rental car company he'd reserved with. Leaving little to chance, he ruled out the possibility of being stuck in a cab. Some people labeled it being a control freak, but Colton called it having a plan.

As he navigated through the congested streets of LA, Colton stared through the windshield, watching the towering skyscrapers give way to the sprawling suburbs. The transition from the bustling city to the serene coastal views was stark, but it was just what he needed. Reminiscent of home, the coastline embodied the simplicity and beauty he desired to integrate into his life and work.

River had clarified that, while Colton was in town, no expense was to be spared and had all but forced Colton to secure a place to stay at the lavish venue that was hosting the weekend's merrymaking. He had booked the room to silence River, but now he was looking forward to indulging in the luxurious accommodations. His focus had been so intensely narrowed on getting to California that everything else faded into the background. Now that he was here, though, he might as well enjoy it.

Colton didn't treat himself to much more than the occasional rare bottle of Scotch or vintage vinyl to enhance his collection. He wasn't a high-maintenance guy. However, as he neared the main drag of Laguna Beach, he had to admit that relaxing in the secluded, Spanish-style guest room he'd checked out online was a more than acceptable alternative to his usual, far simpler arrangements. A moment of tranquility was a scarce treat amidst the typical hustle, and he was ready to embrace it.

Soon, the warm glow of vintage lanterns on each side of an arched entrance came into view. Casa del Refugio, translated "house of refuge," was a beautiful building boasting an unrivaled oceanfront view. A low, red-tiled roof and white stucco walls created an exterior that exuded timeless sophistication, and a covered portico stood stately at the front.

Lush, manicured gardens, filled with colorful flowers and swaying palm trees, lined the drive. The fragrance of blooming bougainvillea seeped through the open car windows. The driveway curved gracefully and the place's loveliness took him aback; he also noted the irony of its name.

As Colton began to leave his vehicle and move onto the terracotta-tiled walkway, the valet service demanded his keys and room number. The gentle rustling of palm leaves created a soothing soundtrack as he lingered outside the large entry doors. He stayed planted there for a few beats, savoring the scent of the Pacific ocean.

Casa del Refugio allowed mobile check-in, so there was no need to stop by the front desk before heading upstairs. There were three stories to the hotel, and he had chosen his room on the top floor with minimal deliberation. Behind the heavy wooden door were antique, hand-carved furnishings, vibrant Moroccan tiles, and a king-sized bed.

Colton laid his suitcase on the provided luggage rack and filtered through the emails and text messages he had missed on the flight.

There was something from his dad:

Hey Colton, just checking in. How's your trip going? Remember to pick up some batteries for the garage remote when you're back. Thanks.

Colton shook his head and guffawed into the silence at his father's never-ceasing ability to get to the point.

The next one was from Axel:

Sup bro? Look, I kinda messed up and need a favor...

Not surprised by this, Colton deleted the message without reading it a second time. Whatever Axel had gotten himself into, he didn't want any part of it. Fortunately, today, he was

2,500 miles away, so he lacked the ability to just drop by the workshop and harass him.

The last correspondence was from Eve Vasquez, the interior designer he was working with here in Laguna:

Colton, I've met someone in town who's doing a piece on sustainability. Nice girl. Anyway, I told her you'd love to do an interview! Call me.

Colton mentally ticked off a list of activities he disliked. Unsurprisingly, being interviewed made the cut.

Wonderful.

He wasn't big on being put in a position to fulfill promises others made on his behalf and he was itching to get the phone conversation out of the way. The line was already ringing as Colton considered how he would refuse the opportunity.

It only took two rings before a raspy, yet feminine, voice answered.

"Colton! It's about time I heard from you!" Eve crooned into the receiver.

"Hey, Eve," Colton began. "Look, we've got a problem. I came out here to see a job site, not to be interviewed by some wannabe reporter." He sounded more like his father than he wanted to, but sometimes bluntness was best.

"Oh, boo! Of course, you'll do the interview," Eve replied with confidence. "I already promised I'd get you to say yes, and I don't want to break poor little Maris's heart. Plus, it'll be good for your brand."

"Yeah, my brand…," Colton mused. "Wait, did you say Maris?"

"Uh-huh. Maris…Oakwood, I think she said her last name was. Anyway, she's doing a nice little article that will make your story the talk of the town."

Colton almost dropped the phone at the second mention of Maris's name, and the clarification of who she was. A writer, from Laguna Beach. His mind fixated on River's nonchalant suggestion to introduce them, and it hit him like an eighteen-wheeler losing control on the highway—this was no mere accident, but something far more deliberate. A sudden wave of unease overcame him, making it hard to focus on Eve's words.

"… and the designs you sent over were brilliant, so I showed them to the spa owner…," Eve continued, oblivious to Colton's lack of acknowledgement.

"Mm hmm, that all sounds perfect, Eve. Just send me the day and time of the interview, okay? I've gotta go," he said without explanation. It was a mystery to him why he had consented to speak with Maris. He hadn't even met her yet and already sensed the weight of new expectations pressing down on him. It was unsettling.

Colton took a moment to collect himself, pushing aside the realization that he was now obligated to a stranger. He unpacked his suitcase, trying to focus on recreating his at-home routine rather than the unforeseen turn his day had taken. After a quick shower and bite to eat, he settled in for the night, the king-sized mattress offering a welcome respite from his racing mind.

The following day, the sound of the hotel phone ringing jolted Colton awake. He groggily reached for the receiver, glancing at the clock—it was 9 AM.

"Good morning, Mr. Vance. This is your wake-up call!" the receptionist chirped.

"Thank you," Colton mumbled, still half-asleep. He rubbed his eyes and sat up, realizing that he had to get ready for brunch with River.

The indulgence of sleeping late wasn't something he had the opportunity for often; yet, from his present feeling, it was a luxury he might grow accustomed to. This morning, however, he didn't have the advantage of dilly-dallying. Colton was already running late.

He freshened up and dressed, tugging an ordinary grey t-shirt over his strong back and replacing it with a crisp, white button down accented with a light gray windowpane design. He grabbed a pair of well-loved khakis and, after a longing look at his boots, decided on wearing sneakers.

The spot where they had chosen to meet wasn't hard to find, just a few miles from the hotel. Its sunlit terrace faced the ocean and, as he entered the courtyard, he spotted River at a small table by a shaded pergola. River's flaxen hair had grown out and bangs hung near his hazel eyes. He was tall, almost as tall as Colton, and he stood with outstretched arms as they greeted one another. As the two hugged, River clapped Colton on the back.

"Good to see you, brother," River stated. He stood back and gave Colton his megawatt smile.

Colton smiled in response. It had been too long since he'd seen his friend. Yes, he received an invitation to the bachelor party last month, but to be honest, he was so wrapped up in himself that he lacked celebratory spirit. His excuse was that he didn't want to dampen the party's mood but, honestly, he found the prospect of an entire weekend centered on conversations about women, love, and marriage unbearable. In fact, he was thankful River hadn't asked him to be a groomsman. River understood that matrimony was hitting close to home these days.

Colton had enjoyed being married and had been a good husband. He had provided a home and love and a sense of security. Heck, he even worked hard to give the relationship a little mystery and romance. It had been seventeen years of being a stand-up guy. He had tried to make her world go 'round, but it hadn't been enough. *He* hadn't been enough.

Put plainly, Colton was disenchanted with love. Resentful and hollow.

"Pleased to see you're still too handsome for your own good," Colton poked, creases forming around his eyes.

River brushed the fringe back from his forehead and feigned bashfulness. He was different since he'd met Liza, in all the best ways, from Colton's observation. He looked smitten, and it suited him; Colton saw his adoration for his future wife. In all the trips they had made east to visit River's family, Colton hadn't seen the spark between them waver. Even the most gifted storyteller would fail to portray how River looked at Liza. Those two had something special.

"Eh," River grunted, settling back into his chair. "So, how's the collab goin' with Laguna Luxe Studios?"

Colton ran his hand through his dark waves. "It's been good, so far. Stressful and challenging, but good. They're really pushin' for more pieces, which I'm all for. It's just balancin' that with everything else, you know? And now I have an interview that's been sprung on me."

"Interview?" River raised his eyebrows. "That doesn't sound so bad. In fact, it sounds like great exposure!"

Colton let his head dip, as he chose his wording.

"Yeah, maybe…," he began. "It's with someone named Maris Oakwood. The interior design rep mentioned she's doin' an article on sustainability and thought I'd be a good fit."

River's interest was aroused. His nose twitched with excitement.

"Maris Oakwood? Remember, I was plannin' on introducing you guys this weekend? What are the odds!"

Colton sensed that River enjoyed his apprehension. Since high school, River had attempted to set Colton up with just about every girl he met. He was a fantastic wingman; Colton would never forget. But something about the eagerness in his voice made Colton wary. He hoped River wasn't staking too much on him hitting it off with a young, artistic, type A and living happily ever after.

"Anyway, you should plan to meet her," River concluded. "And, speakin' of plans, Liza and I are hostin' a bonfire out at Balboa Pier tonight. You should come. Take a load off."

Colton, upon hearing the invitation, was relieved. "Thanks man. I need some fun, and somethin' stronger than coffee. I'll be there."

As Colton chatted with laughter and trash talk, a content River fell back into step, sharing memories and jokes. It was, during that reunion, like they'd never been apart at all. Colton saw them as children, in his mind's eye, taking a blood-brother oath and wrestling on his childhood home's floor. They were always there for each other. In fact, he was more of a sibling than Axel, and Colton was indebted to him for his loyalty.

As they finished their meal, a flutter of apprehension came over Colton. The bonfire tonight was a welcome diversion, if not an unpredictable one. With the ocean as a backdrop and the night sky above, a meeting with Maris Oakwood was sure to be intriguing. He was forced to consider how the evening would turn out and what influence she might exert on his career—on his existence.

Shifting Sands

It was just after seven o'clock when Colton rolled into the parking lot near Balboa Pier. The ride to Newport Beach only took half an hour, thanks to the decent traffic flow. Emerging from the vehicle, he was struck by the spectacular transformation of the sky.

He noticed now that the sun had sunk way down behind the peaks of mammoth waves forming off the shore. The dark, massive swells were backlit by the luminous expanse of color, stretching into infinity. Deep red, lavender, and indigo splashed across the feathery clouds, adding a sense of ethereal splendor to the landscape.

Well, I'll be… The only words he managed to think of faded in his mind before he spoke them.

The vibrancy of the setting sun, he admitted, was a major difference between SoCal and South Carolina. If there was one trump card California could play, it was that sundown here was an awe-inspiring experience, each day. California, but for the earthquakes, wildfires, and high cost of living, might have enticed him to move there.

His gait was purposeful, strides long, as he made his way onto the sand. Colton effortlessly commanded authority, making him appear impenetrable to outsiders. A few folks looked in his direction, then spun back to their lively discussions or chilled drinks. He disliked being stared at, and valued privacy, despite considering himself a social person.

He watched the crowd that had gathered to support River and Liza. It was moving to witness the backbone of their lives in action. A wide range of ages and backgrounds had turned out to be part of this important occasion. Colton recognized River's mother speaking in hushed tones with an eccentric-looking elderly woman. He observed Liza, engaging in a group photo with whom he assumed were her bridesmaids. His examination of the crowd stopped when he noticed a solitary girl by the fire.

While the rest of the gathering thrived on each other's energy, this guest stood alone, like a question mark at a sentence's end. Lustrous strands of sun-kissed hair framed her face, and its length cascaded down her back. She swayed in the dusky twilight, her hips mimicking the dance of a palm tree in the wind. The intriguing stranger, aglow with firelight, captivated Colton's attention with her puzzling presence and how the flames danced in her eyes.

Colton sensed a hand clap against his back. River had approached unnoticed, with Liza in tow, breaking him free from his trance. With a kiss on the cheek and a shoulder squeeze, Colton awkwardly hugged Liza.

"Hey, Colton! Glad you could make it," River said, his cheeks red from alcohol consumption.

"Wouldn't miss it for the world," Colton replied with a grin. "Liza, you look stunning, as always."

"Thanks, Colton," Liza said, tucking an unruly auburn curl behind her ear. "And thank you for coming. It means a lot to us."

"Of course," Colton nodded. "So, how are you two holdin' up? Must be a bit overwhelming with all these people, huh?"

River laughed. "You have no idea. But it's fantastic that everyone came together. Speakin' of which, let's go mingle! There are a few folks I'd love for you to meet.

Walking through the crowd, River and Liza introduced Colton to various attendees. He exchanged polite greetings and small talk with everyone, from longtime friends of River's family to Liza's childhood companions.

"Colton, this is Dalton, an old buddy from college," River explained, gesturing to a round man with an amicable presence.

"Hey Dalton, good to meet you," Colton stated, shaking his hand firmly.

"Likewise," Dalton replied. "River has told me a lot about you. I can't believe it took us these many years to be in the same place at the same time."

They continued to chat, swapping stories and anecdotes about River's history. Liza's laughter was infectious, and River's enthusiasm made everyone welcome. Despite relaxing and enjoying himself, the image of the woman he'd seen earlier that evening lingered in Colton's mind.

Soon, he saw her again, nearer this time. She was wearing cuffed blue jean shorts and her tight-fitting undershirt showed the tautness of her stomach, while the loose flannel she wore over it gave her a sultry lumberjack look. Colton, from this vantage point, observed her intensely blue eyes—shimmering like the sky at twilight. He had seen nothing comparable to it. Her face, speckled lightly with freckles, was free of heavy makeup.

No sooner did Colton blink and the mystery girl was standing next to Liza, whispering something in her ear. Liza, midway through a swig of her second IPA, giggled, and they looped their arms together like a twisted pretzel.

He was determining if he should introduce himself or not when River interrupted.

"Maris! There you are," River said, his voice louder than necessary. "I want you to meet a friend of mine. This is Colton Vance. We grew up together."

Maris faced Colton, her intense eyes meeting his.

"Hi, Colton. It's nice to meet you," she remarked, but her expression was unreadable.

Colton hesitated, feeling a spark of recognition. He recalled Eve mentioning Maris on the phone yesterday, noting that she was the writer interested in interviewing him. He bristled at the thought—just another reporter looking to make a name for herself. Colton had no patience for snoops who pried into his life.

"Nice to meet you too, Maris," Colton returned, his tone cooler than intended. He noticed the delicacy of her skin as he took her hand, and he sensed the slight chill in her demeanor. "So, how do you know Liza?"

"We've been friends forever," she replied with a polite yet guarded smile. "She's practically family."

Noticing the tense interaction, Liza chimed in playfully. "Yeah, Maris here has seen me through all the ups and downs. She's my rock."

Maris, flattered by the compliment, softened her posture.

Just then, River handed Maris a tasty-looking margarita, with an unsalted rim and garnished with a jalapeño, handcrafted at the cocktail cart he and Liza had rented. "Here you go. Thought you might like something to sip on."

"Thanks," Maris said, taking the drink and giving him a grateful look.

Liza turned once again to Colton. "So, Colton, I hear you have a big interview coming up. How are you feeling about it?"

"Uh, yeah…" Colton stammered. "I believe a certain acquaintance might've mentioned that to me. I'm game if Maris is."

Maris opened her mouth wide, shut it, and then opened it again.

"I'm always game," she said coolly. "It's not every day you get to see how well someone handles an interrogation."

Cautiously, Colton proceeded, sensing the change in her expression. "I'm sure it'll be an interestin' experience for both of us."

She took a sip of her margarita, her gaze steady. "Interesting is one word for it."

River and Liza exchanged a glance, noticing the mutual agitation but choosing not to intervene.

"So, Maris," Colton continued, trying to steer the conversation to safer ground, "what do you do when you're not makin' margaritas disappear?"

"Oh, you know, just balancing coffee cups and deadlines," Maris quipped, quirking an eyebrow. "And you? When you're not playing the saint, do you solve world hunger on your lunch breaks?"

There was a brief pause as heads turned to stare at Maris, her voice having risen above the general murmur of the group. The sudden attention didn't faze her, but Colton was taken aback.

"Well, it's not easy, but it's somethin' I'm passionate about. What about you? How did you get into writin'? Run out of crayons?" he responded icily.

A few people nearby exchanged glances and whispered amongst themselves, intrigued by the heated exchange.

"Who's interviewing who?" Maris shot back.

Colton smirked, looking smug. "You know, sweetheart, you've got quite the edge for someone in your line of work. I guess puttin' words on paper must be tough if you can't even handle a little friendly conversation."

Maris's eyes now flashed with anger. "Excuse me?"

He shrugged; his tone dismissive. "Just an observation. Maybe try to lighten up a bit, girlie."

Maris mumbled an insult under her breath, her face a mixture of irritation and shock. "I don't need advice from someone who thinks condescension is charming. And for the record, I'm not your girlie. Enjoy your evening, Colton."

Turning on her heel, she walked away, leaving him with a mix of frustration and curiosity as he watched her go. Confusion penetrated him to the core, as much about his own words and actions as about Maris's. He told River and Liza he needed to leave; they were equally bewildered. Wishing them a goodnight and promising to see them tomorrow, Colton, still smoldering, stalked back towards the car.

What is it with Maris, anyway? He wondered. *She's got some nerve, and I gave her what she had comin' to her. Hmph.*

As he crossed the expanse of the beach, his initial irritation started to wane, replaced by an unsettling feeling in the pit of his stomach. By the time he reached the pavement, remorse for his rudeness had fully set in.

A mix of dread and curiosity about the wedding day flooded him as he stared out at the moonlit ocean. He would try to steer clear of Maris and, if that didn't work, there would be an open bar. No matter what unfolded, he needed to keep his focus on his friends' celebration.

Little did he know, avoiding Maris would be more challenging than anticipated. As he reentered the parking lot to grab a breath of fresh air, he spotted her leaning against her car, holding her sandals and muttering to herself. Suddenly she turned and kicked the tire, but her bare foot caught the edge of the rim, sending her howling in pain.

"What's the matter? Car givin' ya trouble?" Colton asked, strolling over.

Maris glared at him, her frustration evident. "Everything's just peachy, Colton. Leave me alone."

"How 'bout some help?" he offered, against his better judgement. "I happen to be excellent at jump-startin' things."

She crossed her arms and scowled. "I don't need your help. I'm perfectly capable of handling this on my own."

Colton chuckled, ignoring her protest and strode over, popping the hood of her car.

"I'll bet you are, sweetheart, but let's not let a little thing like pride keep you stranded here."

Maris sighed, resigned to the fact that he wasn't going to leave. "Fine, but don't expect a thank you."

"Wouldn't dream of it," Colton replied, his tone dripping in sarcasm. "Just enjoy the free roadside assistance, courtesy of yours truly."

Here we go again, he thought.

"Just hurry up, would you? I have better things to do than stand here with you all night."

"As you wish, princess," he teased. "I'll just grab the jumper cables from my rental. You're battery's probably dead."

Colton walked over to his car and retrieved them, taking his time just to annoy her a bit more. When he returned, Maris was drumming her fingers on her upper arm impatiently.

"Finally," she muttered.

Colton avoided commenting and simply smirked as he connected the cables.

A few minutes later, Maris got behind the wheel and revved the engine. As the car roared to life she turned to Colton, her expression a mix of irritation and reluctant gratitude.

"Alright, I'm out of here," she declared.

Colton gave her a mock bow. "Glad to have been of service, Maris," he said with a wink.

Maris drove off, leaving him standing in the parking lot sneering, and with a growing curiosity about the woman who seemed to be both his nemesis and the most intriguing person he'd ever met.

No one had ever so quickly gotten under his skin before. He experienced relief at no longer being under her scrutiny and felt juvenile and impulsive for having retaliated with sarcasm and mockery.

He resolved to focus on his work with Laguna Luxe, regardless of how uncomfortable it might be to face Maris again. His career was important, and he couldn't afford to let a single person, however infuriating, derail his ambitions. He would approach the interview with professionalism and determination, setting aside his personal feelings.

Undercurrents

Grumpy. Crabby. Testy. All these words could describe Maris as the stifled first light of day permeated her bedroom. As the clouds fought the sun for dominance, she sat in her papasan chair in the corner of the small space. She'd been up for endless hours, pacing and biting her nails down to nubs. She couldn't stop mulling over the head-on collision she experienced with Colton the night before. If ever there was something to be ashamed of, it was herself and the series of stupid comments she had chucked his way.

The definitive term for their interaction: turbulent. Embarrassment applied, but frustration burned brighter. Why had he irked her? Was it something in her demeanor, her reputation, or just his own insecurities peeking out from their hiding places? River treated him as if he was one of the good ole boys, but when she'd entered the group, he'd gotten prickly—similar to a porcupine that felt threatened. Surely Colton wasn't intimidated by her. He was at least eight to ten years older than her and had an established career, friends, and no shortage of physically attractive features.

He was tall and muscular—though not in a meathead kind of way. His strength probably came from long hours of physical labor, each movement carrying the weight of dedication. His dark rebellious waves and matching eyes had bored into her and made her feel exposed.

Colton's reaction puzzled her. She knew from Liza that he had a reputation for being driven and exceedingly loyal to his friends. His success in the business world was well known. He was a man who seemed to have little tolerance. But there was a vulnerability in his eyes last night, something that suggested he carried burdens of his own.

Noting the absence of a wedding ring, she figured River wouldn't have introduced them had he been married. Then again, Liza might've told him she needed the professional boost, and perhaps River believed that rubbing shoulders with Colton would somehow raise her status. It was all so disconcerting.

Maris recalled the frosty reaction she had had when Colton pointed out her inexperience in the writing world. Yet, when he was delivering his snobby comments, there was a flicker of tenderness in his face—almost as if it pained him to bruise her pride. On the flip side, it was gutsy to tear down a woman in front of her closest friends. She wondered what had made him so guarded, so quick to lash out.

There were still nine hours until River and Liza's wedding began. Occupying her time until the ceremony was going to prove difficult in this state of mind. She sank further into the comfort of her seat and grabbed a throw blanket from the basket beside her, wishing she could disappear. If she couldn't escape her reality, could a fairy godmother transform her into an unrecognizable princess for the wedding?

The amount of vulnerability she was going to show by turning up at the ceremony after revealing her obstinance at someone else's event was immense. A knot of worry tightened in Maris's chest at the thought of appearing impertinent. Mercifully, Liza's mother insisted on Liza's cousin, Cadence, being a bridesmaid, forcing Liza to make tricky, last-minute adjustments to her bridal party. Because all the other ladies taking part in the wedding were also family, Maris had bowed out for Cadence to take her place. Now, she wouldn't have to endure being visually dissected by everyone who had been onlookers the previous evening.

Bending forward, she pulled her laptop from where it sat on the edge of the desk. Only three minutes had passed since she previously checked the time. The morning was going to continue forever without a diversion. Reluctantly, she opened the file on her computer that she'd last updated two years prior. Her novel — or the rocky beginning of it — filled the screen.

"Uncharted," the work in progress Maris had abandoned and tried to forget, was a contemporary romance. Set in the fictional town of Haven's Point, marine biologist Ellie Mason returns, hoping for a fresh start after a devastating loss. Instead, she encounters Jake Lawrence, a rugged fisherman with a shady past and a heart as vast as the ocean. Working through the obstacles her plot line throws at them, the two fall head over heels in love.

Maris stared at the synopsis she'd typed at the top of page one.

"…they uncover hidden depths in themselves and each other," it read.

It was the hidden depths that frightened her most. She had attempted to write what she knew, to draw on her own experiences with romance, though they were few. After she developed the main character profiles and was halfway through her first draft, Maris had given up.

Her prose was impeccable, her grammar was perfect, but once love blossomed between the two protagonists, she hit a wall. It wasn't just writer's block; it was as if her own heart refused to navigate the uncharted waters of emotional intimacy. Whenever she tried to write a sensitive moment, her fingers hesitated, paralyzed by the fear of making a mistake or oversharing her personal pain.

Maris's eyes watered, anger boiling within her. She yearned for Ellie and Jake's happily ever after, but their emotions were too close to her own. She couldn't continue writing.

Memories of Hendrix's cruel words after she rejected his advances resurfaced, stabbing at her heart.

"You'll never find someone who truly loves you," he had sneered, leaving her feeling more isolated than ever. To aggravate the wound, Hendrix had spread rumors to all their other friends, claiming that Maris was untrustworthy and had been the one to come on to him. The vicious lies made her feel even more betrayed and alone. Her senior year had been hard to muddle through.

Hendrix had always been charismatic, the kind of guy who could charm his way out of any situation. He was the life of the party, the one everyone wanted to be around. But beneath the surface, he was manipulative and selfish, using people to get what he wanted. His betrayal cut deep, leaving scars that Maris struggled to heal.

As if that wasn't enough, the deceit of her only post-high school boyfriend still lingered. He had been emotionally unavailable, sneaky and talked with other women while they were together. Maris was young and impressionable, always trying to please him. Despite her efforts, he cast her aside and quickly married another woman, painfully reminding her how easily replaceable she was.

The sting of these experiences made it difficult for her to write about romantic relationships. How could she convey the depth of Ellie and Jake's bond when her own attempts at love, both platonic and romantic, had ended in heartbreak? The thought was paralyzing.

The cursor, idle on the screen, symbolized the inactivity of her creativity. It was clear to her, sooner than later, that this emotional and mental blockade she couldn't seem to overcome needed to be moved. She also realized the only way to connect authentically with readers, despite any discomfort, was by letting her guard down.

Gingerly, she tapped out a sentence with staccato rhythm. Then another. It was unrushed, but it was a step forward. By channeling her pain into her writing, maybe she could break free from the chains of days gone by and heal.

Gravitational Pull

Maris immersed herself in reviving her once riveting tale. Taking only a couple of brief breaks — one to make a cup of hot tea and the other to complete ten minutes of stretching before heading back to the grindstone — had kept her motivated without becoming strained. Periodically, she thought of Colton and wondered if perhaps he found their word war as silly as she did. But she couldn't dwell on that and used it as fuel for the story that was flowing out of her.

As more ideas flooded her mind, her speed accelerated. What started out as a sporadic jabbing at the keyboard turned into a true author's pace. Six hours later, she had written over 5,000 words to add to her original narrative. Maris knew that to keep up that kind of momentum, she would have to do a lot of work to outline the remaining chapters and tie up the loose ends of the subplots. Yet, a warm glow of accomplishment washed over her.

Across the room, her phone lit up. Urgently, she ran to see what it was. A series of banners informed her that her favorite web-based retailer was having a BOGO sale, urging immediate action to secure her cart items. Beyond these, Maris found three consecutive texts from Eve Vasquez. Nausea overcame her as she pressed the screen with the pad of her finger to reveal the content of the messages.

Eve: *Hey Maris, just confirming the interview with Colton. I know it's short notice, but it's set for 2:00 PM Tuesday.*

Eve: *I've secured the conference room at Oceancrest Hall for the meeting.*

Eve: *And guess what? Colton said he would LOVE to do the interview with you!*

Lies, thought Maris. *Colton would probably love to do just about anything else than this interview.*

Still, she had to respond, and Eve didn't strike her as the kind of woman who would take it well if she canceled at this late date. It occurred to Maris that Eve Vasquez possessed the power to ruin her career if sufficiently provoked. She likely used hashtags like #girlboss and #bossbabe on all her personal social media posts.

Maris: *Sounds great! I can make Tuesday work. Thank you.*

As she sent her reply, out of the corner of her eye, she noticed the analog clock that sat on an open shelf near the closet.

Observing the time, she gasped. It was already after 1 PM, and she was running behind. She still needed to bathe and dress for the wedding, not to mention hair and makeup. As she put the phone down, she went to the faucet and turned on the showerhead.

Maris stepped into the steamy, soothing shower, letting the hot water embrace her. She stood motionless for a moment, allowing the warmth to lull her into an aquatic euphoria and wash away the remnants of her irritability. The spray ran down her back, pooling at her feet before swirling down the drain, taking with it the remains of her self-doubt.

She reached for her favorite guava-scented body gel, the familiar fragrance filling the small bathroom. Maris lathered it onto her skin, the creamy texture gliding smoothly as she massaged her shoulders, arms, and legs. The scent of the tropics was fruity and sweet, helping her to invigorate herself for the day ahead.

After washing and conditioning her hair, she turned off the shower and stepped out into the humidity. She moved to the mirror, where the steam still clung to the glass, and began her skincare routine. With practiced precision, she used serums and moisturizer, her blurry reflection staring back, a mixture of determination and distress in her appearance.

She dried her tresses, brushing through the damp strands until they were smooth and tangle-free. Opting for a simple style, she wore loose curls that framed her face.

Next, she moved on to her makeup. Normally, Maris kept it understated with a bit of tinted balm and mascara. But today, she upped the ante a little to enhance her natural features. With a light foundation diffused effortlessly into her skin, she added a soft peach blush, achieving a radiant and healthy glow.

Although an amateur, she worked to apply eyeshadow in warm, earthy tones. Beginning with a base of subtle beige, blending in a hint of copper shimmer to add depth. For a pop, she added a touch of eggplant to the crease, creating a look that was both distinctive and elegant. Mascara followed, lengthening her lashes and providing volume.

She finished with an understated gloss in a neutral rosewood hue. The subtle sheen looked youthful and stylish.

With her hair and makeup done, Maris turned her attention to her outfit. The satin dress she'd steamed the wrinkles from yesterday hung on the inside of the bathroom door. A notched vee closed in the back of the knee-length dress, which zipped up one side. It was sophisticated, and the ornate black lace details had made it an irresistible purchase. Adjusting the fabric for the perfect fit, she slipped into the garment, with exhilaration and apprehension coursing through her.

She chose a pair of gunmetal earrings with diamond accents that had been a college graduation gift from her parents; the accessories adding a touch of sparkle. Maris then stepped into some comfortable yet stylish heels. Classic and elegant, they featured delicate rhinestone embellishments that matched her jewelry.

As she looked at herself in the full-length mirror, she felt glamorous. Granted, no one would be looking at her during the wedding—they all were coming to see Liza. Nobody faulted them when she excitedly shared her great deal on a Vera Wang gown from a Los Angeles sample sale. Liza had sent a photo of herself saying yes to the dress, but even Maris was eager to behold it in person.

Despite lacking a date, she thought she would find one of River or Liza's friends to help her release her inhibitions and let loose. Plus, she had above-average dancing skills, which she could be persuaded to show off on the dance floor. Whatever the case, it would be memorable.

An alarm jingled in the other room, signaling that it was now 2:50 PM and Maris was going to be late if she didn't leave within the next few minutes. Unclasping her minaudière bag and filling it with the bare necessities, she glanced one last time at her reflection. Concluding that her hair might've looked better in an updo, she shrugged at herself, and, walking out the door, left the second-guessing at home.

Casa del Refugio, in all its grandeur, was in South Laguna Beach. Maris had never been there before, but knowing her friend's champagne taste, she knew that it would be top notch. She pictured Liza, emerald eyes, and a permanent, demure expression on her pale face. She was going to be every inch the portrait of a bride.

The color palette of the event, as determined by Liza's wedding planner, was amber, sea foam, and olive. As Maris approached the venue, she observed these hues enveloping the entire rooftop lounge, including sheer fabric of each tone that had been loosely tangled and woven around the railing on all sides.

The valet was double staffed in anticipation of the lofty occasion and, while one drove away with the Mercedes in front of her, another opened Maris's door, serving as an attendant. It was a gorgeous day for a wedding. The sugary scent of the tuberose, imported from Mexico, coupled with the freshness of hydrangeas, wafted over to Maris as she turned toward the entry.

As she observed the overall magnificence and wide-ranging ocean vistas, she noticed the ceremony location was rapidly filling. The seating consisted of various vintage couches and armchairs, an aisle dividing the outdoor space. A wooden wedding canopy, draped in fairy lights, stood in the center of the platform stage. Upon closer inspection, Maris saw it was also carved with images of trees, swans, bees, daisies, and other elements from nature.

Lost in appreciation for the surroundings, she was hardly aware when Colton brushed past her, making his way to a seat near the front. It took her a moment to register that he hadn't recognized her, and this made her trill with delight. However, she noticed that, with him only rows away, the veranda that had only moments ago seemed cozy and quaint now looked far too small. Everything appeared to close in on her, and as objects seemingly inched closer, her thoughts spiraled.

Grateful to hear a few taps on the microphone and an announcement that the service would begin shortly, Maris took her own seat on the opposite side of the aisle, a few rows back from Colton. She was aware of being watched by a few guests but stayed focused on the wedding program, concentrating on the string quartet members' names. Still, her cheeks burned, and a squeamishness churned within her.

One by one, family and friends filed in to observe the marriage of River and Liza. They observed each of the lovely bridesmaids, on the arms of handpicked groomsmen, glide down the silk chiffon fabric to their respective places on the stage. Maris began to speculate about why Colton wasn't the man standing on River's left. Why had they selected rotund but compassionate Dalton as best man instead of River's closest friend? It dawned on Maris that perhaps their friendship wasn't as solid as she believed, and she turned her attention to Liza.

The wedding march played in the background as Liza stood stationary, armed with her father as an escort. As the photographer's camera made soft clicking noises, they began their procession toward the altar. Delicate butterfly-shaped hair clips, glimmering in the sunshine, pinned back her mid-length auburn curls. A simple veil hung just past her dark lashes and touched the bridge of her auspicious nose. Liza's high cheekbones jutted out underneath.

Her Vera Wang gown was a genuine piece of bridal artistry. The bodice, adorned with glittering tulle, created a shimmering effect as she moved forward. Slightly below the midsection, the dress flowed gracefully into an A-line silhouette, adding a touch of timeless charm. Not to be missed was the detachable overskirt. Draped across her front, it reminded Maris of a gown from a fairytale. It was the perfect blend of current and romantic, just like River and Liza.

River stood as a statue, save for the broad, uninhibited grin on his face. Watery eyed, he looked handsome and composed, but those who knew him well could see the tremor in his hands as he awaited his bride. His eyes never left his beloved, a testament to his devotion; it was as if she was the only person in the world at that moment.

As they stood under the beautifully carved canopy, their fingers intertwined, the officiant spoke. Maris's heart swelled as she listened to the couple exchange their vows. Adoration, commitment, and a shared vision for the future filled each word. Tears welled up in her eyes, the sincerity of their promises touching a deep chord within her.

River began, "Liza, from the instant I met you, I knew you were my true partner. Today, I vow to always stand by your side, support your dreams, and cherish every moment we share."

Liza followed with her vows. "River, you are the love of my life, my confidant, and my best friend. I promise to care for you unconditionally, to laugh with you in joy, and to comfort you in times of sorrow. Together, we'll weather every storm and treasure every sunny day…"

Maris inevitably replayed her past while observing them. Would she ever find someone who looked at her the way River gazed at Liza? Would anyone accept her for who she was and what she wanted?

She'd never been the girl to put together a thick, fantasy wedding binder as her sister, Alex, had done as a teen. Marriage had seemed like a far-off dream. And now that she was getting older, it appeared even more elusive. Amidst the beauty and passion of this moment, she simultaneously experienced sorrow. Tears flowed, not only for the couple's joy, but also because of the uncertainty about her own future.

As the ceremony concluded and everyone erupted into cheers, Maris clapped and smiled, her eyes brimming with emotion. River and Liza were now husband and wife, beaming with delight as they jaunted back down the aisle together. It was a pivotal moment of collective happiness as each of them waved and blew kisses to guests as they passed by.

With tears streaming down her face, Maris looked around to see that Colton was unable to look away. Her eyes, almost periwinkle in the light, glistened with emotion. His gaze held hers. Never had she experienced such profound understanding in another's stare, yet so much foolishness in displaying such uninhibited feeling.

As the ceremony finished, guests slowly moved to the reception. The transition to a lively celebration was seamless and the atmosphere buzzed with opinions on the décor and other details. Twinkling lights and cylindrical lanterns strung up in every direction, an ochre glow encapsulating everyone.

Peonies, gardenias, ranunculus, and eucalyptus evoked an aura of lush romance in imitation of the bouquets and boutonnieres. Garlands intertwined and draped across the main seating area and around the wedding cake. Abundant floral arrangements using different heights and styles of vases created visual interest. Elegant table settings with fine china, crystal glassware, and polished silverware completed the whimsical coastal garden look.

They considered no cost too great. Liza's father, Julian Whitaker, made his fortune through shrewd investments and developments as a real estate mogul. Starting with a few small properties, he had a knack for spotting undervalued locations with high potential. After his first big break, his portfolio blew up overnight, and Julian had built a successful empire. His success in the property business not only provided financial stability but also influenced Liza's upbringing and opportunities. She was a daddy's girl, living at home, and was spoiled by her father's money.

Opportunity had led her to River. He had earned his master's degree in architectural engineering from Harvard. His passion for creating and industry knowledge garnered him respect and recognition in the field, making him a sought-after consultant. Julian had wanted to expand his business, integrating intelligent technology into his designs, and River was the one to make it happen.

It was during one of Julian's high-profile events that Liza and River's paths crossed. Julian invited River to discuss the future of smart city infrastructure, hoping to inspire potential investors with his innovative ideas. Liza listened to River's presentation and was drawn to his vision and dedication. After the speech, Julian introduced Liza to River, and, as they say, the rest was history.

Maris, coming back to reality, looked for her name on the seating chart that Liza's mother had painstakingly produced. She was a well-meaning woman with many strong opinions and a do-it-yourself attitude.

Ah, there I am… Maris said to herself, as she found her seat assignment. *Table Twelve.*

Table twelve was near the dance floor, and Maris already heard the band playing soft dinner music. She discovered her name, written in metallic calligraphy, on a place card at the circular table set for eight. While she recognized some of Liza's relatives and acquaintances' names on other seating cards around the table, others she didn't. Assuming the groom's side had invited them, she sat down her purse and went to get in line for a drink.

As she weaved her way through the crowd, she almost bumped into someone. Maris sidestepped, narrowly avoiding impact. A chill went down her spine when she realized it was Colton, who hadn't seemed to notice her yet again, in his hurry to reach the bar.

Arriving there a few seconds later, Maris promptly ordered a Manhattan with extra cherries. Two close encounters with Colton were too many for one night. She struggled to reconcile her usual behavior with the need to avoid him.

Cocktail in hand, she turned to find her chair, but a large floral arrangement blocked her path. Thinking swiftly, she ducked behind it, hoping to steal a few moments of composure before having to socialize.

As soon as she thought she was in the clear, she heard a familiar voice.

"Plannin' to hide behind flowers all night, Maris?"

She turned to see Colton standing there, looking smug as ever.

"Just enjoying the décor," she replied, trying to keep her tone light. Confrontation wasn't her aim tonight, though she felt it drawing her in.

"Sure you are, trouble," he said. His eyes, the color of fresh honey, twinkled with amusement.

"Well, what else would I be doing?!" Maris exclaimed, attracting unwanted attention to their corner. She sensed something unidentifiable as Colton shifted nearer.

"Seems like a waste of a perfectly good party," he teased, with a deep, gravelly voice.

Maris took a step back, hoping to change the subject. "I was just taking a moment for myself."

He smirked. "And now you're sharing it with me. What a gift."

Maris ignored the comment and squeezed by him, her arm grazing his as she made her escape. She started returning to table twelve, in hopes he wouldn't notice. As she approached her seat, her heart sank. The name on the place card next to hers was the only one she hadn't read. Bold, gleaming gold lettering spelled out Colton Vance.

"Guess we're dinner buddies," he said, pleased with her misery.

"Great," she muttered under her breath as she sat down.

Throughout the courses of dinner, they exchanged playful barbs. He commented on her choice of entrée, and Maris teased him about his suit, joking that he looked like he was auditioning for a part in The Godfather. Despite their banter, she was unable to ignore the chemistry between them. Every time his knee brushed against hers under the table, her heart raced a little faster.

At long last, no more food was being served, and Maris thought she might be rid of Colton. She'd gotten up to refresh her drink and when she returned, he was nowhere to be seen. A tremendous weight lifted from her chest. The feeling of being around him left her breathless, and it wasn't something she liked.

She extracted her phone from her purse, opening the camera app to take a photo of the extravagant room for her missing sisters and parents. Though her mom and dad had planned on attending, recent health concerns were enough to keep them away. Maris was keenly aware of their absence, but she resolved to enjoy the evening.

As she framed the shot, focusing on the twinkling lights and elegant decorations, she noticed a figure stepping into the frame. Lowering the phone, she realized it was Colton. His back was turned as he spoke to another guest. She snapped the photo anyway, capturing the moment.

As she was about to put her phone away, he swiveled around, catching her in the act. He raised an eyebrow inquisitively.

"Takin' pictures of me now?" he teased, stepping closer.

She felt her cheeks flush, and she rolled her eyes. "Just trying to capture the ambiance," she replied, attempting to sound nonchalant. "Don't flatter yourself."

She turned her attention back to her phone, pretending to review the picture she had taken. The image showed the beautiful décor, glittering bokeh, and, of course, Colton was right in the middle of it all.

"So, what do you think of the ambiance?" Colton asked, trying to see the photo over her shoulder. He leaned in close enough for his chest to skim her back.

"It's lovely," she admitted, endeavoring to ignore the way his proximity made her pulse quicken. "Liza has fantastic taste."

"She does," Colton agreed. "But I think you add somethin' *extra* to the scene."

Maris glanced at him, surprised by his comment. "Are you always this smooth?"

He chuckled. "Only when I'm around you, darlin'."

She couldn't help but let out a laugh, shaking her head. "You're impossible."

Suddenly upon them was a well-meaning guest. "Oh, you two look so lovely together! Let me take a picture of you as a couple." The dainty, white-haired woman looked at Maris expectantly.

Maris blushed. "Oh, no, we're not together," she insisted, waving her hands.

The lady seemed embarrassed but quickly recovered. "Well, you should be! You make a beautiful pair. How about a dance instead?"

Before Maris could protest, the announcement came, all couples were welcome to join River and Liza on the floor for their first dance. The guest, determined to see them together, nudged them towards the floor.

"Go on, you two. It's a wedding! Have some fun!"

Colton, unperturbed, extended his hand to Maris.

Maris hesitated but then placed her hand in his. "Just one dance," she warned.

As they moved to the music, the discomfort between them was clear. But, Maris couldn't deny that Colton's grasp on the small of her back felt both electrifying and terrifying. She sensed ridicule rising into her mouth like bile.

"This certainly wasn't my idea of fun," she blurted.

Colton's brows furrowed. "Believe me, it wasn't mine either," he replied, his voice lowering a register.

"Guess we're both unfortunate, then."

"Or maybe it's a giant hoax. We're gettin' Punk'd and Ashton is out there watchin' right now."

She snorted at the dated reference. "I'm sure that's it," she said sarcastically. "He's having a laugh at our expense."

They stayed silent for the next few seconds and Maris dared to close her eyes. The distance between her and Colton closed, and she could hear his steady breathing. The song the band was playing spoke about finding your place in the embrace of your sweetheart.

In your arms, I've found my forever, where every moment feels like home…

"Ya know, you're pretty good at this," Colton said into her ear.

Maris opened her eyes. His face was just inches from hers, and she couldn't find her words. The sensation of their palms pressed together seemed to intensify. The music slowed, then shifted to an upbeat melody, breaking the spell as Maris looked up into Colton's eyes and opened her mouth to speak. She withdrew, and bit the inside of her cheek to stop herself from saying something she might regret.

"Thank you for the dance." Colton's tone was more formal now, though he gazed at her. Maris felt a twinge of annoyance.

"Of course," she said, breaking eye contact and looking down at her feet.

"It's not like me to be so abrasive, so you know," Colton took a step toward her as she retreated. "You just… get under my skin."

Maris's head shot up and her eyes narrowed. "Join the club. You're not exactly my favorite person, either."

Her emotions were welling up, and she didn't want him to see her cry. She clenched her fists, trying to rein in her frustration. Without another word, she spun around, planning to leave him standing there alone. But before she could run off, Colton caught up to her and seized her by the arm.

"Maris, wait," he said, urgently.

She stopped, but didn't turn to face him. "Let go of me, Colton."

"Not until you hear me out," he insisted, his grip firm but gentle.

Maris took a deep breath, trying to steady her trembling voice. "What do you want?" she asked, barely keeping her tears at bay.

He stepped closer, his tone softening. "I'm sorry. I didn't mean to upset you."

"Too late."

She turned to look at him, her eyes glistening. She saw the genuine remorse on his face, but it did nothing to soothe her wounded self-esteem.

She yanked her arm away from his grip. "I can't do this," she said, her voice cracking as she whirled around and rushed towards the ladies' room, leaving Colton standing there, stunned, his hand still hovering in mid-air where her arm had been.

As soon as she reached the safety of the bathroom, she locked herself in a stall and let the tears flow freely and grasped at her burning chest. She needed a moment to gather herself before facing the world again. As she sat on the closed toilet seat, her emotions swirled like a hurricane. Maris dabbed at her face and tried to compose herself. The confrontation with Colton had shaken her, stirring up old wounds she thought she had buried.

Her mind raced with thoughts of past failures and heartbreaks, each one feeling like a fresh cut.

She clenched her fists, feeling a surge of frustration mixed with sadness. The vulnerability she felt in front of Colton was a harsh reminder of how fragile her self-esteem truly was. She felt as though she had been stripped bare, her insecurities exposed for all to see.

One thing was certain, though—this night had only added fuel to the fire. And she sensed that dealing with Colton would be complicated.

She knew she couldn't stay hidden in the bathroom forever. With a final, shaky breath, she straightened her dress and exited the stall. She glanced at herself in the mirror, fixing her makeup before stepping back into the reception. For now, she had to focus on getting through the rest of the evening. The night was still young, and she would not let Colton get the best of her. With firm resolve, Maris joined the guests, putting on a brave face and vowing to keep her distance from him.

Yet, at her core, she knew their strange encounters were far from over.

Low Tide

If the human mind is an abyss, Colton had disappeared into it. Imprisoned by his memories of the way Maris smelled—a sweet blend of candied guava and creamy coconut—as they drifted at the edge of the dance floor. A serendipitous moment, and a small amount of coaxing from a stranger, had placed her, peculiarly relaxed, in his arms for a solid three minutes. And, Colton admitted, he didn't dislike the way it affected him.

He replayed those three minutes again and again, unable to shake the impact her presence had on him. Self-control, and the management of his feelings, were things he always took pride in. Even more so after his wife had abandoned what they'd built together. But Maris could unravel that control with effortless ease.

Last night, after River and Liza's wedding, he remained awake. Every infernal hour's passing brought a flood of images; the dim lighting had cast a halo around them and Maris's full, rosy lips, curved into an indecipherable smile. Her dress was dark and snug—delicate lace details tickling her tawny, sun-soaked skin, kissing her collarbone. The cinched waist caused the fabric to spread tightly across her midsection and, when it brushed against his fingers, it sent a tremor through him. Unable to help himself, he questioned if she felt it, or if it was only another figment of his overactive imagination.

Despite Maris's harsh persona, she had captured Colton's curiosity. Though he had been a fool, he was sure, to think she would value his honesty. Colton had wanted to express his frustration to Maris about their strained first encounter, but the confession had only led to a second, worse one. Her hasty temper was maddening, her lack of patience and humility enraged him. Why then did he get a tingly feeling in his chest when he thought of her?

Every detail, the lightness of her hand on his shoulder, the gentle bend of each thread of her hair, and the mischievous glint in her eye, was etched into his mind. It was unclear to Colton if the music's slow pace or the unspoken words were the cause of his intoxication. Was he simply swept up in the celebration? Had he had too many old fashioneds? One thing he knew for certain was that the chasm of his mind was far from offering any simple answers.

As he stared at the ceiling, Colton's thoughts drifted to his own failed marriage. The wedding had unearthed long-buried memories. Cruelly, the vows and promises of forever served as a reminder of his loss. His wife leaving had shattered his trust in love and commitment, and seeing River and Liza so blissfully happy had only deepened the wound.

Colton's mind flashed back to the conversation he had with River at the reception. He clenched his jaw; the anger rising again as he conjured the moment.

He had found River by the bar, a smile plastered on his face. Colton approached him, drink in hand.

"Hey, man. Congrats again," Colton said, forcing a smile.

"Thanks, Colton. Grateful you're here for it," River replied, signaling the bartender.

As their conversation shifted from one topic to another, River dropped the bombshell.

"So, I have some news," River started, hesitating. "Liza and I decided we're stayin' in California. I got an offer that doubles my current salary."

Colton's disingenuous smile faded, replaced by a frown. "What?! You were supposed to move back to Charleston."

"I know, I know," River said, putting his hands up, mimicking surrender. "But this opportunity is too good to pass up. It's a game-changer for us. I want to provide a good life for Liza.

Movin' out of her parents' home and out of Carlsbad to Morro Bay is goin' to be a hard enough change for her. I'm not a millionaire like Julian; money's gonna be tight even with the pay increase."

Colton sensed the hot knife of betrayal sticking out of his back. "So, that's it? You're just goin' to stay here and leave me behind?"

"It's not like that," River protested. "We can still stay in touch, visit each other. This doesn't change our friendship."

"Doesn't change our friendship?" Colton echoed, his volume escalating. "You promised you'd come back. We had plans, River. We were gonna start BioHaven together. Remember? Design and consulting—what happened to that? Plus, I can't offer workshops and seminars on my own."

River's expression softened. "I'm sorry, Colton. I really am. But this is the best decision for us right now."

Colton set his jaw, anger mixing with a deep sense of loss.

"Right. Well, congratulations on the new job," he said tersely before walking away, leaving River standing alone filled with guilt.

Back in the present, the sting of River's treachery was apparent to Colton, simmering beneath the surface. His decision to stay in California seemed like another act of disloyalty, another relationship that hadn't gone the way he had hoped. The plans for BioHaven were now just another casualty of broken promises. Because of the wedding, reflections on his divorce, and River's bad news, he felt directionless.

He had invested time, energy, and resources into this project. It had been a symbol of hope, a positive sign that he could build a better future. River had ripped the rug out from under him with the news he would be relocating to California permanently. And that announcement had only exacerbated Colton's feelings of desertion and loss.

Needing distraction and to attend to his business, Colton dragged himself out of bed and got ready for the day. He had a lunch meeting with Eve, and he hoped focusing on work would help clear his mind.

Arriving at the upscale restaurant, Ocean's Edge Bistro, Colton spotted Eve at a corner table, already immersed in paperwork. Her no-nonsense demeanor had always impressed him, and today he needed her level-headedness more than ever. However, with nagging confusion about Maris and trepidation of what was to become of his future settled deep inside of him, the last thing he wanted was food.

"Eve," Colton greeted flatly as he approached the table.

"Colton. Just the man I wanted to see," Eve oozed, barely looking up from her documents. "Have a seat. We have a lot to cover."

Colton took a deep breath and settled into the chair opposite her. A waiter appeared to take their order.

"I'll just have a raspberry iced tea," Colton said.

"C'mon, you need more than that," Eve urged. "Order something to eat. It's the company's money."

Colton grimaced. "I'm not that hungry."

"Fine," Eve sighed. "But don't blame me when you pass out."

He tried to pay attention to the matter at hand, but his thoughts kept returning to recent events.

"Let's start with the financials," Eve began, pushing a spreadsheet towards him. "The spa you're furnishing has requested a line of credit. Here's a breakdown of the amount that's been paid out versus what they're asking for."

With a struggling mind, Colton scanned the numbers. Eve's voice seemed distant, like background noise. He was lightheaded.

"Colton?" Eve's voice snapped him back to reality.

"Yeah, sorry. Just a lot on my mind," he admitted, trying to shake off his distraction.

Eve arched an eyebrow. "Well, try to focus. This is important. We need to decide if the spa's request is reasonable or if we need to renegotiate terms."

With a nod, Colton tried to focus on the figures before him. But Eve's next words made the hair on the back of his neck stand up.

"By the way, I scheduled your interview with Maris," Eve said, her tone casual. "It's tomorrow at 2 PM at Oceancrest Hall. I'll text you the address."

The news hit like a punch to the gut. His fragile composure began to crumble. The last thing he wanted was another meeting with Maris, especially in a formal setting where he couldn't afford to lose his cool. It made his queasy stomach churn.

"Dadgummit," he muttered, unable to hide the bitterness in his voice.

Eve glanced up, noticing his change in demeanor. "Is there a problem?"

Colton forced a smile as the waiter returned with his raspberry iced tea and Eve gave him a pointed look.

"No, it's fine. Just... not lookin' forward to it."

Eve sighed, leaning back in her chair. "Look, I know things have been strenuous lately. But you can't let whatever personal issues you have interfere with business. Maris is a professional, and so are you. Just get through the interview and move on."

As the lunch continued, Colton struggled to maintain his professionalism. His mind kept wandering, hashing out scenarios of the upcoming interview. With his anxiety gnawing at him like a persistent itch, he could barely endure the conversation with Eve.

By the time they concluded the luncheon, Colton was drained. He knew he had to get a grip before Tuesday, but the looming interaction with Maris was like a dark cloud hanging over him.

Colton took a deep breath, steeling himself for the days ahead. Looking out at the sun-drenched sand below the deck of the restaurant, he decided to take a solo walk on the beach. The tranquil sound of waves crashing against the shore offered a welcome respite from his tangled thoughts.

As he made his way down the sandy path, Colton found himself drawn to the tide pools, their aquamarine waters glistening in the midday sun. He knelt, intently observing the vibrant underwater life within them. Tiny crabs scuttled across the rocks, and small fish darted through the shallow puddles, their scales catching the light and reflecting a kaleidoscope of colors. Sea anemones swayed gently with the ebb and flow of the water, their finger-like tentacles moving from side-to-side.

Briefly, Colton escaped from his worries within the marine world. Left behind as the tide went out, these small bodies of water were teeming with vibrant life. He watched as kids splashed in the pools, their laughter and excitement adding to the picturesque atmosphere. The simplicity of the moment allowed him to find a sense of peace until it was once again lost by the buzz of his phone. Reluctantly, he pulled it from his pocket and glanced at the screen. A text from Axel.

Hey, little bro. Can you send me some cash? I'm in a bit of trouble.

Colton's neck tensed. He was too annoyed by Axel's ignorance to respond. Axel's constant need for rescue was a source of an ongoing grudge. He felt bitter towards the burden of it. The acidic taste of resentment surfaced in his mouth.

Just as he was about to put his phone away, he looked up and saw Maris walking along the shoreline, her bare feet kicking the surf absentmindedly. She seemed lost in thought, unaware of his presence; her usual guarded expression was soft. Colton was caught off guard by her sudden appearance.

Maris was carrying a camera with a mid-range macro lens and occasionally stopped to capture a few shots. It was clear she was deeply engrossed in her hobby and, fearing disturbing her, Colton started to sneak away. But he had already been noticed, and she was headed in his direction with a blatant look of surprise on her face.

"Colton," she said, her voice carrying a hint of genuine curiosity. "What brings you here? Are you stalking me?"

Colton hesitated, shuffling his feet in the sand. "Needed some fresh air," he replied, trying to stay casual. "And you?"

Maris held up her camera. "Just taking some photos. It's a good way to clear my mind."

Colton nodded, unsure of what else to say. Just then, a seagull swooped down and, to Maris's dismay, relieved itself on her head. She froze, her eyes wide with shock.

Colton had no choice—he burst out laughing. "Well, that's one way to make a memorable photo."

Maris glared at him. "Glad you find this so amusing," she said, as she looked around in desperation.

"Hey, it's not every day you get a free souvenir from a seagull," Colton teased, still chuckling.

Maris rolled her eyes and snatched the handkerchief he offered. "Thanks. I'll keep that in mind," she muttered, her voice tinged with irritation.

She projected an unspoken tension. Yet, Colton found himself drawn to her, his feet moving closer almost involuntarily. He noticed the way her eyes softened when she looked out at the ocean, its depth shimmering in their reflection. She held her camera protectively to her chest as she struggled to maintain her grace.

"So, what do you do with all these photos?" he asked, returning to the topic.

Maris glanced at him, looking vulnerable. "Sometimes I use them for my articles. It's... just a hobby. But it helps me unwind."

He nodded. "Big shot photographer. That's pretty cool."

Maris shrugged, the corners of her lips twitching upwards.

"Thanks. It's nothing major. But I thought these beach photos might be cool for showing how beautiful the area is and the diverse life supported here. I want to inspire people to be more sustainable. Plus, I read about a local surfer who's been leading efforts to clean up the beach. I think it's a story worth telling."

"That's brilliant," Colton said, impressed. "You're doing more than just takin' amazing pictures. You're raisin' awareness."

Maris looked down, fiddling with her camera strap. "It's just a small effort, but every bit helps, right?"

He noticed the unshielded look in her eyes and sensed an undeniable connection. "Absolutely. Sometimes the small efforts can make the biggest impact."

Their eyes met, and for a moment, it seemed to him that something deeper than disdain for him flashed across her pretty face.

Colton cleared his throat, breaking the moment. "So, tell me more about this surfer. What's his story?"

Maris lit up, and she launched into a passionate explanation. "His name is Ripley, but he goes by Rip. He's been surfing these beaches since he was a kid. A few years ago, he started noticing all the trash and decided to do something about it. He organizes beach clean-ups and even turned it into a community initiative. He's making a real difference."

As she spoke, Colton admired her dedication. It was clear that her passion for photography and storytelling went beyond the surface. He found himself drawn to her intensity, the way her eyes sparkled when she talked about something she cared about. He scolded himself for ever having belittled her line of work.

"So, are you gonna interview Ripley?" he wondered aloud.

"I'd like to. I think his story could inspire a lot of people."

"Aspiring journalist. I dig it."

"Oh. I don't want to be a journalist. These freelance articles are just a way to make a living right now. Keep my head above water, ya know?" Maris confided.

Colton noticed the waver in her voice and had an unexpected pang of sympathy. "I get it. Sometimes you just do what you have to so you can get by," he said softly, reflecting on his now squashed ambitions for BioHaven.

"Yeah, exactly. But it's hard sometimes, trying to find the balance between doing what I love and making enough to live," Maris admitted.

Colton found himself captivated by the sincerity in her words and instinctively moved even closer.

"Well, from what I've heard, you're doin' a pretty great job. Raisin' awareness, tellin' important stories… I'm impressed."

"Thanks. My dream would be to load up an old VW bus, windows down, and road trip from here to Acadia National Park. Stopping wherever the light feels right, capturing it all, and sharing those moments at local festivals and farmers' markets."

"You should one day. What's holdin' ya back?" Colton asked.

"Oh, I don't know," Maris said, her fingers tracing shapes in the sand. "Maybe I just haven't been brave enough. Plus, it's not like I have a travel partner. My sisters are doing their own thing. Someday though."

Colton's gaze didn't waver, but the way his expression softened told her he wasn't judging—just listening.

A strange, almost magnetic pull toward Maris came over him as she traced patterns in the sand. Drawn to the quiet determination in her voice, the breaking waves filling the void between them. Colton was unable to dismiss the hope that something had changed between them. If they weren't mortal enemies anymore, maybe they would at least be friends.

"You know, despite everything, I'm glad we ran into each other today. It was kind of…good?" Maris said with uncertainty.

He smiled at her hesitant admission. "Yeah, it was. A lot better than I expected, honestly."

Maris raised an eyebrow, a hint of her usual sarcasm creeping back. "Better than you expected? Wow, high praise coming from you."

Colton chuckled, as the strain between them eased. "Hey, I call it like I see it. And today was... good."

"So, I guess I'll see you at the interview," Maris speculated, shielding her eyes from the sun.

He nodded, a half-smile still playing on his lips. "Yeah, I'll be there. Try not to scare me too much with your questions."

Maris smirked. "No promises."

As they prepared to part ways, an awkward silence set in. Neither knew whether to extend a hand for a handshake or go for a friendly hug. They both shifted uncomfortably.

Colton rubbed the back of his neck. "Well, uh…"

Before he finished, Maris turned and stumbled on an uneven section of sand. On impulse, he reached out to steady her, his hand gripping her waist. The contact sent a jolt through him, and for a few seconds, they both stood still, caught in the unexpected intimacy of the moment.

"Thanks," Maris said. Her voice was a breathy whisper.

Colton nodded, his hand lingering for a moment longer than necessary. "Anytime."

Reluctantly, he let go, his fingertips tingling. "See you tomorrow, Maris."

She gave him a small nod before turning and walking away, her steps more cautious now. Colton watched her go, feeling a strange mix of emotions. He was unable to pinpoint it, but something in their dynamic had altered. As he returned to his hotel room, he thought about her.

Once inside his room, he sat down at the small desk by the window. He pulled out his sketchbook and flipped through the pages, stopping at the logos he had designed for BioHaven. The sight of them brought a pang of disappointment.

With a resigned breath, he picked up a pencil and sketched thoughtlessly. Visions of Maris resurfaced. He revisited the way her eyes had lit up when she talked about her photography and the beach clean-ups in his mind, and it filled him with a mix of admiration and regret. He let those fleeting moments and pent-up feelings guide his hand across the paper.

He set the pencil down, leaned back in his chair, and ran his fingers across the stubble of his perpetual five o'clock shadow.

Outside the window, a lone osprey searched diligently for its next meal. It didn't have to wait long before spotting its prey. The stealthy bird dove into the water and, a second later, returned with a dogfish shark in its beak.

Colton glanced down at the sketchbook and found himself staring at a detailed drawing of Maris. Expressive and full of life, she gazed back at him from the page. Her hair, captured in mid-movement as if caught by the sea breeze, framed her face. He traced the outline of her with his fingertip. Perhaps, amidst all the chaos, he had found an unexpected ally in Maris. At that moment, for the first time that day, Colton felt a glimmer of hope.

Breaking Barriers

Tuesday arrived with the swiftness and majesty of a pronghorn antelope, racing over the rugged California landscape, running toward the horizon. Maris imagined herself, with incredible speed, dashing to a goal of her own. She would interview Colton today and was resolved not to ruin it.

Granted, after yesterday's chance meeting with him at the beach, she was feeling less like his aim was to make her life a bottomless pit of suffering and more that he was just as scarred as she was. One second it was almost as if he was flirting with her and, the next, he seemed to have it out for her. Their brief interaction had left her unsettled yet intrigued. She had to remain focused and not let the memory of his perfect white teeth or the firm, reassuring grip he had on her waist during their previous encounter cloud her thoughts. Today was too important to be sidetracked by the mystifying charm of Colton Vance.

Stay calm, Maris, she told herself. *You've got this.*

The only problem was, she doubted herself. If there was one thing that never failed her, it was her ability to recall the finest and most minute details of even the most mortifying moments. This included, of course, the first time she ever conducted an interview.

In middle school, as the leading reporter for the media team, getting the scoop on trending topics was her responsibility. To a bunch of thirteen-year-olds, who were being pressured by the guidance counselor to join clubs to build social skills and develop friendships, popular issues consisted of which teachers gave the most homework, the latest cafeteria menu changes, and the ongoing debate over who had the best locker decorations.

A staff member was occasionally selected by the school to present an in-depth exposé on a self-chosen topic. During the spring of her seventh-grade year, someone asked the principal to speak on the school's recycling program, giving Maris a few days to prepare an outline of questions. Like a real newscast, they would video record the session live and play it on a large monitor in each classroom. But when the time came to begin the questioning, she choked, forgetting what she planned to ask.

Her heart had pounded in her ears as she stammered through, while the principal's encouraging smile did almost nothing to calm her nerves. With a fumble of her notes, 3x5 cards scattered as they fell to the ground. Little Maris, who thought she'd let down her entire school, cried under the bleachers at the athletic field until her mom came to pick her up. Even at this moment, her face turned red, remembering it.

Maris's phone sounded with a new email notification, and she came back to the present. She saw it was from Alex and braced herself before opening it.

Hey Maris,

I know things might seem rough right now, but remember, you're stronger than you think. Trust your instincts and stay true to yourself. You can do this!

Love, Alex

She released the breath she'd been holding, experiencing a bit more confidence and thankfulness for the encouragement from her sister. After sending a brief, appreciative reply she still felt the need for connection, and sent a text to Jemma:

Hey, guess what? I have to meet Colton for the interview this afternoon. He's such a dingleberry!

With a sigh of relief, she silenced her phone and drained her coffee mug.

A mint green silk blouse and a pair of black, wide-leg trousers rested on the bed. Maris changed and tying her hair into a high chignon, spritzed on her most-liked perfume. As she caressed the tear shaped, crystal-clear glass bottle examining the pale pink liquid inside, she recited the name to herself.

Veiled Yearnings.

That name was fitting, in a way that tugged at the corners of her mind. Maris had chosen it for its delicate, beguiling scent, but now, it held a different significance. She recognized the irony. Here she was, standing on the precipice of a professional milestone, yet her thoughts were becoming cloudy, lingering on Colton.

Just yesterday, his enigmatic presence had stirred something within her—a longing she hadn't expected. Her emotions, hidden desires and unspoken questions veiled by professionalism, were seemingly captured by the perfume. She shook her head, trying to dispel the distraction. This was not the time to indulge in such musings.

Maris put the bottle down with a decisive clink and smoothed the fabric over her toned thighs. A hurried glance in the mirror revealed a mix of grit and ambiguity. But, despite any reservations, she knew she needed to hurry and get to Oceancrest Hall.

Azure Vista Drive wound along the coastal cliffs, offering astonishing three hundred sixty degree views of the sparkling Pacific Ocean. Abundant, technicolor ixora bushes lined the road and stately palm trees moved back and forth in the mild breeze. Well-maintained, historic buildings, reflecting Laguna Beach's rich heritage, lined the road, each telling its own unique story.

Oceancrest Hall stood, tall and proud, on this picturesque street, looking both classic and coastal. While she walked the path, past an expansive water garden to the giant, double doors fitted with ornate brass handles, butterflies rose in her belly. Above the entrance, large arched windows allowed natural light to flood the interior, illuminating the polished wood floors, as Maris stepped foot inside.

Proceeding down the hall, she saw several partitioned and co-working spaces. Wrought iron sconces from the 1930s hung uniformly on the walls beneath the ceiling, adorned with beautiful frescoes inspired by Spanish heritage. On her left were the stairs to the conference space.

Approaching the second floor, she found an inviting coffee station designed for hard-working guests. It featured a high-end espresso machine, a variety of teas, and an assortment of snacks. Productivity and relaxation were both priorities here.

In the middle of the conference room, a large, round table took center stage, surrounded by elegant wooden chairs. Smaller rectangular tables provided additional workspace for individuals or small groups around the room. Stylish desk lamps and ergonomic seating adorned these. Since Colton hadn't turned up yet, Maris decided to set up at one.

Settling into the library-like silence, she organized her outlines and opened her phone's voice recorder application, ready to tackle the inevitable. Just then, she heard footsteps. She looked up to see Colton entering the room, looking as confident as ever. He offered her a polite smile, displaying straight, dazzling teeth. She sought to echo the expression, but it appeared artificial.

Scanning him, she noticed details her eyes had missed at the wedding. His perfectly tailored navy suit accentuated his broad shoulders and athletic build. The pristine, celadon shirt he wore was open at the collar, revealing just a hint of tanned skin. Without a tie to distract, the ensemble made his amber irises stand out even more, a mesmerizing contrast that Maris found hard to ignore.

His deep chestnut hair, slightly tousled, gave him an effortlessly polished charisma. She noticed the subtle flecks of gold in his curls when the light caught it just right. Captivated, she was left weak in the knees by his chiseled jawline and stubble, which gave him an air of rugged sophistication.

"Good afternoon, Maris," Colton greeted, setting his satchel down on the table. "Ready to get started?"

"Yes," she replied, her voice unintentionally curt. She straightened her posture, trying to project authority, but it appeared stiff and awkward.

Colton subtly flinched at her tone but chose not to comment. Instead, he took a seat across from her, close enough for her to catch a hint of his cologne—an enticing scent that only added to her distraction. "Then, let's dive in."

Glancing at her first question, Maris began. "You've made some controversial design choices in the past. How do you justify them?"

The query sounded bratty, and Colton was visibly offended. He frowned but answered, leaning forward, the closeness making her acutely aware of his presence.

"I understand the criticism, but each choice was made with a specific purpose in mind. I believe in pushin' boundaries, even if it means facin' scrutiny."

He paused, gathering his thoughts. "For instance, folks were skeptical about my decision to incorporate reclaimed materials in luxury furniture. They said it compromised the aesthetic, but I saw it as a statement on sustainability. Then there was the time I opted for bold, unconventional color schemes in corporate office designs. Some found it jarring, but I wanted to challenge the idea that workplaces need to be sterile and uninspiring. Each choice was driven by a desire to innovate and redefine standards. I don't expect everyone to agree with my methods, but I stand by them."

Maris pressed her lips together, jotting down his response. She had a pang of guilt for being so gruff, especially after their more personable interaction the previous day.

"Some critics say your work lacks sustainability. How do you respond to that?" she asked, her tone still sharper than she intended.

Colton's frown deepened, but he kept his composure. "Sustainability has always been a priority for me. I constantly try to improve and learn from my mistakes."

As the interview continued, Maris's stiffness thawed, but she remained overly formal. The questions flowed, but her demeanor still seemed off-putting. However, Colton answered each question candidly, maintaining his poise.

After a few particularly tense exchanges, he excused himself to grab a coffee from the station.

"Do you want anything?" he asked as he turned toward the door.

"Not unless you know how to make a caramel macchiato," Maris responded.

"Sheesh …" Colton mumbled.

"And I suppose you like your coffee black?" she speculated.

"Like my soul," he countered. "I'll be right back."

As he walked away Maris was relieved. Her eyes went heavenward, and she mouthed, "*Why me?*", to the coffered ceiling.

Maris's phone glowed beside her, alerting her to a text message from Jemma:

Hey sis! Just wanted to remind you that you're awesome and I believe in you. Go knock 'em dead! Also, guess who just started learning how to play the ukulele? Yep, this girl!

A grin touched her lips as Colton returned with his coffee, now glad she'd told her sister about the interview.

"That must have been a good message. Anything worth sharin'?" he pried.

After a moment, Maris decided to share. "My little sister just wanted to tell me that she started playing the ukelele. One of Hawaii's official state instruments," she said with an air of light humor. "And she wanted to cheer me on. It's a nice break from the seriousness of all this."

"It doesn't have to be so serious, darlin'," Colton ventured.

She blinked, caught off guard by the comment. At first, she bristled. Then a subtle warmth spread through her face, and redness rose to her cheeks. His words lingered in the air, suggesting she had been taking this too seriously. Maybe she could afford to relax a little.

"You're right," she admitted, her voice softer. "I guess I just get caught up in my own head sometimes."

The stiffness in the room seemed to lift, replaced by a more comfortable, almost friendly atmosphere. And, with that, Colton plopped back into his seat.

As they took off into the rest of the interview, he shared a mishap he once had.

"One time, I tried to incorporate a livin' wall into an office lobby. It was supposed to be a serene green feature, but it ended up infestin' the place with spiders. You can imagine— everyone was freakin' out, and we had to call in pest control!"

Maris laughed, picturing the scene. It sounded similar to something from one of those exaggerated arachnophobia movies. Their shared laughter broke the ice further, and she sensed a connection forming. "Sounds like quite an ordeal," she remarked, still smiling.

"It was," Colton replied, chuckling. "But I learned a lot about carefully choosin' materials and the unexpected challenges of ambitious projects."

Maris realized he had quite a bit of sincerity and a willingness to learn from his mistakes. This fresh perspective helped her to see him in a different light.

Feeling more at ease, she continued. "Can you tell me more about your inspiration for your latest project — sustainably furnishing the spa?"

Colton's eyes ignited as he spoke about his work. "Honestly, the idea was to create a luxurious and serene environment while usin' eco-friendly materials and practices. We incorporated bamboo, organic fabrics, and energy-efficient systems to ensure the space was beautiful, in addition to bein' environmentally conscious."

Maris admired his enthusiasm and devotion, quietly overturning her initial judgments. She found herself drawn to him, an undeniable attraction taking root. Her gaze lingered on his mouth as he spoke, and she fought the sudden urge to reach for his arm when he revealed his thoughtful methodology.

As they continued talking, Colton casually mentioned, "I also built the carved wedding canopy for River and Liza."

Maris's eyes widened. She reached out, lightly touching wrist as her resolve faltered. "You did that? It was beautiful," she said, moved by his work. She couldn't help but wonder if he was a hopeless romantic deep down.

Colton smiled, appreciating her gesture. "Thank ya. It was a special project for me."

Maris reflected on her own bias and realized she may have misjudged him. This revelation deepened her respect for him.

Deciding to ask her final question, she looked at Colton with reverence. "You've mentioned that your work has been a way to channel personal challenges. Can you share more about that?"

He hesitated for a long moment, and she feared he might not answer.

"I went through a tough divorce last year... It was a painful process—I felt like my world was falling apart. I channeled my feelings of worthlessness and loss into my designs, hoping to find some sense of purpose again," Colton disclosed.

A tidal wave of empathy and discomfort washed over Maris. She hadn't expected such a forthright response, and felt momentarily unsteady, unsure of what to say. "I'm sorry to hear that," she consoled, her tone soft and careful, as though trying not to disturb the rawness of his words.

He offered sincere thanks, not knowing the lasting effect his authenticity would have on her.

"Once, I was watchin' baseball with my dad—the one recreational thing we ever did together. Our team was on their way to a completely defeated season. After another loss, my favorite player said, 'Rock bottom has built more heroes than privilege'. That stuck with me. Whenever times get hard, I repeat it to myself, and it keeps me goin'," he finished.

"Rock bottom… hmm. Is that where you feel like you are?"

"Maybe not right now. Not completely. When things don't go your way for a few innings, you start to feel like a losin' streak is all you'll ever know. But then, sometimes, one good hit can turn it all around."

She hadn't expected him to open up so honestly, and it stirred something within her—an agonizing admiration she couldn't quite put into words.

"Well, thank you for your time, Colton," Maris remarked.

"I appreciate the opportunity to share. I'm not without faults but I try to keep it real."

With that, they both stood up, gathering their things. As they walked out of the conference room, a comfortable silence hung between them.

They exchanged a brief, somewhat clumsy goodbye outside Oceancrest Hall before going their separate ways. Maris got into her car, intending to drive home, but her mind was abuzz with thoughts and theories about Colton. She drove towards Victoria Beach instead, almost on autopilot.

As she arrived, the sight of the Pirate Tower against the backdrop of the late afternoon sky came into view. The bright blue background paired with the medieval structure was a postcard of a relic. A reminder of a bygone era. Her imagination was captured by the weathered stone and the careful design of its turrets.

Tourists milled about, taking pictures of the iconic landmark. Some posed with the tower, while others admired the view of the ocean. Maris maintained a safe distance and walked along the shoreline collecting shells. The salty breeze filled her senses, her footsteps leaving imprints on the wet sand.

As she bent over to pick up an iridescent abalone shell, she spotted a large, weathered oyster half-submerged in the sediment. Curious, Maris shifted to reach it. The rough texture of the oyster shell was cool against her fingers as she carefully pried it open. It resisted at first, but with a firm twist, she managed to unseal it. To her surprise, she found a tiny, rare yellow pearl nestled inside.

The pearl was not perfectly round. It had an irregular shape that only added to its uniqueness. In the fading sunlight, it gleamed, a symbol of beauty and value under the surface. Maris held the small orb in her hand, reflecting on how it mirrored her realization about Colton. Just as the oyster shell hid its treasure, Colton's true self was hidden beneath her initial impressions.

He was more sincere and transparent than she had observed, which made her admire his trustworthiness. Also, he was creative without boasting about his success. Colton seemed to have more integrity than she had originally assumed, and he was thoughtful—proven by his creation of the huppah. She hoped

that, in time, he could see the same inherent worth and charm
in her.

Hidden Truths

Ugh! I should've gotten a new laptop with that last paycheck, Maris confessed to herself.

A glitch in her computer made her doubt she had managed to save the final bit of manuscript writing before the program crashed. She had attempted to reboot it three times and now, on the fourth try, she wasn't hopeful. Her heart sank as the screen froze and turned black yet again, threatening to erase hours of hard work.

Finding a priceless treasure inside an oyster shell inspired her. She rushed home to record her new ideas. Completion of the book had become Maris's renewed obsession and, with the interview with Colton behind her, she now had plenty of energy to delve into it. As she wrote the scenes in today's sprint toward the finish line, she couldn't help but be grateful to Colton for adding some spice to her main male character's image. Though she hoped he'd never find out.

Suddenly, the laptop hummed back to life, and the dim light from her monitor illuminated the room once again. She exclaimed her happiness aloud as she checked to make sure that her document was preserved. Content with her word count and chosen stopping point, she turned off her computer. Then she strolled to the kitchen, hungry for a late-night treat.

As she looked inside the refrigerator, she surveyed her choices. The shelves were nearly bare, and as much as Maris hated grocery shopping, she wished she hadn't put it off quite so long. The bottom drawer contained oranges, and some milk was on the shelf, with questionable leftover Thai food. Grabbing an orange, she made a mental note to stop at the market tomorrow and get a few essentials.

In the main living area, furnished with low armchairs and thick gingham cushions, she lit a large three-wick candle sitting on the antique coffee table. Beside it were several magazines, a set of agate coasters, and a small potted plant. Maris retrieved the remote from a crack in the chair and settled in for a binge session of the newest Netflix drama.

As she peeled the orange and sifted through titles on the television, looking for the one she wanted, she heard her ringtone. Raising herself up from the seat, she began the search for her cellphone. Finally, she saw a video call request from her mom amongst the blankets on her unmade bed.

They didn't normally phone this late, and she worried that something was amiss. She swiped the screen to answer and observed her parents' serious faces appear.

"Mom, Dad, you both look stressed. Is everything okay?" she asked, her voice filled with concern.

"We're okay, Maris. The doctors are keeping an eye on Dad. Things have just been busy with a lot of appointments, but so far, nothing we can't handle," her mom explained, trying to sound reassuring. "Sorry we didn't call sooner, but we didn't want to worry you during Liza's big day."

"Thanks, but I still wish you would've let me know. I could've come over and helped. Everyone was concerned when they didn't see you there. Did you at least get the photo I sent?" she replied, hoping for some comfort.

Her mom sighed, glancing at her dad before continuing. "It's only a minor issue, Mar. It was important for you to enjoy yourself. And, yes, the wedding looked lovely. I hope you'll give Liza and River our love."

"It's hard not knowing what's going on," Maris said, her voice softening. "And, of course, when I'm with Liza next, I'll tell her you're thinking of her."

Her dad cleared his throat, looking uncomfortable. "Maris, there's something else we need to talk about. It's about Jemma."

Maris's brow furrowed. "What about her?"

Her mom exchanged a quick look with her father. "We've noticed she has been acting a bit differently lately. Spending a lot of time with Hendrix, for one. We're not sure what's going on, but it seems like she's hiding something. Have you heard from her? Did you know she was visiting and staying with us?"

Maris felt a pang of confusion. "Hendrix?! No. And why would she hide a visit from me? She told *me* she couldn't come home because of work."

Her dad sighed. "We wanted to make you aware, in case Jemma has cause for concern. Your mom and I don't know of all the details about what happened between you and Hendrix, but we trust you and just want her to be careful."

Maris nodded, her thoughts racing. "I'll talk to her after I wrap my mind around this. Thanks for telling me."

They chatted for a few more minutes about Maris's work and the fact that she was finishing her manuscript. They had nothing but support and love to share as her obvious excitement spilled over. Though she was careful to leave any details about Colton out of the conversation.

"Maris, we're so proud of you. Trust yourself. You've always had good instincts. Listen to your intuition," her mom advised.

After hanging up, she sat on her bed, her thoughts swirling. She couldn't shake the feeling that there was more to the story about Jemma and Hendrix. Determined to get to the bottom of it, she grabbed her laptop and opened Facebook. She navigated to Jemma's profile and began scrolling through recent photos.

And there it was—a picture of Jemma and Hendrix, smiling at the camera in some beautiful Hawaiian location. Hendrix wore a ball cap and sunglasses, but there was no doubt it was him. A cocktail of surprise, confusion, and a twinge of hurt washed over Maris. Why hadn't Jemma told her about this?

A closer look at the photo showed Hendrix's veiny muscles wrapped around Jemma's narrow shoulders. His face, once smoothly shaven, was now covered with a short, well-kept beard, and his black, curly locks had grown long enough to peek out from under the edges of his hat. In an orange sleeveless shirt and bright board shorts, he appeared relaxed.

Resentment, jealousy, and sadness coursed through her as the photo mocked her from the open internet tab. A lump formed in her throat, making it hard to breathe. Jemma wasn't just her friend; she was her sister. They told each other everything! This secret situationship, or whatever it was, that she was hiding, left Maris feeling deceived.

She realized she needed to confront Jemma, to get the facts. She didn't want to jump to conclusions. Maybe there was a reasonable explanation. But the hurt was real, and she couldn't ignore it.

She closed her laptop with a soft click and lay back on her bed, staring at the ceiling fan spinning around and around. The questions in her mind circled in the same manner. How long had this been going on? Why hadn't Jemma confided in her? And what did this mean for her and Hendrix? Would their paths cross again in the future?

Her phone buzzed beside her. She turned onto her side, glanced at the screen and saw a message from an unknown number. Curiosity piqued; she opened it.

Today seemed to go better than we thought it would. Truce?—Colton

Maris's heart skipped a beat. Where did he get her contact information? Surprise and giddiness coursed through her as she read the text. A grin on her face, she replied.

Truce. Looking forward to seeing what comes next.

Creative Synergy

He paused, taking in the nearly finished job site. The high-end spa, Paradise Palms, that was collaborating with Colton, was almost ready to welcome its first guests. Natural sandstone elements, native to Santa Barbara, blended seamlessly with the calming water features and nature-inspired designs.

Positioning each piece perfectly to create a tranquil atmosphere, Eve and the spa's owner carefully placed the custom-designed furniture. He watched them work, appreciating Eve's keen eye for detail and her zeal for the project. The coffee table he had admired in his workshop was now front and center in the lobby, complemented by barrel chairs upholstered in organic, hemp fabric.

"Do you think the guests will like the layout?" Eve asked, stepping back to take in the view.

Colton nodded, a surge of pride welling up within him. "I think they'll love it. It's exactly what you envisioned—a place where people can come and rejuvenate."

As they continued discussing placing a large cedar bench near the entrance, Colton's mind returned to the previous day's interview with Maris. Her probing questions had made him uneasy, and he couldn't help but feel he had revealed too much by talking about his divorce. Yet, he was unable to deny how undeniably linked he felt to her. Her sincerity and genuine interest had left a powerful impression on him, one that persisted even as he focused on his work.

He was overcome by an urge to text Maris again. The warmth he sensed from her response the night before made him hopeful that they could resolve the damage done by their initial rudeness. He took out his phone, his thumb hovering over the contact info he had weaseled out of Eve, but decided against it. He reminded himself that he was supposed to be working, trying to push the thoughts of her to the back of his mind.

The early hours of the morning and the first part of the afternoon passed as Colton and Eve worked side by side to make the spa look its best. But, as the hands on the clock signaled it was nearing 4:30 PM, the spa's owner had dismissed the entire crew and told them they would start fresh the following day.

After wrapping up at Paradise Palms, he headed to pick up some groceries. Laguna Luxe had asked him to stay a couple of extra days to oversee the rest of the furnishing process, so he decided he should restock the mini fridge in his room. As he wandered through the tiny, brick-floored store, he found himself in the warm light of the wine section, picking out a bottle to have on hand.

That's when he saw her—Maris, standing a few aisles over, examining a selection of cheeses. His heart leaped into his throat. Should he say something or just keep browsing?

Remaining unsure, he watched as she read the label on a container of brie, smelled a sample of Camembert, and settled on a vacuum-sealed pouch of goat cheese. Her deliberate movements and the way her hair fell over her shoulders made him want to reach out and touch her. However, rooted in fear, his feet refused to move.

It wasn't like he had never talked to a woman before. But after years of marriage—and not having to navigate the dating field—his nerves were getting the better of him.

Maybe Maris was the kind of woman who swiped right on guys in spandex workout shorts with names like Chad or Chuck. Colton was the kind of guy who wore beat-up blue jeans and didn't belong in the Gossip Girl world.

She carefully maneuvered her shopping cart around a display of charcuterie meats, and he realized she was heading toward him. He panicked, picking up a random red blend from the live-edge wood shelf and pretended to examine the description. She was now only a few feet away, perusing the Napa Valley whites. This was his chance.

"Studying to be a sommelier?" he asked playfully.

Maris, startled, whirled around in alarm. However, noticing that it was Colton whose voice she'd heard, her demeanor softened, and she flashed a carefree smile.

"Oh, hey, Colton. I was just picking up a few necessities."

He peeked over at the bottle she was holding. "And a bottle of Far Niente Chardonnay is a necessity, huh?" he asked, giving her a teasing nudge.

Maris giggled nervously. "It's my favorite. How about you?" she said, nodding at the red blend he was carrying under his arm. "Shopping for a special occasion?"

"Just restocking the hotel refrigerator. Eve asked me to stay a couple more days and I just can't get the hang of starving to death," he replied, feigning hunger.

Maris threw her head back in genuine amusement and allowed a laugh to escape. Then, as if she had suddenly realized what he said, her eyes widened, and she looked at him with something he couldn't seem to interpret.

"So, you're not going home yet?" she asked hesitantly.

Colton shook his head. "No, not yet. I have some things I'd like to see through here first."

"Oh?" Maris said, curious.

"Yeah…" Colton whispered, getting lost in her intense gaze. "I, uh….um…have a few more design ideas I'm workin' on and they need a bit more brainstormin'. Anyway, I was goin' to show them to Eve before I left and see if she has any clients who might be interested."

"That's great. I'm really happy for you," replied Maris. But her tone told another, sadder story. She looked away and back at the dazzling bottles before her.

Noticing her dejection, he wondered if she felt upset about his eventual departure or if something else weighed on her mind. Then, an idea hit Colton like a bolt of lightning.

"Any chance you'd want to give me your opinion on some of my ideas?" he blurted out after a brief hesitation. He hoped she would accept without further explanation, because he didn't exactly have a plan.

She looked at him for a moment, like he had two heads. He worried she might not let him down easily. What if she wanted nothing to do with him? What if he had read their previous chemistry wrong?

She swallowed hard and he could feel the long seconds filling the space between them.

"Sure," Maris exhaled, giving him relief. "I mean, I have to stop by home to put things away first, but I can meet you somewhere."

Colton's heart raced. "You pick," he said. "I'm not from around here, remember?"

"How about we meet at Shaw's Cove?" she suggested. "In about an hour?"

The cove was a secluded spot, with postcard perfect, crystal-clear water and stunning rock formations. The locals knew it as a place to unwind from the cares of the day, and it was a snorkeling hot spot. Colton, on his first visit to the area, was overcome by its beauty.

He grew up near Kiawah Island and was familiar with its sandy beaches and world class golf courses. River's dad had managed timeshares there when they were young, and the boys often accompanied him so that they could fish or look for shark teeth as he attended to his business.

Shaw's Cove differed from the pomp of South Carolina luxury. It was laid back and peaceful, not crowded, with fine, golden sand. Cobalt and lilac frolicked at the edges of the sky, and the bright, gilded sun reflected on the ocean.

Exactly an hour after they had planned to meet, Maris strode up to him in the parking area, armed with a picnic basket. As it happened, Colton carried a blanket and his sketchbook. The coincidence was uncanny, and they walked side-by-side like two cheshire cats. Grinning from ear to ear.

"Wow, so you really went all out!" he exclaimed as they approached the long staircase to the beach.

"Not really," she said. "But every brainstorming session needs something to munch on."

He watched her as she got to each step. Bracing himself to be her anchor if she needed it. Maris needing him was a thought that made his heart swell with tenderness.

Fifty-eight steps later, they had arrived on the soft sand, gentle underfoot. They surveyed the empty beach and selected a spot. He spread his blanket on the ground, his sketchbook resting beside him. Maris emptied the picnic basket, carrying the bottle of chardonnay and goat cheese, as well as a package of prosciutto and crackers. She also pulled out two dixie cups with a delicate leaf pattern overlapping on the outside.

Colton couldn't help but let his eyes slide over her easy movements as she set everything up. The simplicity of the moment, the sound of the waves, and the calm environment seemed like something straight out of a Nicholas Sparks novel. Not that he'd ever read one, or admit it if he had, of course.

Clearing his throat, he reached for his sketchbook, flipping it open to a blank page. He didn't think he should feel this nervous around a woman he had hardly begun to know. Nevertheless, being alone with her spiked his blood pressure. Sometimes it was her careless words; other times, it was the way the ruffles of her sundress brushed her thighs. Did she know what she was doing? How much she was getting inside his head?

He turned toward her, a spark of excitement lighting his face—perhaps a bit too bright. "Ready for some creative thinkin'?"

She poured them each a cup of chardonnay, handing one to Colton. "Absolutely," she replied, taking a sip of the wine.

He also tasted the cool liquid, noticing the light pear and oak flavors. As he set his cup down, he picked up his pencil and sketched. The ideas flowed freely in the inspiring setting.

As they brainstormed, Colton and Maris discussed several designs. Sketch after sketch filled Colton's notebook, but none of the concepts seemed feasible. The dimensions were off, or the designs lacked stability. Maris's brows furrowed deeply, and Colton sighed each time he canceled out a possibility. Eventually, they took a break.

Together, they wandered down to the water's edge, where the turquoise surf broke against the shore. They stood in the coastal air, watching the bright orange garibaldi fish darting through the clear water. The placid setting seemed to pull them closer.

Colton's hand brushed against Maris's, sending a surge of energy through him. It was obvious that the brief touch stirred their senses, and the newness of it hovered between them. As their eyes locked, the shore blurred, leaving only the unspoken longing between them. The desire to explore new territory suddenly within reach.

Time stretched out, every second filled with the thudding of his heart and the soft crash of the waves. He noticed the way Maris's breath hitched, her chest rising and falling in a rhythm that matched his own growing anticipation. He leaned in, pulled to her as if by an unseen current.

Her eyes searched his, and for a fleeting moment, Colton could see the same desire reflected in her eyes. Her lips parted, a hesitation in her gaze, as if she wanted to say something but couldn't find the words. Their nearness, the tension, the possibility of what could happen next—it all hung in the balance.

Just as he felt himself edging closer, ready to bridge the gap between them, Maris turned back to the water. Colton's enchantment shattered, leaving him standing there, the moment slipping away like a tide retreating from the shore. He chastised himself for letting it pass, the regret seeping into his bones.

What-ifs spiraled through his mind. Had he read the signals wrong? Or should he have been bolder? He was consumed by the passing of their longing look, a reminder of the almost and maybes that remained unfulfilled.

They continued to walk without speaking, each lost in their own thoughts.

"Hey, look at that!" Maris said, breaking the silence. "Look at that piece of driftwood," she said, pointing to a large arched fragment lying in the sand. "Doesn't it look like it could be the perfect beginning of a bookshelf?"

Colton's eyes widened as he took in the driftwood's natural bend. "Yeah, exactly! We could incorporate that curve into the design," he commented, excitement returning to his voice.

They raced over to it, examined the driftwood, and discussed how its shape could be transformed into a unique piece of furniture. The flash of inspiration revived their creative energy, and they hurried back to the blanket.

They pondered over the additional materials they would need: perhaps some sturdy planks of reclaimed wood for the shelves and a few metal brackets for extra support. The thought of sanding and sealing the timber added to their animation.

Would the bookshelf be tall and slender, reaching up to the ceiling to maximize storage space, or short and wide, doubling as a display for cherished items? They imagined different designs, each one more intriguing than the last, and the possibilities seemed endless.

Colton grabbed his sketchbook and pencil, eager to capture the new idea. Maris sat beside him, watching as he sketched out the design. The conversation flowed easily between them. Their earlier near-miss moment was forgotten in the thrill of creation.

As the sun dipped lower in the sky, casting a golden glow over the beach, Colton and Maris paused to rest. They were seated side by side on the blanket, the soft rustle of the surf grass providing a gentle backdrop to their conversation.

"You know, I've always struggled with facing my problems head-on," Maris admitted, her voice tinged with vulnerability. "It's easier for me to run away and avoid them. But I've been trying to change that."

He turned to look at her, his eyes soft and attentive. "I admire that you're workin' on it," he said sincerely. "It's not easy to confront things that scare us. But you're strong for even tryin'."

"Thanks, Colton. I've noticed how you channel your frustrations into your work, and I really admire that. It's inspiring. The way you handled your divorce with such grace and turned that pain into creativity is incredible. You face criticism from strangers with no issues and use it as fuel to improve. I wish I was more like that."

"It's been my outlet," he admitted. "But it's not always easy. We all have our battles." He paused, his eyes searching the horizon as if seeking answers in the fading light. "Sometimes, it feels like a constant tug-of-war inside me, tryin' to balance my emotions with my ambitions. There are days when the weight of expectations, both my own and others', feels overwhelming. But I've learned that pourin' my energy into my work helps me process it all. It's not a perfect solution, but it keeps me grounded."

"You're dedicated to creating and that's a powerful way to cope. I guess we're both just trying to make it through what life throws at us," Maris replied. Then, with bravery, continued.

"I've been feeling stressed lately," Maris said, taking a deep breath. "Jemma, my little sister, is in a relationship with my ex best friend, Hendrix…, things took a turn in high school and ended pretty badly between us. On top of everything else he felt he had to gossip about me and attempt to ruin my reputation. I thought I had moved on but seeing him with Jemma has been bringing up a lot of unresolved feelings. It's like I'm back in that painful place all over again, and it's hard to see them together when I'm struggling with my own emotions."

Colton silently prayed that the unresolved feelings she spoke of weren't romantic. But, of all people, he understood complicated situations.

"That sounds tough, Maris. It's no wonder you're stressed. You gotta give yourself time to process. I know because it took me everything to get through last year. My workshop has been my sanctuary. After my divorce, I poured myself into my work to find some semblance of control. There were days when I didn't think I could make it through, but creating gave me a way to channel my emotions and keep goin'. It wasn't easy, but it helped me reclaim a part of myself. You just have to try and take one day at a time."

Maris nodded, appreciating his understanding. "Thanks, Colton. I'm doing my best. I guess it's just hard to see Jemma with Hendrix, knowing all that history and feeling like it's happening all over again. But hearing about your experience... it gives me hope. I know it must have been insanely hard for you to go through a divorce. I can see how much strength it takes to come out on the other side and still find a way to create beauty in the world. I'm really inspired by that."

He reached out and gently squeezed her hand. "Thanks. And listen, you're doin' great. If you ever need someone to talk to, I'm here."

Maris looked at him, her eyes filled with gratitude. "That means a lot to me."

He glanced down at his sketchbook, a renewed sense of purpose washing over him. "You know, I think we've got somethin' special with this driftwood bookshelf idea."

The beach, whimsical and mesmerizing, seemed to offer them a fresh start, a chance to create something meaningful together. Eventually, though, the wind picked up and swirled around them, signaling that it was time to go.

Reluctantly, they began to pack up, savoring the last moments of calm. Colton bent down to gather his things, not knowing that a sudden gust had caught the pages of his sketchbook and torn a leaf loose. The paper fluttered free and landed near Maris's feet.

She reached down to pick it up, her mouth falling open in stunned surprise — it was her face, captured in a moment of serene beauty, with a hint of a smile playing on her lips. Maris looked up at Colton, who was still busy packing. She quickly slipped the page back into his drawing pad without a word, but her heart raced with the discovery.

Colton turned around, realizing the wind had disturbed his prized possession. He stepped forward and carefully secured it.

"Sorry about that," he said with a sheepish grin. "The wind has a mind of its own."

Maris smiled, hiding her surprise. "No worries," she replied, her voice calm but her mind racing with thoughts of the drawing.

Heading back to their vehicles, she noticed a lone poppy growing, tangled in the grass beyond the steep staircase. It swayed in the breeze—a splash of gold against the deep blues of the Pacific in the distance.

"Wow," she murmured, crouching to examine it. "You don't see these around here, not this time of year. Poppies are my favorite flower. Growing up, my parents used to take us to the fields every spring—acres of orange as far as you could see."

She glanced at Colton wistfully as he knelt beside her, plucking the delicate bloom with care.

"This might be breaking some botanical rule, but…" He paused, leaning closer as he tucked the poppy behind her ear. His fingers brushed her cheek, his voice low and teasing. "Looks like it was meant for you."

It wasn't just the gesture that caught her off guard—it was the unspoken kindness in it, the way it made her feel unexpectedly seen. She glanced away, pretending to adjust the poppy in her hair, but her heart gave a quiet, steady ache she couldn't quite define.

The air between them was charged with new possibilities as they parted ways. As Colton watched her drive away, the tension of their initial judgements gave way to a shared understanding, and a warm, comforting feeling bloomed inside him. Buoyant optimism replaced the weight of uncertainty. He headed home; his mind filled with images of their time together.

Affinity

Maris sat; her entire room illuminated by the natural light coming through the large window. Crossed legged on the bed, she proofread her freelance article and the interview with Colton for the last time. The four walls, painted a calming pale grey, adorned with framed pictures, were her safe place to review her work before sending it out to be criticized.

Her bed itself, with a bronze, spindled headboard, was neatly made with delicate pink bedding and a blue throw blanket draped over it. Several pillows in various shades of teal and coral added to the inviting escape. She left her brass reading lamp on despite the abundant sunshine, and a full glass of water remained on one nightstand. A little vase with fresh flowers was on the other and, next to it, a small jewelry box.

As she read through the last paragraph, her eyes scanned each line for any errors. The deadline loomed dangerously close, but she felt a sense of pride in the sustainability piece she had crafted. The article had become one of her passion projects. It was important to her that every word conveyed the urgency and importance of the topic.

Taking a deep breath, she saved the document and attached it to an email for submission. She hit send and tipped over onto the comforter, relief and anxiety washing over her. The article was out of her hands now, and she hoped it would resonate with readers.

It turned out better than I imagined, Maris thought to herself. *Colton's interview is really gripping, too.*

She felt drained but also relieved. Feeling the urge to call Colton, in the spirit of celebration, she dug her phone out from under the pile of papers, previous drafts, on her desk. Instead of navigating to Colton's contact though, she absentmindedly scrolled to Jemma's.

Staring down at her sister's name on the screen, Maris paced the room, her mind circling back to the photo she'd discovered of Jemma and Hendrix looking happy and close. A mutual friend had commented on the post, saying, "Love these two together!" accompanied by an emoji with heart-shaped eyes. That tiny punctuation mark confirmed what she'd already feared. Their smiling faces unleashed a torrent of memories, anger, and confusion she had been struggling to suppress. Her stomach twisted at the uneasy thoughts, the image branding itself into her mind.

It was clear that the pair were more than just friends, and Maris knew she couldn't ignore it any longer. Jemma's charm had always drawn people in, and for Maris, that charm now felt like a dagger cloaked in warmth.

Pressing Jemma's name apprehensively, the phone dialed and rang.

While waiting for her sister to come to the phone, she contemplated hanging up. But she decided to wait it out and, after a dozen rings, Jemma answered, sounding bright and carefree.

"Hey, Maris! What's up?"

Maris decided to match Jemma's energy, even if it felt forced, and plastered on a smile. She knew Jemma couldn't see her, but if her tone seemed off, her sister would instantly pick up that something was wrong.

"Hey, Jemma! Not much, just thought I'd give you a call," Maris replied, hoping her voice didn't give her away.

"That's nice of you! How's everything going? You sound happy today. Wait! Did something happen with Mr. Designer Dingleberry?!" Jemma asked, her pitch light and upbeat.

"Oh, stop it!" Maris dismissed. "We brainstormed some ideas together the other day, that's all. He's… surprisingly easier to have a conversation with than I thought."

Jemma laughed. "Well, I'm glad to hear that! Maybe he's not as much of a dingleberry then."

Maris chuckled, feeling a bit more at ease. "Yeah, maybe. Anyway, there's actually something I wanted to talk to you about."

Jemma's tone shifted, becoming more serious. "Sure, what's up?"

Maris took a deep breath, gathering her thoughts. "I saw a photo on Facebook the other night, of you and Hendrix. You both looked really happy. And I noticed a comment about how people love seeing you two as a couple. I just wondered what that was all about…"

There was a pause on the other end of the line. "Yeah, Hendrix and I have been spending a lot of time together. We're… we're trying to see where things go," Jemma said carefully.

Maris felt her pulse increase, her emotions impossible to contain. "So, you're dating him now? After everything that happened between us? You know how much he hurt me!"

Jemma sighed, clearly tense. "Maris, I'm sorry. I didn't plan for this to happen. It just did. We reconnected and one thing led to another. Chatting in the comments of a mutual friend's post turned into something more."

Maris's voice grew sharper. "Did you even think about how this would affect me? How could you be so insensitive?"

"Do you think this is easy for me?!..." Jemma began.

Maris's anger flared. "It's not supposed to be easy! You didn't even consider my feelings, Jemma," she said, cutting her sister off.

Jemma's frustration matched Maris's. "I can't put my life on hold because of your past, Maris. I deserve to be happy too!"

Maris felt tears welling up, her voice breaking. "And I deserve some respect! Hendrix was my best friend! He broke me, and now you're with him. He slandered me and made me miserable. But you're fine with that?! You're a traitor!"

The silence on the line was deafening, both sisters processing the hurtful words exchanged.

Maris realized she'd started something she couldn't stop. She didn't want to have this conversation anymore. She wanted to hide under her covers and disappear.

"People change, Maris. I didn't mean to betray you, but I can't undo what's happening. You need to deal with your issues and let me live my life."

"You know what, Jemma? Do what you want. You usually do."

With that, Maris tapped the red button on her phone to end the call. The unresolved conversation left her feeling hollow and conflicted. She knew they needed to address these issues sooner than later but, right now, it would have to wait.

Needing a friendly face, and with River and Liza still away on their honeymoon in Tuscany, she returned to her contact list and selected Colton's name. She hesitated for a moment before hitting the call button, unsure if he'd be available but hoping for distraction.

The phone rang just once before he picked up, his voice mellow and familiar. A low hum she found reassuring. "Hey, Maris!"

"Hey, Colton," she replied lightly, masking her feelings. "I was wondering if you're free to hang out. I could really use some company right now."

"Of course! I'm just finishin' up some sketches, but I was about to head over to Paradise Palms and check on some things. Wanna come along? I could use a second opinion—it's always better with company." he offered.

She gripped the phone tighter, hesitating for a moment. "That sounds perfect. I'd love to see what you've been working on," she resolved.

"Great! I'll pick you up in about twenty minutes," he said energetically.

Maris freshened up and grabbed her bag. Her heart fluttered with excitement and nerves. As she waited for Colton to arrive, she reflected on how much she appreciated his newfound emotional support. Though, she couldn't deny her feelings for him were developing into something more—a warmth that was both invigorating and frightening. A sense of security that went beyond friendship lurked under his thick skin.

Why was it that he could be absolutely maddening one minute, and agreeable the next? Charming comments contrasted with quick wit. It wasn't fair how well he pulled off a t-shirt and simple denim. The way he fidgeted with his gold chain when he thought no one was looking was definitely *not* something she thought was endearing either. Definitely not.

Okay, maybe the slightest bit.

When Colton pulled up outside her bungalow, Maris hopped into his car with a smile. "Thanks for inviting me along," she said as she buckled her seatbelt.

"I'm glad you're comin'," he replied, with genuine excitement. "I think you'll enjoy seeing the final touches we're puttin' on the spa."

The drive to Paradise Palms was pleasant, filled with light conversation and peaceful quiet. Even with the disagreement with Jemma on her mind, Maris was thankful for the company. The desire she'd had to hide under the duvet slowly dissipated as they approached the wellness center.

Upon arriving, Colton led her inside, greeting the manager. The woman behind the welcome desk, with round metal-framed glasses, was engrossed in paperwork. Maris, however, immediately noticed the harmonious atmosphere, shaped by the striking details of Paradise Palms. Soft lighting, calming scents, and soothing music created an oasis of relaxation. The beauty of the surroundings anchored her wandering thoughts in the present.

"This place is amazing," Maris said, surveying the room in awe.

"Thanks," Colton said with a smile. "C'mon, let me show you around."

He guided her through the various rooms, explaining the purpose and design of each space. In the Zen Den, she admired the elegant lounge chairs and the massive, no-grid windows that allowed sunshine to flood in.

Colton noticed her lingering in the sprawling relaxation area. "I wanted to bring the outside in—it felt important to create a space that feels alive, using natural materials and organic shapes."

"It's beautiful, Colton. You've really outdone yourself." She was struck by the care and detail in every aspect of the exquisite designs. "I can see how much heart you poured into this project. I'm impressed."

A rosy color came to his cheeks. "Hearing that from you makes me feel like I might actually know what I'm doin'. Thanks, Maris."

His bashful smile tugged at her heart, but she quickly shook it off. This was all strictly professional... wasn't it? Before she could sort through her thoughts, the tour came to an end.

As she settled in the cozy corner of the café, the peaceful surroundings and soothing aroma of herbal tea eased the tension she'd been carrying.

"This was just what I needed," she said, as Colton handed her a Borbone mug. "Thanks for bringing me here."

"I'm glad ya came," he said with a smile, "and that you called me."

His words made her chest tighten, though she wasn't sure if it was from relief or something else entirely.

"I'm glad, too. Oh! And I submitted the freelance article today! I'm really proud of how it turned out. You're not a bad interviewee after all," she said with a smile.

Colton looked pleased with the compliment, returning her happy gesture. Then, Maris took a deep breath, deciding to share what had been weighing on her mind.

"I had a pretty intense argument with Jemma this morning, and it's been hard to shake off. Hanging out here has been a very welcome turn of events," she revealed.

Colton's expression turned serious; his concern on full display. "I'm sorry to hear that. Do you want to talk about it?"

She sighed, her shoulders slumping. "I don't know. I guess, I just don't want this to come between us. Jemma means everything to me, but it's hard to see her with someone who caused me so much pain."

Colton listened intently, his expression encouraging her to continue. She inhaled again, gathering her thoughts.

"It's not that Hendrix and I dated or anything," she began. "He was my best friend for years. We did everything together, and I trusted him completely. But the situation changed when he told me he was interested in me, as more than a friend. I let him know that I didn't feel the same way and, later, he started making some terrible decisions. He got involved with the wrong crowd and began doing things that went against all the things he once stood for. The whole time he made me feel like I was the problem. Anyway, we had a big falling out, and we haven't spoken since."

Now that Colton understood the full situation, he nodded, encouraging her to open up.

"I don't have romantic feelings for him. It's more about the betrayal and losing someone who was like a brother to me. And now, seeing Jemma with him... it just brings all those emotions back," Maris said, her voice heavy with defeat.

Colton placed his hand gently over hers. The warmth of his touch seemed to melt away a fraction of the pain she carried. And, without thinking, she intertwined her fingers with his, drawing relief from their connection. The contact felt natural, like a lifeline grounding her in the present moment. She looked up at Colton, his eyes reflecting genuine compassion.

This is definitely not strictly professional, Maris thought frantically. *But, he's the one who started this… Am I supposed to pull away?*

She decided against moving, uncertain yet unwilling to break the moment, and tried her voice once more.

"It's not just about Hendrix. It's also about my own insecurities—feeling like I'm not enough, like I'll always be second best," she said, but her words faded. Her fingers tightened slightly around his as her mind raced.

As Maris's words hung in the air, Colton's jaw tightened. He leaned forward slightly, his voice low but laced with anger.

"Darlin', who made you feel like you aren't worth the trouble? Whoever it was must have been a real piece of work."

Maris blinked, surprised by the edge in his tone. Her gaze dropped to the floor, words catching in her throat before she murmured, "It doesn't matter now. It was a long time ago."

"That's a bunch o' hooey and you know it," Colton said firmly. "Someone made you feel like you weren't enough, like you didn't deserve love. That's not okay, Mar. You've got to know that's not true."

She stared at him and bit her lip, as the intensity in his gaze pinned her in place. A knot tightened in her chest, the truth in his words almost too much to bear.

"In college, I was dumped for another girl by someone I thought I had a future with. It really shattered my confidence and made me doubt my worth. Sure, he was a scumbag for talking to other girls when he was with me. But I swore I could change him. Tricked myself into thinking we could be happy, and that he'd stop going out and flirting at bars every night. I was wrong. Now, I'm afraid of not being good enough, whether it's in my writing or in my relationships. It's hard to let go of that feeling, no matter how much time passes."

Colton's face was carved in stone. His hand clasped hers with unyielding strength. "Then I'll remind you every day if I have to. Maris, you are more than enough. Anyone who made you feel otherwise was a fool. There are too many mediocre things in life. Love is meant to be extraordinary. If it doesn't burn like wildfire, sweetheart, it's a waste of your time."

As they continued to sip their tea and held tightly to one another, he shared more about himself as well. He opened up about the struggles that had shaped him—the moments that had hardened him, but also those that had taught him to go after what he wanted.

"You know, I've been workin' on this project called BioHaven. It's my dream to create sustainable, nature-inspired places for people to fill with memories."

Maris's eyes lit up with interest. "That sounds amazing. Tell me more about it."

Colton smiled, feeling encouraged by her enthusiasm. "It's been a long journey, and there have been a lot of challenges along the way. But I'm kinda obsessed about it because I believe in the power of design to improve people's well-being. It's not just about the furniture but about creatin' spaces that feel like home. I was goin' to run the design side of the business and contribute to building projects and someone else would worry about the finances and logistics."

Maris listened, admiring his vision. Eagerly she waited for him to go on.

"My divorce, ironically enough, is what made me realize how important it is to build peaceful places that bring people together."

Colton, savoring the bond they were forming, reached out and gently ran his thumb over her freckled cheek.

"Although," he continued, "meetin' you has shown me there's more to life than just work."

"You're doing something truly special, Colton," Maris replied, her admiration for him taking root and flourishing. A wistful expression flashed across her face.

Colton's phone suddenly rang, interrupting their blissful cocoon. He glanced at the screen and saw River's name.

"Sorry, I need to take this," Colton said, giving Maris an apologetic look before answering the call. "Hey, River. How's the honeymoon?"

Concern filled River's voice, a stark contrast to his honeymoon's carefree atmosphere. "Hey, Colton. I'm sorry to bother you, but I've been thinkin' a lot, and I wanted to talk to you."

Colton's brow furrowed. "Okay…"

"I know you were upset about BioHaven and all the plans we made, and I want to make things right before you go home," River said, his tone sincere. "I have an extra key to my apartment. Why don't you take it and stay there until we get back? It'll give you a place to sort things out about the business. Unless you have to get back to Charleston right away."

Colton glanced at Maris, who was watching him with curiosity and concern. "Are you sure, River? I don't want to intrude. I've been thinkin' quite a bit too and I know you have a lot on your plate."

"It's no trouble at all," River insisted. "Plus, I've been tryin' to come up with a way to stay involved. If that's still alright with you?"

Colton took a moment to process River's offer, feeling a mix of relief and gratitude. "Of course, River. I'd love to work somethin' out."

River's tone softened. "I'm glad to hear that. You're more than just a business partner to me, Colton. You're family. I want to make sure we're on the same page. For now, you can pick up the key from the office in my building. I'll let them know you're comin'."

"Thanks, brother. We can discuss everything more when you get back. Have an awesome time."

Colton put his phone down and sighed, feeling a weight lift off his shoulders. He looked at Maris, who was still holding his hand.

"Is everything okay?" she asked.

"Yeah," Colton said with a small smile. "Or, at least, it will be. River just offered me his apartment to stay in until they get back. I didn't tell you I had my own tug of war goin' on. My partner in BioHaven was supposed to be River. We were set on playin' to both our strengths. But now that he and Liza are movin' to Morro Bay, we have some things to figure out."

Maris squeezed his hand.

"Thanks for bein' here, Maris. You've helped more than you know."

"Well, then, you wouldn't mind doing me a favor?" she inquired playfully.

Colton looked at her as if she'd asked a trick question. "What do you need?" he replied, overly cautious.

Maris hesitated for a moment, then trusted him. "I've been working on finishing a novel manuscript. It's always been my dream to become a bona fide author, but I could use some feedback from someone who's not afraid to give me some constructive criticism," she teased. "Since you're staying, would you mind being my first beta reader, and giving me your thoughts? I mean, it's not a thriller or anything, but a pair of fresh eyes on it couldn't hurt."

"I'm happy to help," he answered.

She smiled, grateful for this affinity. Colton took a deep breath, his eyes meeting hers with sincerity. He reached out and affectionately tucked a loose strand of hair behind her ear.

"Maris," he began. "I must admit, I'm sorry we started out on the wrong foot. Now that I'm startin' to really see you, I realize how stupid I was to attack you that first day. The more I've gotten to experience, the last few days, your passion and determination… It makes me feel like I might be able to move past all the hurt."

Maris looked at Colton, impatiently waiting to hear his next words.

"I've been hesitant to open my heart again. To take any real risks. For a long time, I thought I had it all figured out. But when my ex left, it shattered my confidence and made me question everything I believed in. I was confused and hurt, and didn't know if I could ever trust someone like that again. As you know, I threw myself into my work, tryin' to fill the void and rebuild some kind of normalcy. But, in doing that, I forgot what genuine connection was like. I'm a friendly enough guy, I guess. But, deep down, I've been keepin' people at arm's length, afraid to let anyone get too close."

He paused, looking into Maris's baby blue eyes. They were clear as a summer sky. "These last few days, though, spendin' time with you, I've felt somethin' shift inside me. I feel like every moment with you is bringin' back a part of me I thought was gone forever."

Maris had a lump in her throat, moved by his honesty. "You've brought a lot of perspective into my life too, in just this short time," she said. "Somehow, even when I was at odds with you, you made it easy for me to be honest and open. That's not something most people do. And I'm sorry that you got hurt last year. I can't imagine what that must have been like for you."

Colton reached out and cupped her cheek. His palm was warm against her skin. "I guess we both have our scars," he said.

Still not professional. Still not mad about it, her brain signaled.

After a quiet moment that seemed to stretch forever, they stood up to leave, hand in hand. Maris felt that, while the days ahead held their uncertainties, the two of them had found strength in each other, and she dared to long for the bond between them to grow.

Convergence

It had been a couple of busy days since she had last seen Colton. He was so wrapped up in sharing designs with Eve and landing a new client, not to mention his plans for BioHaven. And Maris, though longing to spend time with him, had used the duration apart to do research on getting her manuscript published. She had worked diligently to make sure every "i" was dotted and every "t" was crossed. Querying literary agents was going to be a lot of work and effort. Maris hoped she was able to rise to the challenge.

Perched on a stool at Driftwood Shelves, her feet dangled as she waited. Colton had said he would rendezvous with her there after his meeting at Laguna Luxe Studios. It was a rare rainy day, and light showers hit the glass of the bookstore's display window, creating an intimate mood. The rain engulfed the coast in a dreamlike mist, blurring the lines between reality and fantasy. The soft patter of raindrops provided a soothing soundtrack as she lingered, wrapped in the comforting embrace of the shop's warm, wooden interior.

Chrissy, in jeans, a cream sweater, and suspenders, was busy stocking shelves with new arrivals and creating eye-catching table presentations. As she worked, she and Maris traded book recommendations and chatted about the store's upcoming events.

"I always find the best reads here," Maris declared, thumbing through a historical fiction novel.

"We do everything we can to stock the gems!" Chrissy replied, standing on her tiptoes to reach the top shelf. "Hey, you wouldn't want to help me plan a book swap event, would you?"

She looked up from the paperback, captivated. "A book swap event? That sounds fun! What do you have in mind?"

Chrissy smiled, pleased with Maris's enthusiasm. "Well, I was thinking we could invite people to bring in books they've read and loved and then exchange them for something new-to-them. It would be a great way to build a sense of community and introduce everyone to different genres and authors. I've noticed a lot of bookstores doing that these days."

Maris nodded, already envisioning the possibilities. "I love that idea! We could set up tables with various categories, have some snacks and drinks, a small reading nook for people to start their new books immediately."

Chrissy's eyes danced with joy. "Exactly! And we could have some local authors come in for signings and readings. It would be a great way to support the literary community and make it even more special."

Maris's excitement grew. "Count me in! I'd love to help. When were you thinking of having it?"

Chrissy considered for a moment. "How about in a few weeks? That should give us enough time to get the word out and finalize all the arrangements."

"Perfect," Maris agreed. "Let's start planning. I'll do whatever you need."

The exuberance was contagious as they thought up more ideas for the book swap. They discussed potential themes, decorations, and ways to make the event engaging for all attendees.

As they continued to plan, the bell above the door jingled, signaling another customer. Maris glanced up and saw Colton walking in, bringing a smile to her face. He shook the dampness from his hair and hung up his jacket. His moisture-wicking shirt clung to his brawny biceps.

She couldn't pull her eyes away. His dark curls, wet from the rain, fell slightly into his warm brown eyes. His strong jawline and stubble contributed to his rugged charm. He wore well-fitted jeans that accentuated his build and a pair of worn-in work boots that underscored his down-to-earth charm.

Something about the way he strode in, casual yet commanding, sent a current through her.

She greeted him cheerfully. "Perfect timing!" she called.

Colton crossed the room and embraced her. "Hey," he began, "I'll be with you in a minute. I just need to make a quick call."

Chrissy noticed the dreamy expression on Maris's face. Colton excused himself, and Chrissy came closer to Maris with a more serious demeanor than before.

"You two seem to be getting along well," she said, cupping her hand around her mouth, for fear Colton might overhear.

Maris blushed; happiness and shyness combined within her. "He's just been there for me lately. Especially since Liza isn't around. It's actually been pretty great."

Chrissy nodded approvingly. "It's wonderful to see. You deserve some happiness. And hey, if you ever want to talk—or just need someone to remind you how amazing you are—I'm here for you."

Advice on how to make a man stay in my life… for keeps. Do people like me ever get that fortunate? Maybe this is all too good to be true, she scolded herself.

Colton returned and his expression was noticeably lighter after his call. He caught Maris's eye and gave her a reassuring smile, as if silently conveying that everything was okay.

Maris tilted her head slightly, and her lips curled. "So, did you get summoned about a new project that needs your magic touch?"

Colton grinned. "You could say that. Eve found a client for me, so I called their office to set up a virtual meetin'. It's a tech startup in Boulder, Colorado. I'll admit, I'm excited about the prospect."

"A tech startup?" Maris repeated, confused. "What does a computer company want *you* to do for them?"

Colton laughed. "They're designing software to help people live greener lives —trackin' carbon footprints, reducing energy use, stuff like that. And they want me to create office pieces that embody those principles. It's right up my alley."

Maris smirked. "Ah, the life of a hero carpenter. Must be exhausting, being in such high demand."

Colton laughed, his damp curls bouncing. "Well, it's tough, but someone's got to do it. Besides, I always make time for the important things."

Just as she was about to respond, the door swung open once more, drawing her attention. She glanced up and saw Jemma and Hendrix walking into the store, arm in arm. Jemma looked radiant in a trendy outfit. Her hair was perfectly styled and her makeup, as always, was flawless. Hendrix looked even more handsome than he did in the Facebook picture Maris had seen. His laid-back demeanor was clear in his relaxed posture and amiable smile.

Jemma's laughter echoed as she stepped inside, catching the attention of everyone in the store. Hendrix appeared exceedingly calm, while Maris felt an immediate tenseness wash over her. She straightened up, no longer focused on Colton.

He noticed the change in Maris's behavior and followed her gaze as it became more guarded.

"Is everything okay?" he whispered.

"Yeah, just...unexpected company," she said, though she sounded strained.

Colton put a hand on her shoulder, offering silent support as he glanced between Maris and the surprise guests.

Jemma spotted Maris and Colton and approached them. On her face was a mix of determination and defiance. "Maris," she greeted, her tone cool. "Fancy seeing you here."

Maris managed a polite nod. "Jemma. Hendrix."

Hendrix gave a nod in return. "Maris."

There was an awkward silence before Jemma spoke again, her eyes flicking to Colton. "Who's this?"

Colton extended his hand, his smile polite but reserved. "Colton. Nice to meet you."

"Nice to meet you," Jemma replied curtly, her attention shifting back to Maris. "We were looking for you, actually. When you weren't at home, we decided to check out the town. Didn't expect to find you here."

Maris forced a smile, the tightness in her chest refusing to ease. "Small world, I guess. And why were you at my house?"

Jemma crossed her arms, unwavering. "We wanted to talk. I thought we could clear the air, maybe try to understand each other better. Thought in person might be better so you couldn't hang up on me again."

Maris's smile tightened. Her voice was edged with frustration. "I believe we've covered everything, Jemma. But if you really wanted to talk, you could have let me know before you just showed up.”

Hendrix remained silent and steady, in an unspoken contrast to the tension between the two women. Colton stood with devotion beside Maris, offering support.

Jemma sighed, her eyes flicking to Hendrix before returning to Maris. “Look, I know you don’t approve, but this is important to me. We can keep butting heads, or we can try to move forward.”

Maris, now trembling, felt Colton’s arm wrap around her back and his warm hand slip onto her waist. He drew her to his side protectively.

“Maybe a surprise run-in isn’t the *best* time to discuss this. It might be better if you both take some time to think,” Colton started, but Jemma cut him off.

“And who do you think you are?” she said, her voice snarky.

Colton remained calm, but his grip on Maris tightened. “I’m just someone who cares about Maris and wants to make sure she’s okay,” he said, his eyes meeting Jemma’s with unfaltering collectedness.

Jemma's face hardened. "This is between me and Maris. You don't get to interfere."

The tension tightened around Maris like a vise. She took a deep breath, trying to gather her thoughts. "Colton's right. This isn't the place to hash things out. If you really want to talk, we can set up a time and place that makes sense for both of us."

Hendrix finally spoke but his voice was gentle. "Yeah, taking a step back and thinking things through might be good. There's no point in escalating this here," echoing the sentiment.

Jemma glanced at Hendrix, then back at Maris. "Fine. Let's talk later. But this conversation is far from over."

Maris nodded, having no other choice than to agree. With that, Jemma pivoted and walked away, Hendrix following closely behind. The bell above the door jingled as they exited the bookstore, the tension in the air beginning to dissipate. Maris resembled a deflated balloon.

"You okay?" Colton asked.

"Yeah," Maris managed, lacking conviction.

Colton guided her to a nearby chair, his touch both secure and soothing. "Take a minute," he said softly.

As she sat down, contemplating the interaction with Jemma, Chrissy noticed and walked over. She approached with worry in her eyes.

"Everything okay?" Chrissy asked, kneeling beside her.

Maris sighed, burdened by her emotions. "Not really. Jemma and I… we're in a rough spot. She's seeing someone who hurt me deeply in the past, and she just won't respect my feelings about it. I feel so betrayed."

Chrissy placed a comforting hand on Maris's shoulder, her expression empathetic. "That sounds tough," she admitted. "But it's important to stay true to yourself. Focus on your own happiness. You can't let others dictate your emotions, and you can't control the choices other people make. Jemma's decisions are her own, but you have the power to choose how you respond and what you prioritize in your life."

Maris nodded, absorbing Chrissy's words. "You're right. It's just hard to see past the hurt sometimes. I'm not sure time heals all wounds."

Chrissy squeezed her shoulder. "I know it is. But I've got at least ten years on Colton here and even more on you, young lady. I've seen my fair share of difficulties, but here I am. I own a bookstore I love, live in a town that's incredibly beautiful, and I know I'm worth more than getting my panties in a twist over someone else's problems. Don't lose sight of what makes you happy and what you deserve."

As the comforting climate of the store enveloped them, Maris experienced peace returning. With Chrissy's sage advice and Colton's staunch support, she saw a glimmer of hope amidst the turmoil.

"Thank you both," she said, with newfound confidence in her voice. "I needed that more than I realized."

"That's what friends are for, Maris. Tough love. Remember, you've got people that care about you," Chrissy soothed, winking at Colton. "Stay in your energy. Let people meet you there."

Maris, surrounded by their commiseration, looked out the window as they spoke and realized the rain outside had eased, hinting at clearer skies ahead. The three of them sat together, Maris desiring to turn the page and start a new chapter.

Beach Evening Primrose

It took her exactly fifty-eight minutes to reach her parents' house from Laguna Beach. Maris had gotten up early and felt out of place in her own home. The silence was deafening, and today she was uncomfortable relying on Colton or Chrissy. Normally, she would've called Liza and asked her for a girls' luncheon or movie night, but she and River were halfway across the world, meaning no one to share mimosas or a pint of Ben and Jerry's with.

So, Maris had resolved, she would drive to her parents', make them a big breakfast and cry on their shoulders. The talk she'd had with Chrissy and Colton at the bookstore, following Jemma and Hendrix's departure, had been reassuring enough to get her a good night's sleep. However, disquieting thoughts had returned since her waking, and the sudden ache to see her mom and dad's faces was irrefutable.

She had sent Colton a brief text before she left:

Spending the day at my parents'. All is well.

Then, despite the early hour, sent a text to her mom.

Thought I'd come by and spend the day. Headed your way!

Thankfully, traffic on I-5 wasn't congested, and as she sped along, she felt homesick. The thought of Jemma staying with their parents—and the uncertainty of whether she'd be the one to answer the door when she got to Bressi Ranch—filled her with dread.

The Bressi Ranch community was family-friendly, just over six miles from North Ponto Beach, and surrounded by parks and natural beauty. Her family moved into their new construction home in 2003, when she was only seven years old. Alex was nine and Jemma was two. Pedestrian walking paths and many amenities filled the community. Maris's parents had fallen in love with it right away.

Passing the high school, she continued her route, anticipating her parents' reaction to her arrival. Sure, they would be happy to see her, but would they wonder why she was stopping by?

She drove around the town square, luscious rose gardens, and community green space, making her way to the street she knew so well. Pulling into the driveway, she turned off the engine and took a moment to compose herself. The house looked just as she remembered it— steadfast and inviting, with the familiar scent of sweet osmanthus wafting through the air.

Taking a deep breath, she left her car and approached the front entrance, anxiety coursing through her. She knocked and waited, her heart pounding in her chest. Moments later, the door opened, and her mom's shocked face appeared, framed by the familiar glow of the hallway light.

"Maris! What a lovely surprise," her mom exclaimed, pulling her into a warm embrace.

"Hi, Mom," Maris said quietly. "I hope it's okay I came by. I sent a text."

"Of course, it's okay!" her mom reassured, ushering her inside. "I didn't see the text but, this is fantastic! Your dad's in the living room. He'll be so happy to see you."

As Maris stepped into the house, the sights and sounds of her childhood home greeted her. Her dad looked up from his newspaper and his face lit up with a smile.

"There's my girl! What brings you here so early?" he asked, getting up to give her a hug.

She embraced him tightly, feeling the familiar strength in his arms. "I just needed to see you both," she admitted. "I've been a bit overwhelmed."

Her parents exchanged a concerned look, but didn't press her for details.

"Let's get some coffee and talk," her mom suggested, leading her to the kitchen.

As she helped her mother with breakfast preparations, she started to be more at ease. Cherished memories and a sense of normalcy returned from the simple act of cooking together.

"So, what's been on your mind, honey?" her mom asked, handing her a bowl of eggs to beat.

Maris sighed, her focus on the steady rhythm of the whisk. "It's just... Jemma and Hendrix. They showed up at the bookstore yesterday, and it was tense, to say the least."

Her dad looked up from his coffee, a look of concern consuming his face. "Hendrix? I thought you two weren't on speaking terms."

Setting down the whisk with a clatter, Maris nodded. "We're not. That's part of the problem. She's seeing him despite everything he did to me, and she just doesn't care how I feel about it."

Her mom placed a reassuring hand on her shoulder. "I know it's hard, sweetie. You can't control Jemma's choices. You can only control your reaction to them", she said matter-of-factly.

"That's exactly what my friend, Chrissy, said," Maris recalled.

Her dad nodded approvingly. "It's good to have friends who offer solid advice."

Maris smiled faintly. "There's been someone else there for me lately too," she mentioned. "His name is Colton Vance, a friend of River and Liza's from South Carolina. He's a carpenter, and I actually ended up interviewing him for my last article. He was there when everything happened with Jemma at the bookstore."

Her mom's eyes lit up with curiosity, and a knowing smile spread across her face. "Colton? Tell us more about him."

"Honestly, we *really* had trouble getting along when I met him. He seemed conceited and egotistical. But the more I was around him, I realized that he's kinder and more thoughtful than I expected. I guess I didn't give him a chance at first."

Her dad let out a low chuckle, shaking his head in amusement. "Sounds like a good man—and a stubborn woman," he added with a teasing grin.

As they continued to talk, Maris felt the weight on her shoulders lift even more. The supportive words from her parents and the opportunity to share her thoughts provided a sense of relief and clarity.

After breakfast, she spent some time with her dad, checking in on his health and expressing her concerns. He reassured her, placing a hand on her shoulder, emphasizing that he understood and appreciated her care. The medical team had determined that his breathlessness was likely due to overexertion, rather than a more serious issue. He was sixty-one, he reminded her. Though Maris still saw glimpses of her dad's youth in his actions, she couldn't argue with the doctors' advice and felt relieved that his breathlessness had a relatively simple explanation.

"Just promise me you'll take it easy, Dad," she said, her voice tinged with worry.

"I promise, sweetheart," he replied with a gentle smile. "And don't you worry about me so much. You've got your own life to live."

Her mom joined them, wrapping an arm around Maris. "Your dad's right. We're here for you, no matter what. Just remember to take care of yourself, too. You know, you've always reminded me of the beach evening primrose that grows around here, Mar.

It thrives in harsh conditions. It's resilient, flourishing and bringing beauty into the world. Even in the driest sand, it blooms, bright and unyielding, just like you. You have so much to offer, sweetheart. Don't let the hard times hold you back."

"I'm so grateful for you both," Maris said softly, her voice trembling with emotion. "I honestly don't know what I'd do without you."

When she left, Maris felt more grounded and stable. And as she drove back home, the comforting expressions of her parents, Colton, and Chrissy resonated within her. She would have to concentrate on cultivating her own joy. Happiness, she decided, didn't have to be elusive. She could capture it, like a butterfly in a net, and admire its beauty for the time she possessed it.

Shaping Tomorrow

Colton's rough, calloused hand held the jagged steel key to River's apartment. He rested his forehead against the laminated wood door and sucked in a lungful of air before loudly releasing it. Closing his eyes, he repeated the action. Slowly this time, more intentional. His thoughts formed a tangled mess, and he needed to steady himself before stepping inside. Recent events left him overwhelmed, but also protective of Maris. He wanted to shield her from her pain.

After a moment, he turned the key and stepped into the apartment. Unlike Colton's loft, the peak of single life, River's place appeared magazine-ready. The suite was fit for a king. It boasted floor-to-ceiling windows with a view of the dunes and ocean, and low, beige tweed couches with colorful throw pillows. It was clear Liza had decorated for him.

A large bird of paradise stood in the corner of the spacious, main living area and lanterns guarded either side of the tall stone fireplace. An enormous flat screen tv was mounted above the mantle and sheer drapes were arranged neatly, casting a soft, ethereal glow across the room. Colton was obliged to admit it was a pretty great place to crash.

He sat his bag down, plopped down on one of the firm couches, and glanced around. His mind wandered back to the intimate moment he had shared with Maris at the café, wishing she'd appear in the doorway. The way her eyes softened at his touch, the connection that sparked between them—it was all significant. The start of something meaningful.

She had sent a brief text earlier that she was spending the day at her parents' house. Colton hoped she was alright, but the memory of the clash at the bookstore refused to leave him. Seeing Maris and Jemma face off had stirred something else in him—a growing sense that he was in over his head.

He leaned back against the cushions and put his hands over his face.

"What have I gotten myself into?" he muttered under his breath. Then, realizing he'd forgotten to text Maris a response, he pulled out his phone and typed a message:

Take as long as necessary. Just let me know if you need anything.

River's meticulously decorated apartment, however stiff it might've seemed, became more appealing to him each minute. He kicked off his shoes and made himself comfortable. The curated room started to seem less like a museum and became more of a welcoming retreat. He found the sound of the waves crashing against the shore outside his window soothing, and let it wash over him. His shoulders gradually relaxed, yet his mind remained restless.

He thought of the way Maris looked in the flickering firelight the evening he first saw her and of the heat in their exchange later that night. Now, a different heat simmered beneath the surface, a constant presence that ignited whenever she was near, stirring feelings he couldn't ignore.

It had been ages since he was so blinded by his feelings for someone else. Despite the surrounding chaos, he felt a powerful pull toward Maris. Maybe she was unsure of her future and easily wounded, but the way she wore her heart on her sleeve was also something he liked about her. He had been unable to do the same until recently. She had unlocked something inside of him.

But with those feelings came a flood of memories he'd tried to bury. Images of his ex-wife, Tori, rushed back to him. They had married young, filled with dreams and idealistic notions of what the future would be like. But life hadn't handed Tori what she was hoping for. She'd said yes to Colton with the idea that he would be rich by the time her five-year plan was up, they'd have two kids, and he could make her every whim into a reality.

When his love wasn't enough and her patience ran out, so did she.

He remembered the day Tori left like it was yesterday. He could still see the tears in her eyes as she packed her bags and hear the way her voice quivered. She had apologized, still trying to convince him it was all for the best. Feeling forsaken had cut deep, leaving scars that hadn't fully healed and the fear of a repeat experience had always held him back.

He had tried to move on, to bury his suffering and focus on his work. The physical labor of carpentry had been a refuge, a way to drown out the noise of the trauma. But now, with Maris, those old wounds were being reopened. He was letting himself feel again but it was a mix of pleasure and pain. She made him want to take a risk, while a part of him wanted to get on the next plane back to Charleston.

The city loomed around him like a shadow of his past mistakes, but within its streets lay the comfort of the familiar. It was a place he could disappear into, escaping the tangled web of his current emotions. But running away wasn't an option. Not this time. He couldn't just walk away from Maris the way Tori had left him. She deserved better, and he wanted to be the person who stood by her, even when things got tough. As he let this determination sink in, Colton's thoughts drifted back to a moment that had marked a turning point in his relationship with Tori. The shadows of it hung around like a dark stranger, ever-present and impossible to ignore.

It had been a summer evening, the type where the air held a gentle warmth and the sky stayed blue until 10 PM. Colton, covered in sawdust and sweat from a long day of work, arrived home only to find Tori sitting on the porch steps, her face fixed in an unreadable expression.

"Colton, we need to talk," she had said. Those five words had ended his world.

He attempted to argue, but she had already made up her mind and was slipping through his fingers. It was like trying to hold on to a fistful of water. The image of her leaving, the box of her belongings tucked into the trunk, burned itself into his memory.

He remembered how he had stood there, feeling helpless and numb, watching as the woman he had once loved drove away. Her parting words, "We want different things," had echoed in his mind for months afterward. Everything they had built together had crumbled, leaving him with nothing but the bitter taste of loss.

Reaching back from where he sat to pull one drape closed, he decided to tackle things with Maris step by step. He vowed to support her, regardless of how intense things seemed. While he couldn't manage the chaos surrounding them, he could remain constant and dependable. Maris was worth fighting for.

Deciding he needed a distraction, he got up and wandered into the kitchen. He rummaged through the cabinets, finding nothing but a few rice cakes and an almost empty jar of peanut butter. Clearly, River hadn't been expecting company. He leaned against the cold countertop, taking a reluctant nibble of a rice cake.

Suddenly, he stood up straight and looked at his watch. Only 11:12 AM. There was still a lot of the day left, and Colton knew what he needed to do. He had to act. Making note of the lack of supplies he had and the space he would need to execute his plan; he dialed up Eve.

As the phone rang, he grabbed his keys and headed out the door. Getting started right away was his only option, and the joy he hoped to bring to Maris with his creation spurred him on.

"Eve? It's Colton," he said when she answered. "Could you do me a favor? Can I use that shared makerspace today? I've got a project in mind, and I need the room and tools to get started."

With an affirmative answer on the other end of the line, he drove to Pebble's Nook. It was a bright, open air, natural light studio with high beam ceilings and a large brick courtyard.

Although the setting was a bit fancy for a carpenter, he was thankful for the privacy.

He parked his car and quickly unloaded the materials he'd picked up during a brief pit stop. He was relieved he hadn't been pulled over on his way, especially since his hatchback was only secured with a bungee cord. Now, he could hardly contain his excitement. The studio, filled with sunlight and scattered tools, had been designed for artists and makers of all kinds. Today, it would be the birthplace of something special.

Colton set up his workspace, laying out the driftwood pieces he had collected and arranging his tools within easy reach. As he surveyed the array of materials before him, he realized this project was more than just a distraction—it was a labor of love.

Love, Colton mused, was a strange and fragile thing. To hand your heart to someone—trusting them to hold it gently, knowing they might break it—felt like the ultimate gamble.

He picked up a piece of wood, its surface smooth from years of being shaped by the ocean. He ran his fingers along its contours, imagining the potential it held. With steady precision, he began sanding and shaping the wood, each stroke transforming it closer to his vision. Time blurred as Colton lost himself in the rhythm of his work, the repetitive movements becoming almost meditative.

Hours passed and the sun set. The sound of sandpaper against wood faded, and the distant cry of seagulls called him to leave his work behind for another day. As he packed up, the shapes of his project began to take form, subtle but promising. Though the finite details of his creation remained a mystery even to him, he felt the spark of something extraordinary beginning to emerge, as if the piece itself was still deciding what it wanted to become.

The project was far from complete, but the strides he had made filled him with a sense of accomplishment. He knew that each accurate measurement, each piece of driftwood he carefully soaked in a concoction of oxalic acid and hot water, was bringing him closer to creating something deeply meaningful for Maris.

As he locked up the studio, a quiet determination settled within him. This wasn't just about completing a project; it was about building something enduring—for her, for them. Would they take the leap and explore the depths of their connection, or would they remain in this delicate balance?

Ebb and Embrace

Malachi's Beach Brew was abuzz with chatter, as Maris and Colton sat sequestered at a table for two in the far-right corner. After taking the previous day to deal with her lingering dismay, Colton's company was bewitching. As the sounds of grinding espresso beans and the smell of sweet coffee cake wafted between them, Maris felt like she was in a movie. The Lumineers, circa 2016, rained down from the overhead speakers while Colton tenderly traced circles on her soft hand with his thumb. Contentment settled over her like a warm blanket.

Colton's touch made the cinematic moment more intense as she blushed, a delightful shiver running through her.

"This place always feels like a second home," she told Colton, brushing the foam from her cappuccino off her lips.

"I can see why," he replied, adding, "It's got a great vibe… just like you."

Maris had reached a point where she accepted cheesy compliments like this, amused by the fact that he was showing her more adoration than any other guy ever had. She took another sip of her coffee, savoring the rich flavor.

Colton's eyes never left hers, and she felt a sense of security and affection that was new and exhilarating. She smiled at the thought, her heart swelling with emotion. She couldn't help but think about their first meeting. Who would've imagined that it would lead to this genuine closeness?

Is this what it feels like to belong to someone? To trust them with your heart and feel safe in their presence? she wondered.

As he emptied the contents of his warm mug, he bent over the tabletop. Hunching forward, he signaled for Maris to come closer. As if drawn by an invisible thread, she too leaned in.

"I have a surprise for you," he whispered. A hint of mischief was in his voice.

Maris's eyes widened with curiosity. "A surprise? What is it?"

Colton grinned, his eyes twinkling with orneriness. "You'll have to wait and see. But I promise, it's somethin' special. Patience is key," he informed, wagging his finger at her.

Maris enjoyed the tease and shook her head innocently in return. He knew by now that patience wasn't her strong suit. Procrastination, in contrast, was her art form. She would have to find a distraction to busy herself and forget about this gift until Colton wanted to reveal it to her. Maybe Chrissy's book swap would be enough to keep her occupied.

Malachi, fond of Maris, noticed their endearing moment and walked over to them. Placing a hand on Maris's arm, he gave a hearty hello. With his free hand, he shook Colton's and asked if there was anything he could get them. Declining politely and fawning over how amazing everything was, she thanked him.

"I couldn't help but notice you two over here," Malachi said. "Of course, Maris is one of my all-time favorite customers, but it makes me doubly as happy to have her in here when she's smiling from ear to ear because of more than just how I make her coffee."

She saw Colton's expression shift from wary to elated as he absorbed Malachi's words.

"Reminds me of myself and my beautiful bride back in the day. You've got a good one here, man. Don't let her get away," he added.

"Thanks, I won't," Colton replied confidently.

Moved by his sincerity, she tightened her grip on his hand. Kindness and warmth radiated from his honey-colored eyes. There was a commanding strength to his presence that made her feel safe. For the first time, she trusted the loyalty Liza had so often described.

Malachi bid them farewell and headed to another table where an acquaintance was waving. As Maris and Colton resumed their conversation, she couldn't help but feel that, for the first time, she had finally found someone who truly saw her, flaws and all. Yet, despite her imperfections, Colton still made her feel treasured and completely at home. Regardless of knowing each other for only a couple of weeks, she felt good about their future as a couple.

The sight of them sitting there together was far from how she had imagined passing the time while waiting for her next freelance job. But when Colton was around, it was easy—almost effortless—to set aside her worries about money and bills, even if just for a while. Her thoughts had only just started to drift back to finances when Colton's voice pulled her from the haze.

"So, Maris," he began, his tone gentle yet inquisitive. "How's your manuscript comin' along? You haven't mentioned it lately."

She looked up, embarrassment flashing across her face. "It's progressing...slowly," she admitted. "I've been so caught up with everything else that I haven't had much time to focus on it." There was uncertainty in her eyes.

Propping his elbow on the table and resting his cheek on a fisted hand, he considered her excuse.

"I get it. I just think maybe you're goin' about this the wrong way. Have you ever thought about self-publishing? I mean, I'm no writer, but it seems like the approach to take if you want to get your content out there.

"Self-publishing?" Maris repeated, unsure she'd heard him correctly. "I always dreamed of getting a contract with a big publishing house. It's what I've been working towards for so long."

"I know," said Colton. "And that dream is absolutely valid. But self-publishing could be a means of getting your work out there faster and on your own terms. Plus, you'd have complete creative control over your book." He offered a supportive nudge.

Maris cringed, considering his words. "I guess I've always been cautious of the idea. It seems so daunting, and I wouldn't even know where to start. Especially trying to do all the marketing and promoting by myself."

"Well, you're incredibly creative. Plus, you're not alone. There are so many resources and communities out there for supporting that kind of journey. My search engine history could show you," he joked.

"You really think I can do it?" she asked, unsure.

"I know you can," Colton replied. "But we are gonna need to pick this back up later, Mar," he continued, checking the time on his phone. "I'm goin' to be late for that client meetin' I told you about the other day."

He stood up and kissed her on the forehead, as if he'd been doing it forever. Maris felt a flutter in her chest. His confidence in her abilities gave her a renewed sense of self-worth. She watched him gather his things, a warm smile on her face.

"I'll see you later," Colton said, giving her one last squeeze before heading out the door.

Her mind buzzing with thoughts of self-publishing, she leaned back in her chair. She had always envisioned her book on the shelves of a major bookstore, but perhaps it was time to reconsider her approach. The idea of having complete creative control was enticing.

Finishing her cappuccino and walking out of Malachi's Beach Brew, Maris decided it was too nice of a day to spend it in the library doing research and making pros and cons lists about the avenues of publishing the manuscript she hadn't even finished writing yet. She was nearing the final chapter but wasn't sure what the ending would be. The two fateful lovers in her book had gone through their share of trials and she wanted to make certain the resolution felt earned.

Basking in the warm sunlight and with an entire day ahead to avoid her novel, what would she do?

Instead of heading to the library, an idea sparked in her mind. It had been a lifetime since she'd last taken her surfboard out and today was the ideal time to change that. She could almost feel the rush of the sea calling to her. The thought of being out in the ocean, feeling the power of the waves beneath her board, brought a sense of freedom she hadn't felt in years.

Maris's footsteps quickened as she made her way back home. The prospect of hitting the waves filled her with anticipation, the kind that made her heartbeat quicken, in sync with her hurried steps. Right now, the idea of being in control of something—anything—felt like just what she needed.

Reaching her house, she wasted no time slipping into her wetsuit and grabbing her longboard from its resting place in the garage. Stepping back outside, the sun warming her skin, she moved with purpose.

The beach was just a short walk away, and with each step, Maris felt the anticipation building. When she reached the shore, the familiar sight of the rolling waves and the salty sea breeze greeted her like an old friend.

She paused for a moment, toes buried in the sand. Watching other surfers paddle out and wait for the right wave, perfecting their drop-in technique, and making smooth, powerful bottom turns inspired her. She loved the way their movements looked; resembling an interpretive dance where everyone plays a specific part. A dance she knew how to perform very well.

Her board, painted in white and parakeet green with pink hibiscus flowers, hung at her side. She ran her fingers along the smooth fiberglass surface as the sea breeze rustled through the trees, tiny particles of sand brushing against her legs.

It's now or never, Maris thought, her feet in motion.

She waded into the water, the coolness refreshing. It soaked into the neoprene she wore and reached her skin. Paddling out, she was present in a way she hadn't experienced in a long time. The simple joy of being in the moment washed her mind clear and renewed her spirit.

A rush of adrenaline coursed through her as she balanced on her board, riding the first wave with confidence before jumping off in the surf's break. For the next few hours, Maris lost herself in the rise and fall of the waves. The ocean had a way of helping her find clarity and perspective.

Exhausted, she paddled back to shore. Calm and worn out, like a child after a long day of play, she sat on the sand with her board beside her. Ocean waves crashed on the shore, as they had done for centuries, and Maris contemplated the idea of self-publishing once more. For the first time, it didn't seem so daunting—perhaps because she was learning to trust herself, or perhaps because the endless rhythm of the waves reminded her that persistence could shape even the most stubborn obstacles.

As she rested there, lost in thought, Maris noticed a familiar figure emerging from the water with a surfboard under his arm. Her heart skipped a beat as she realized it was Hendrix. He hadn't seen her yet, so she took a deep breath, stood up, and brushed the sand off her wetsuit.

I need to confront him, she thought. *I can't keep running away from these feelings. Maybe if I talk to him, I can finally get some closure and move on.*

She jogged towards him, the soft ground giving way under her feet. When she was close enough, she called out, "Hendrix!"

He turned, surprise flashing across his face as he recognized her. "Maris?" he said, a mixture of emotions in his voice. He walked over to her, his expression shifting from shock to something more subdued. "Hey."

"What are you doing here?" she asked, trying to keep her voice even.

"We decided to stay in town for a while," Hendrix finally stated, his tone quiet. "Jemma's working on a collaboration with a local brand. She's doing photoshoots and stuff. So, I came to the beach to surf while she's busy. I'm kind of between jobs right now…" his words trailed off.

Maris nodded. Conversation between them used to be friendly and easy. Now it was strained and uncomfortable.

Hendrix looked down at the sand, kicking at it with his foot. "I understand if you can't stand the sight of me," he said, his voice barely above a whisper. "After everything that happened… I wouldn't blame you. Honestly, I'm surprised we're having *this* conversation."

Maris sighed, her heart aching at the vulnerability in his words. "Hendrix, it's not that I don't want to see you. It's just… complicated."

Hendrix looked at her, their eyes meeting briefly before looking away. She fidgeted with the leash of her surfboard.

"I was hurt, ya know?" she went on. "But… I think it's time to let go of the past and look forward. I haven't been so good at that, but I'm realizing that all holding on to pain does is damage my mental health and my relationships with other people."

"I just want a chance to make things right. I understand I've made mistakes. I'm not perfect but that's not an excuse. I regret everything that happened between us, and I wish, every day, that I could take it back."

Maris appreciated his honesty, the way he was willing to face their tainted past and reach out.

They stood there for a moment longer, the weight of their shared history hanging between them. Suddenly, another person joined them. Before she could respond to Hendrix's last remark, Jemma, looking stylish as always, walked up wearing large designer sunglasses and an oversized sunhat. She carried a dozen boutique bags. Her overproduced ensemble was in stark contrast to the natural beauty of the beach, making her stand out more like a tourist than an influencer.

"Hey, babe!" Jemma called out, her voice merry and loud. She approached Hendrix, giving Maris a fleeting, almost dismissive, glance. "I got some amazing shots today. You should see the new collection. It's going to be fabulous!"

Hendrix offered Jemma a weak smile, his conversation with Maris still weighing on him. "That's great, Jem," he said, his voice lacking enthusiasm.

Without even acknowledging Maris's presence, Jemma addressed Hendrix. "We should head back to the hotel," she announced, her tone curt. "I've got a call with the brand rep in an hour."

Hendrix gave Maris a sad, apologetic look. "I'll see you around, Maris," he muttered, filled with regret.

She forced a smile, nodding in response. "Yeah, see you around," she replied, barely audible.

She could've initiated an interaction with Jemma, but she didn't want the progress she'd made that day to go to waste. So, instead, she counted her conversation with Hendrix as a win and would deal with Jemma later.

Watching as he followed like a lost puppy behind Jemma as she led the way to their, no doubt, trendy and expensive accommodations, Maris wondered what drew them together.

But, feeling the need for a mid-afternoon nap, she headed home and rejected the thought. Her bed beckoned, and she needed to recharge.

Making her way to her front step was more of a challenge than it should've been, given that she was in good shape and tried to keep up somewhat of a workout routine. But the familiar achy feeling in her arms and the cumbersome board she was carrying weren't a great combination. She regretted having waited so long to take the opportunity to surf. Now, she was paying for it with sore muscles and a growling stomach.

By the time she had sprayed herself and the board off with the hose, showered, and changed, she was too tired even to eat. She climbed into bed, feeling the soft sheets against her skin, and let out a contented sigh. As she closed her eyes, she began thinking of Colton.

She imagined their life together — full of laughter and shared ambitions. The idea of waking up next to him every morning, sharing quiet breakfasts, and building a future filled her heart with happiness. She pictured them traveling, exploring new places, and creating countless memories.

As she slipped into a peaceful slumber, her dreams took over, weaving vivid images of their shared life. They were discovering tropical sun-drenched beaches, their fingers intertwined as they strolled along the shore. The world around them fading into a blissful blur. The visions felt so real.

Maris's dreams carried her to a place where love and contentment reigned. She slept soundly, her heart full and her spirit at peace. But each day has its own anxieties.

Ties That Bind

"…and he was standing there telling me how much he regretted everything that happened between us when Jemma had to show up and botch the whole thing!" Maris finished.

Colton, blown about by the abundance of words that she had just poured out, processed the information slowly. He reached out, placing a comforting hand on her shoulder.

"Wow, Mar. I'm not sure what to say. Do you think he wanted to talk more? In private?"

"I don't know," Maris confessed. "He didn't seem like he wanted Jemma to be a part of the conversation, that's for sure. But who could blame him when she's acting like such a witch? I mean, she completely ignored me!"

Colton frowned, his protective instincts kicking in. "You deserve better than to be treated like that. But that probably sounds hypocritical comin' from a guy who judged you before knowin' you," he shrugged.

Maris sighed, frustrated. "I just don't understand how they're a couple. I mean, she's all about herself, and he doesn't even have a job!"

Colton squeezed her shoulder gently, trying to offer some comfort. "People can get stuck in complicated relationships for all sorts of reasons. It doesn't excuse their behavior, but it might explain some of it."

She nodded, and her lips curled into a wicked grin. "You should've seen her trying to trek across the sand in her four-inch espadrilles!"

He soaked in the way she looked when she was amused. And he couldn't help but chuckle at the mental image. "I can only imagine…" he replied, shaking his head.

A smile rested on his face as he watched Maris. He loved seeing her like this, her eyes sparkling, animated gestures, and hilarious facial expressions. However, within a few moments, she grew serious again.

"Part of me wants to give him a chance to explain, but another part just wants to move on and focus on the future," Maris stated. "I just don't feel right being at odds with my little sister. I don't know what to do about it. It's never easy to make the first move."

He reached out, placing a gentle hand on her back. "I get it," he said. "It's tough when you're caught between wanting to give someone a chance and needing to protect yourself. And it's even harder when family is involved."

Maris stared at him expectantly, waiting for him to continue.

"My older brother, Axel… I haven't mentioned him a lot. He's a total loser, always getting himself into trouble, sticking his nose where it doesn't belong. Our relationship has been on the rocks for years because he constantly drags me into his messes. I'm the guy who makes his worries disappear. The last little while, I haven't responded to any of his attempts to reach out because I just don't want to be the hero anymore."

Colton took a deep breath, feeling the weight of the memories he was sharing. "It's hard to cut ties with family, even when it's for our own well-being. But sometimes, we have to take a step back and think about what's best for us. Maybe you don't want to cut Jemma completely out of your life, but that doesn't require you to fix things right this minute either. I had to make a choice for my own sanity. It doesn't mean I don't care about Axel or want him to get better. I just can't be the one who always runs to the rescue. Jemma needs you. She might not know how much yet."

Maris offered a nod of recognition. "You're right. I guess I need to give myself some time to figure things out," she conceded.

Colton gave her a reassuring smile. "Let's take a break from all the heavy stuff for now. How about I make us a couple of drinks and we talk about somethin' lighter?" he suggested, headed toward her mid-century modern mini bar.

"That sounds perfect."

He got up and grabbed a couple of copper mugs, gingerly maneuvering around the various shelves and ingredients. Soon he waltzed into the living room and joined Maris on her loveseat, a deep shade of mustard, and presented her with a drink. They settled back into the cushions, the atmosphere becoming more relaxed as they sipped their drinks and chatted about their interests and dreams. He rested a rough, warm hand on her thigh, grounding himself in the moment.

As the night wore on, the conversation flowed, uninhibited. They shared stories, laughter, and even discussed their hopes for the future. Maris rested her head on Colton's shoulder, feeling the steady rise and fall of his breath. His arm wrapped around her, pulling her closer, and she felt a sense of security she'd only imagined. Their fingers intertwined, and he gently brushed his thumb over her knuckles, a silent promise of his presence.

The night seemed infinite, brimming with the promise of something beautiful blossoming between them.

Just as Colton was about to launch into another story, a sudden knock at the door interrupted him. He shared a curious look with Maris as she rose to answer it.

She found Jemma standing outside, looking both worried and determined. "Jemma?" she said, her voice filled with surprise.

Jemma didn't waste a moment. She rushed past Maris and into the house, then swiftly turned to face her.

"Maris, we need to talk," she said urgently. "I couldn't sleep. Hendrix told me about your conversation, and I feel so guilty for letting this come between us."

Maris set her mug down on the entry table, her heart racing as she processed Jemma's words. "Jemma, what are you talking about?"

Jemma's hands trembled as she began to speak. "Hendrix told me how much he regretted everything that's happened. And I realized that I've been so focused on myself that I haven't considered how my actions have affected you. I'm so sorry, Mar."

Colton watched for Maris's reaction. For a moment, she seemed frozen in time, unable to respond. Jemma waited, looking for acknowledgment from her sister.

"Hendrix broke my trust," Maris finally said. "Seeing you with him initially felt like a dagger twisting in my heart.." Her voice broke with the onset of tears. Nevertheless, she pressed on. "To be honest, it still does. You and Hendrix are saying all the pretty things you think I want to hear, but it's not that simple."

"I never meant to hurt you, Maris. Hendrix let you down, but it was a long time ago. I'm not asking you to forgive him. I just think he deserves a second chance. He's changed. I wish you could see how much."

Maris sighed as a tear slid down her cheek. "For the longest time, I didn't think that my best friend turning his back on me was forgivable. Then, to turn around and date my sister?! Maybe he's different now… I know I am. But that doesn't change the fact that you hid your relationship from me, Jem. We're sisters. And, on top of it all, you waltzed in from Hawaii acting like an entitled brat. Like I owed *you* something for being upset about all this."

"And now, I'm giving you a heartfelt apology. I don't know what more I can do."

"It's not about the words, Jemma. It's about proving them. I get that you want things to go back to normal, and so do I. Maybe I just need some time to consider everything."

"You're seriously gonna continue with this grudge?" Jemma asked, perturbed.

"It's not that," Maris replied. "I love you. And despite what you might think, I do want you to be happy. I just think it's best if I at least sleep on what you've said, and then we can talk again. I'm not in the mindset to process all this tonight."

"Fine," Jemma huffed, unsatisfied. "But I'm going back to Maui next weekend, so don't think too long." With that, she reached for the handle of the door.

As she left, they exchanged uneasy goodbyes and, when the door closed behind her, Maris turned to Colton, her eyes shining with a mix of emotions.

"You've been amazing tonight," she breathed. "I don't know how I can ever thank you."

Colton pulled her against him, pressing his lips to her forehead. "You don't have to thank me. I'm proud of you for standin' up for yourself. You deserve a life that feels good. However you get there. And if takin' your time with Jemma makes that happen, I'm all for it."

They stood there for a moment, wrapped in each other's arms. Maris felt a sense of peace, resting her head on Colton's chest, listening to the steady rhythm of his heartbeat.

"I'm so glad to have you here with me," she whispered.

In the quiet, Colton gently tilted her chin up, their eyes locking in a tender gaze. He whispered back, "This is exactly where I want to be." Then, leaning down, he kissed her lips with a gentle, unwavering love, just beginning to bloom.

Unraveled

I don't know if I ever knew what feeling complete was like, Colton considered as he left Maris's. *Until now.*

The evening had built to the most fiery first kiss he'd ever experienced, and he couldn't stop thinking about the way Maris melted into his embrace It felt as though she were the puzzle piece he'd been missing all along. Something in the way she said his name was quietly enchanting. The way her mouth moved when she spoke was hypnotizing. Reflecting on it made him want to storm back in and kiss her again.

As he walked to his vehicle, the cool night air did little to cool the warmth that had spread through him. Fireworks were still going off behind his eyes and his heartbeat assaulted the inside of his chest. Everything about Maris was something to get lost in—her gentleness, her voice, the way her eyes sparkled when she looked at him. He was willfully drowning in all of it.

Sliding into the driver's side, Colton attempted to steady himself. But every imprint of what had just happened between them left a sweet ache that he didn't want to fade. It had been innocent enough. However, as he started the engine, his mind was still in Maris's entryway, drunk with the moment they'd spent together.

He smiled into the darkness as he pulled away and drove down the empty streets. As the city lights blurred past, he relaxed into his seat and let out a contented sigh. Being with Maris was unlike anything he'd ever experienced. It was real and natural; nothing about it felt forced. The magnetism he felt pulling him to her made him feel alive and optimistic. She created a world he couldn't control or micro-manage and its intensity gave him a rush of emotions that he hadn't experienced elsewhere. Just the way her hand fit perfectly in his drove him wild.

Colton recalled vividly the enchantment he felt, before coming to California, with the idea of Maris. Then they'd met, in an idyllic setting no less, and sparks had flown—but not the romantic kind. He chuckled at the thought of their assessments of each other at the bonfire. How wrong they'd been! Colton thinking she was a snobby, career-seeking know-it-all. And now, all he wanted was to make her happy in a million little ways and make a grin play on her lips the way it did when she was up to no good.

At first, she'd seen him as narcissistic and patronizing. Now, she appeared to wilt whenever he was nearby. The journey from misconception to connection amazed him. How two people could misjudge one another so harshly and then come to an understanding led to an immense gratefulness that was difficult for him to contain. The evening's magic and the anticipation of the next time they would see each other lingered as he drove on. It was as if tonight had solidified the shaky ground they once stood on. They were no longer at odds and, instead, were cultivating a budding relationship.

It was hardly something he could put a label on. But he knew it was a direction he wanted to take. A path he wanted to finish walking, to see where it led. Of course, he hadn't planned on licking the wounds inflicted by Tori indefinitely. Nevertheless, he admitted, he would never be open to new love if he waited until he was ready. If he did that, he'd be waiting for the rest of his life.

Colton wasn't a risktaker. Maris made him want to change that.

She was all pretty things and witty words. He was calculation and introspection, mixed with a little dry humor. Yet, they worked. And he wanted to learn all the ways to turn that happy accident into something constant. Because, when she walked into the room, his heart beat differently. She was beautiful and sun-drenched and everywhere he wanted to be.

Maris, he realized, had cast a spell that transformed his reality.

When Colton let himself into the apartment, upon arrival, it was as if his whole world, even amidst the darkness of night, was technicolor. Charleston had never seemed as distant and monochrome as it did now that he had found Maris. She was the vibrancy that made everything else pale in comparison.

He had come to Laguna Beach hoping for inspiration and possibilities professionally. He had put his personal life on a shelf. There it had stayed, collecting dust and cobwebs, until someone had deigned to get it down and brush it off. Maris had swooped in with infectious energy and an effortless smile and, suddenly, the walls that once seemed suffocating now felt like a canvas for new memories. Light now shone in his darkest corners and flowers bloomed in his deepest recesses. It was as if he was a magnet for miracles.

Wow, Colton thought, getting into bed. *I've been unraveled by a kiss.*

The man who boasted in restraint found it all washed away by a tall, blonde enchantress with ocean eyes. And yet, he welcomed it. The uncertainty, the spontaneity, the rawness of it all—it felt right in a way he hadn't anticipated.

He closed his eyes and replayed the night's events. It was the best thing he'd ever not planned for.

Outside, the moon rose high into the sky and Colton counted his blessings. It wasn't just being in the right place at the right time that he was thankful for, but the active participation he was having in his own life. He wasn't just existing anymore. His senses were reawakened; a part of him restored. The memory of her touch remained, a ghostly presence that refused to fade and left him yearning for more.

Perhaps he'd spent too long loathing his circumstances and being the victim. Now, he felt empowered and genuinely peaceful.

With a final, satisfied sigh, Colton allowed himself to drift towards sleep. The thought of Maris whispering goodnight settled in his heart. His soul, once tied up in knots, was untangled and relaxed. As he succumbed to the embrace of slumber, he felt confident that every moment with her held the potential for euphoria.

In The Hereafter

Washing her face and brushing her teeth had never seemed as mundane before as they did that night. Every nerve stood on end and every breath hitched at the thought of Colton. The kiss they'd shared before bidding one another goodnight was perhaps the most romantic and intoxicating thing Maris had ever experienced. And now, everything that was normal seemed boring. Each task she needed to perform after he'd left was underwhelming. None of it compared to his devilish grin and the electricity that flowed between them.

She stared at her reflection, as she dabbed her face with a towel. A small smile tugged at her lips as she played back the evening's end in her mind. It had been like a dream, and she was still on the verge of pinching herself to make sure it had really happened.

As she moved through her nightly routine, the memory of their kiss echoed around her like a sweet whisper. It had fully awakened a longing inside of her that she had been trying to lay to rest. There was no hope of that now. She was enslaved to whatever spark had just exploded between them. A raging fire now burned in its place and its brightness illuminated parts of her soul she didn't know existed.

She slipped into bed, pulling the covers up to her chin, her mind lost to the way Colton looked at her and the ease of his arms around her. She marveled at how quickly he'd crumbled the walls she had desperately tried to fortify. They now lay in broken parts around her swollen heart and, for once, she didn't feel the need to rebuild them. She wanted to let him in.

The connection she felt with him defied logic and explanation. A man she had despised only a short time ago had swiftly caused her suit of armor to fall to the ground in a heap. As they'd stood in her entry, the world outside continued to move, but in her heart, time stood still.

How could someone she once viewed with disdain now make her feel so full of life? So vulnerable and yet so secure? Colton had a way of seeing through her defenses, reaching the parts of her that she had long hidden away. She regretted that their first meeting had gone sideways but, in a small way, she was happy it had led to the slow undoing of their misjudgments. And Colton was also gradually conquering her inhibitions.

Would she ever tell him that even when he was a total jerk at the bonfire that she found him alluring? Probably not. Would she ever confess that the way he called her "darlin'" ignited a flame in her that refused to be extinguished? Maybe.

The slow burn of their relationship was both gratifying and frightening.

As she lay there, Maris felt a surge of longing. The future with Colton was uncertain, but it was also filled with endless possibilities.

Yes, he had initially thought she was an underqualified wannabe filled with sarcasm-soaked stubbornness. But now, she knew that those rough edges were just the façade of a man who was nursing stab wounds from the past. He had proved that his character was deeper than someone who covers over their scars with humor and ridicule.

Oh, how his arrogance at the bonfire had grated on her nerves! And yet, there was something about him that had intrigued her from the start, something she couldn't quite put her finger on. Now, that intrigue had blossomed into something much deeper, something she wanted to explore.

She pulled the covers tighter around her and closed her eyes. Her thoughts shifted to Jemma and her unexpected arrival at the bungalow that evening. Jemma's presence had added a layer of complexity to the night, but it had also brought clarity to Maris about her sister's motives.

Maris knew that Jemma wasn't typically spiteful, even if she did throw a fit when she didn't get her way. And from the look in her eyes when she was offering her winsome apology, she likely did feel bad for letting something like her relationship with Hendrix come between their bond. But, still, it was hard for Maris to understand why, of all people, Jemma had to fall for this one.

She tossed her head against the pillow, trying to reconcile her feelings for Colton with the unease brought on by Jemma's relationship with Hendrix.

Jemma had said all the right things when she turned up on Maris's doorstep, but was she willing to prove that there would be no additional drama? Maris couldn't help but wonder if her sister truly understood the gravity of the situation. Could she trust Jemma to navigate her relationship with Hendrix without causing further rifts?

Ultimately, she wanted to forgive and move on. She knew it wouldn't be easy, but there were too many things holding her back emotionally. And, if she could let go of these negative emotions, maybe she could more easily tackle the other obstacles that no doubt lay ahead. Her book, her relationship with Colton, and closeness with her family were worth putting herself out for. This conflict with Jemma just wasn't worth fighting about anymore. If Hendrix had truly made changes for the better, only time would tell.

Resolve settled over her, clear and steady, as she decided to speak with Jemma again when she woke up. And, with that, allowed a restful sleep to overtake her.

Only a few hours passed before the morning announced its arrival with a soft brilliance engulfing Maris, stretched lazily on the bed. Despite the lack of sleep, she felt her mood brighten with the events of the previous night flooding back to her. Within moments her feet hit the floor, and she was searching for a shoe here and a hair tie there.

She quickly typed out a message to Jemma to meet her at Table Rock Beach. She hoped her little sister was already awake and would open the text soon. The conversation they needed to have could wait no longer and she wanted to hurry and get to the shore before it happened so that she could hash through her thoughts once more.

By the time Maris arrived at the beach, the sun was already climbing higher in the sky. The sand and waves were overtaken by a beautiful golden hue and called her to the water's edge. As she dipped her toes into the cool surf, she rehearsed what she wanted to say to Jemma.

A few minutes later, she saw her sister approaching from a distance, her figure silhouetted against the bright morning light. Maris waved, and Jemma quickened her pace, a tentative smile on her face.

"Thanks for meeting me," Maris said as Jemma reached her. "I know it's early, but I felt like we needed to talk. Especially after last night."

Jemma nodded, her expression earnest. "I agree."

They walked along the shoreline in silence for a moment, the soft crunch of sand beneath their feet blending with the crashing waves. Maris tried to find the right words to express how she felt.

"I know things have been tense between us, and I hate that," Maris began. "And I've been a bit strong with my words…"

"You're not the only one, Mar," Jemma said, resting a hand on her arm.

Maris offered a genuine smile. "I've realized—with the help of others—that, for my sake, I have to make peace with this Hendrix situation. I want us to be sisters again."

Jemma's eyes now welled up with tears, her relief palpable. She stepped forward and wrapped her arms around Maris. "I've missed you, Mar."

"I love you, Jem."

Jemma pulled back slightly, wiping a tear from her cheek. "I love you too, Mar." Then, a mischievous grin spread across her face. "By the way… You and Mr. Designer Dingleberry looked pretty cozy last night when I showed up. Was that another 'brainstorming session'?" she laughed, and poked Maris in the rib. "For real, though, it's good to see you happy."

"Thanks. He's different than I thought. I was completely blind to who he really was when we first met."

"And…? You're glowing like a moonstone!"

"Alright, alright. I'll tell you all about it," Maris conceded. "But first, let's go get a coffee."

At a nearby café, over steaming lattes and huevos rancheros, Maris and Jemma instantly reconnected, mending their kinship. The atmosphere was light, filled with the warmth of reconciliation and renewed hope, as Maris gave her all the details of her growing relationship with Colton.

Jemma listened intently, her eyes sparkling with excitement as Maris recounted the previous night's events. They laughed and reminisced and shared dreams and current goings on, each of them feeling content in the renewed effortless conversation.

By the time they finished their coffee and left, heading to their vehicles arm-in-arm, Maris couldn't help but feel grateful for her clear mind and open heart. Now, all the was left to do was seize the day and all that life held out before her.

Still Waters

Glad Colton hadn't mentioned when he was leaving for South Carolina and, waiting impatiently for River and Liza to return from their last few days in Siena, Maris slid into an easy routine of waking early to write and edit, spending the long mild day with Colton, and falling into a restful sleep at night. In the wee hours of the morning, she worked on her manuscript or the new freelance article she was outlining about work-life balance in Southern California. By mid-afternoon, she was hand-in-hand with Colton enjoying a snuggly brunch or a mellow walk along Avenida del Mar in San Clemente.

Sometimes he would take her to Pebble's Nook, and she would observe him working on miniature samples and prototypes for Eve to have on display in her showroom at Laguna Luxe. She glowed with envy watching him, easily making something recognizable out of a chunk of unfinished wood, with only his hands and a few tools. There was an intimacy about being allowed to see his creative process for each project. It was as if someone gave her a ticket to a private performance of a highly esteemed show. Maris would pack them lunch and they would sit at the oversized wooden table with bulky metal legs, drinking Cactus Cooler and swapping anecdotes.

She would sneak her camera out of its case and snap a few photos of Colton hard at work. Jokingly, she told him that if he posted them on his Instagram business profile, he'd have hundreds of DM's from women across the country, fishing to find out his relationship status. He would roll his eyes, brushing off her comments with a wave of his hand. Yet, whenever she showed him the pictures, a hint of a smile would tug at the corners of his mouth, proud of the projects he was so passionate about.

Other times, they would spend romantic days at Treasure Island Beach, building sandcastles and wading in the waves. The natural cliff-side arch provided them with shelter from the midday sun and often, they sat in its shade, sharing their deepest secrets and biggest regrets. The beautiful moments they collected, trademarked by the salty breeze tousling Maris's hair and the soft laughter that echoed between them felt timeless.

Her favorite thing to do with Colton was to drive out to Aliso Beach on a clear night, and watch the stars dazzle in the inky, black sky. They would put Bon Iver on the car stereo, roll down the windows, and dance under the moonlight, their silhouettes swaying to the music's soft melodies. In those moments, surrounded by the beauty of the darkness and each other's presence, the world seemed to pause, leaving only their love illuminated by the glittering lights above.

"This feels like a scene out of your novel," he'd breathed into her ear as he held her close.

She looked up at him in the dark. "I guess life can be even more beautiful than fiction sometimes."

Afterward he had twirled her as she giggled into the onyx evening air.

Occasionally, they would end their midnight escapade sitting alongside one another on the packed sand. Woven together like the tight knit of a fabric and backlit by the headlights of Colton's car, they'd savor the stillness and listen to the sounds of the ocean. Colton's eyes gleamed like liquid gold in the white light, as he peered down at her knowingly. And Maris, pink-cheeked under his steady gaze, found herself more enamored with him than ever. Her every fear seemed to vanish in those precious moments and love felt infinite.

"Okay…where's the most romantic place you've ever been?" Maris probed.

"Eh… next question," Colton chuckled.

"Fine. I'll *rephrase* the question. Besides right now, what's the most romantic thing you'd like to do with me?"

"Truthfully? I don't think we need fancy plans, as you can see," he said, gesturing around them. "But, if I had to choose, because you'd likely force me to… I guess I'd take you horseback riding. My neighbors growin' up owned a horse farm and I always loved watchin' the horses out of my bedroom window. S'pose it'd be peaceful to take someone I care about out and ride through the oaks with the Spanish moss hangin' down everywhere, or out on the beach and just glide down the shore on these huge, majestic animals."

Maris tilted her head, her lips curling into a smile. "Horseback riding, huh? I knew I sensed a hopeless romantic! No tailgate down, lukewarm beer kind of date for you, huh?"

Colton laughed, shaking his head. "You wound me, Maris."

But her teasing softened as she glanced at him, her voice lowering. "Honestly, that sounds amazing. The beach, the oaks, all of it. I can see why you'd think it's peaceful—feels like it's straight out of a dream."

She paused for a moment and he playfully nudged her chin. "I think I'd like that. Just… being there. With you."

That was the thing about Colton, Maris thought—he made even the simplest moments feel like magic. She knew then— this wasn't just fleeting affection. It was something she could let herself believe in.

Over time, their days began to blend together. They each reveled in the simplicity of their togetherness, finding bits of joy in each one. Maris loved sharing her world with Colton—the quirky rituals she followed before starting a new project, the way she meticulously arranged her workspace to spark creativity. The way he lit a candle in her workspace without asking, or how he always seemed to notice when her favorite mug was empty. She found comfort in his quiet presence—the soft scrape of his pencil on paper as he sketched, or the warmth of his laughter when he teased her about her color-coded notebooks. Often, she caught him stealing glances at her while she wrote, and though he never said a word, his eyes spoke volumes—like he was quietly memorizing her, one moment at a time.

One morning, as she was chipping away at her work-life balance piece, Colton placed a steaming cup of coffee next to her laptop and gently kissed the top of her head. "Good mornin', beautiful. Thought you could use a little pick-me-up."

She looked up from her screen, a grateful smile spreading across her face. "You're officially the best."

They spent the morning side by side, Maris typing away on her computer while Colton sketched a compact sofa structure for the waiting area in the Colorado tech startup's office. It would be the perfect statement piece for a space where they would meet clients and investors. Sleek and modern with built-in charging ports, and durable fabric, it was quite a marvel.

By mid-afternoon, she stretched and looked over at Colton. "How is the sofa design looking?"

Colton held up his sketch, a proud grin on his face. "What do ya think?"

Maris examined the drawing, her eyes lighting up with admiration. "It's awesome! Truly, I think they'll love it!"

"Thanks, Mar," Colton said, his grin widening. "And how's your article comin' along?"

"It's getting there," she replied, taking a sip of her cold coffee. "I think I need a change of scenery to get the creative juices flowing again."

"Ya know, if we were back in Charleston, Maggie and I would pick ya up and take you out. You've only seen a fraction of my gentlemanly ways."

"Oh really? Is part of those mysterious ways taking me out with whoever Maggie might be?"

"Yeah. Maggie wouldn't give ya any trouble. She's my best girl," Colton replied mischievously.

"Call me old-fashioned, but I don't think taking another woman on a date counts as chivalry," she teased, though her crinkled nose betrayed genuine disapproval.

Colton's shoulders began to shake as he tried to hold back his laughter. But soon, his whole body joined in and the sound of his amusement filled the room.

"Mags is my truck, Maris," he said, finally catching his breath.

"Your truck has a name?"

"Sure does. 1979 Ford F-150. She's quite the cougar, with paint that gleams like black silk—most days. I've kept her roadworthy for ten years, even when she's thrown a tantrum or two," Colton remarked with a knowing glance.

"And Maggie is…?"

Colton's grin softened as his eyes grew misty, the playful banter giving way to quiet nostalgia. "That was my grandma's name. Saint of a woman. But a real vixen too, back in the day. She passed when I was sixteen and just gettin' my license. Always said I'd name my dream car after her."

"That's the sweetest thing I've ever heard," Maris noted.

Colton cleared his throat. "Hey, I have just the thing for ya. Come with me."

Maris followed him to the car, curiosity bubbling as she wondered what kind of surprise a man who named his truck after his grandmother could have in store.

"Where are we going?" she asked, intrigued.

"You'll see," he said with a playful smile. "It's a surprise."

They drove through the scenic streets, the anticipation building with each passing mile. Dense clouds cloaked the world around them. Maris couldn't help but wonder what he had planned. The foggy day added an aura of enchantment to their cruise across town.

Soon, they arrived at Laguna Luxe Studios, a place she had heard Colton talk about but had never visited. He parked the car and led her inside, guiding her through the studio and past Eve prattling into the phone at her desk, until they reached a room in the back.

"Close your eyes," he instructed. "Keep them shut, and no peeking."

She complied, adding the extra measure of placing her hands over her eyes. She was essentially blind. He then guided her by the shoulders through the doorway and positioned her in the center of the space, facing the east wall. Maris could hear the gentle rustling of fabric and wondered what he was up to. The wait seemed like an eternity, and Maris's eagerness made it nearly impossible for her not to steal a glance.

Finally satisfied with the conditions, Colton hesitantly told her to open her eyes. When she did, he gestured towards a beautifully crafted bleached driftwood bookshelf, resembling the one they'd dreamt up on the beach. The natural grain and knots of the weathered wood gave it a rustic and organic look, making it truly unique. It was beyond anything she could've imagined.

"Surprise!" Colton sang out.

Maris's jaw dropped in awe as she took in the bookshelf. The weathered wood, its texture and color, the labyrinth of overlapping pieces. There were fourteen offset shelves in total and a giant arch forming the top section of the bookcase itself, perfect for displaying art or trinkets of all kinds. She also noticed a small set of intricate wave shaped carvings on either side. The care and effort Colton had put into every detail was clear.

"Colton, this is incredible," Maris said, her voice filled with emotion. "You made this for me?"

He nodded, joy on his face. "You can fill it with your favorite books and anything else that inspires you."

She stepped closer, running her fingers over the smooth surface of the driftwood. "It's perfect. I can't believe you did this."

Colton wrapped his arms around the front of her. She placed her hands over his and relaxed into his caress.

"I'll always have a piece of you with me now," she said, reflecting on the fact that he would have to go back to Charleston, eventually.

Noticing the sadness in her tone, he squeezed her tighter. "Hey now, sweetheart. None of that sad stuff," he stated, spinning her around to face him. "I don't allow depression to accompany gifts for people I care about. Happy tears only."

Maris couldn't help but laugh at Colton's playful insistence, though her eyes were watering.

"Alright, alright, happy tears only," she agreed, her voice catching.

"That's more like it."

On the way out, Colton swung by to ask Eve if the company's delivery service would bring the bookshelf to Maris's the next day. Having been assured it could be arranged, Maris waved goodbye and thanked Eve for any part she might have played in concealing such an enormous gift.

As they drove back to the house, the mist lifted, revealing the rolling hills bathed in the soft, golden light of the evening sun. The landscape transformed before their eyes. The fog had diffused to unveil vibrant colors.

"So, what's on the menu for dinner, chef?"

Maris chuckled and playfully nudged him. "Oh, you're the guest chef tonight. I thought we'd make something together. How about pasta?"

"Perfect," Colton said, rolling up to the house. "Let's get to it."

They made their way to the kitchen, and Maris began gathering the ingredients while Colton filled a pot with water and set it to boil. They moved around the kitchen in a comfortable rhythm, the evening filled with lighthearted teasing and topped off glasses of wine.

"Think you can handle grating the cheese without eating half of it?" Maris teased, handing Colton a block of Parmesan.

"Deal," he said with a grin.

They continued working together, chopping vegetables, sautéing ingredients, and mixing everything into a delicious pasta dish.

We should open our own restaurant," Colton joked. "We'll call it 'Pasta by the Pacific'."

They both laughed at the idea of opening a bistro, imagining the chaos and fun they would have running it as partners. With dinner ready, they set the table and served themselves ample helpings, the aroma of their cooking filling the cozy kitchen.

As they sat down to eat, Maris took a bite and closed her eyes, savoring the flavors. "This is amazing. We really do make a great team."

Colton nodded in agreement. "Absolutely," he said, without looking away from her.

She smiled, her cheeks burning. "You're just saying that because we made it together."

"Maybe," he admitted with a lopsided smile. "You make everything that much better."

"You know, we could call our restaurant 'Saucy Duo' instead," she played back, giving a little shimmy.

Colton couldn't help but tilt his head upward and burst into laughter. Maris joined him. The combined cackling echoed through all 889 square feet of her small home.

After dinner, Colton volunteered for dish duty, and Maris curled up on the couch with a happy sigh. She yawned and snuggled into the throw pillow behind her neck.

Once he had finished cleaning up, Colton looked in on her with a soft smile, feeling a deep sense of contentment. He kissed her forehead and whispered, "Sweet dreams, Mar."

As Maris drifted into a peaceful slumber, he sat down in the armchair nearby, pulling out his phone to check messages. A series of texts from Axel lit up the screen, each one more urgent than the last.

Hey, Colt. I need to talk to you.

Please, it's important.

Colt, c'mon, man. I'm sorry about everything. I really need your help.

Then, a final text appeared with a plea that tugged at Colton's heartstrings:

Colton sighed, mussing his waves. He knew he couldn't ignore these messages from his brother, no matter how complicated their relationship was. Glancing at Maris to make sure she was still asleep, he slipped out the door. It creaked softly behind him. Maris rolled over, groaning at the sound.

He stepped outside into the cool night air. A starry sky hung above. Colton found a quiet spot on the porch and dialed Axel's number, his heart heavy.

Riptide

River's apartment had seemed more like Colton's the more time he spent there. And now, standing in the immaculate kitchen, he felt a strange bittersweet sensation at the thought of leaving it. Axel had made his point clear in their discussion on the phone. Colton needed to come home.

The cooking area was enormous, the largest room in the house by far. It had trendy black cabinets, veiny quartz counters and matching backsplash, and a huge navy island that held the sink and seating for three. Leather barstools, globe pendant lights, and a shiny range hood gave it a state-of-the-art essence, but the photos and letters on the fridge lent the place character.

There were polaroids and postcards all featuring either River and Liza's smiling faces or places they'd visited together. It stunned Colton how his friends could sell this condo after so much of their relationship had developed while making a home here. Maybe he was sentimental, but something told Colton there was ample reason to be. The rooms seemed to echo their laughter, and the air was still thick with the scent of the vanilla and vetiver candles Liza loved. It was like the walls held a part of their souls; a living scrapbook of memories that felt too precious to abandon.

It was clear to him that letting go of this place meant more than just selling a property. It meant moving on to a new chapter of life. And, after his conversation the previous evening with Axel, he wondered what the future might hold for them all, not only Liza and River.

Bile burned the back of his throat, and his head throbbed from a restless night. Maris was on her way over. She'd sensed something suspicious in his tone earlier that day and insisted that Colton let her do what she could to soothe him. What she didn't know was that she was the one going to need comfort.

Anger and frustration rose inside of him, and he clenched his fists at his sides. His workshop in Charleston had been closed for weeks now and, although he'd stopped taking local orders before coming out to California, it was supposed to be temporary. People were counting on him. Axel was counting on him. The sound of Axel's desperation was etched deeply into Colton's memory of their conversation.

Here we go again, Colton thought. *Little brother to the rescue. How many times can this play out the same way?*

Yes, he had pressed pause on real life and morphed into a different person in Laguna Beach, with Maris. But the reflection of himself he saw when he looked in the mirror in the Golden State was the version he longed to be. Not a cynical divorcé, forcing a smile for the neighbors who left lasagna on his front step every other week, and constantly commented on his loneliness. Instead, he wanted to be a man with hope, a person who embraced new beginnings, and someone who believed in the possibility of love and happiness once more.

"Hello?" Maris's voice called from the direction of the door. Absorbed in his thoughts, Colton hadn't heard her knock.

"Sorry! C'mon in," he hollered back, not moving from his spot in the kitchen. Dread was coming over him.

Maris immediately noticed his unkempt appearance. Frustration from pacing the morning away had mussed his hair, wrinkled his clothes, and slumped his shoulders. Even Colton knew he didn't look like himself. He didn't feel like himself either.

"You look terrible! Colton, what's wrong?" Maris asked fearfully.

He couldn't summon the courage to meet her worried eyes. Their beauty and brightness, roaming over him, filled him with guilt before he even spoke.

"It's my brother… He's… been havin' some issues again. And I guess I can't keep puttin' this off…" his words petered out.

"Putting what off? What are you not telling me?"

Colton took a deep breath, trying to gather the courage to explain. The enormity of the truth bore down on him, and he knew he couldn't keep it from her any longer.

"I called Axel last night," he began, his voice trembling. "He's in trouble, Maris. He's been sendin' me messages here and there, hintin' that he needed help, and I ignored him, until I couldn't anymore."

"I see," she said, struggling to find words. "So that's why you snuck outside last night when I was on the couch? Axel needed to talk?"

"Yeah…" Colton managed.

"Well, did you get everything figured out? Is he going to be okay?" Maris inquired, moving closer to him.

Colton's heart ached, knowing what he had to say. "I have to go back to Charleston, Mar. At least for a while. My workshop's been closed for weeks, and Axel… he depends on me. And I hate it, but I don't have a choice."

She stepped back, her expression more hurt than shocked. It was as though a bullet had passed clean through her, and she was only just beginning to realize she'd been hit. Maris's eyes widened as she withdrew further, the distance between them growing.

"So... you're leaving," she said, her voice faint.

"I don't want to, Mar. Believe me, this is the last thing I want to do. But Axel... he needs me. I can't turn my back on him. Plus, we both knew I couldn't stay indefinitely."

Tears welled up in Maris's eyes, but she fought to keep her composure. "Yeah... It's just... it's so sudden."

He approached her, reaching out to grasp her hand. "I promise I'll come back as soon as I can."

"So, you don't know how long you'll be gone?" Maris asked, searching his face for answers.

Colton scowled, feeling defensive and overwhelmed. "I'll be honest, Mar. I have no idea how long it's goin' to take to help Axel get back on his feet. He's in real financial trouble. He's always been reckless, but he's my brother."

"But you said yourself that you were always running to fix his problems, and that you didn't want to do that anymore!" she exclaimed, confused.

"You don't understand!" Colton snapped. "He's blood. I can't just desert him!" His face flushing with frustration, he closed his eyes. But it was too late to take back what he had said, and she had already headed for the exit.

He stood frozen, his outburst hanging in the air like a leaden cloud. His heart pounded, and a tsunami of regret washed over him. He felt helpless to change the way Maris was reacting, but he had to make her see.

"Maris, wait," he called out.

She paused, her hand resting on the doorknob, but she refused to turn around.

He crossed the expanse, his voice breaking. "I'm sorry. I didn't mean to hurt you. It's just..."

"It's just what?" Maris began, turning to face him. "I understand you feel obligated to your family, Colton. But you can't just lash out at me because you're stressed. This isn't only about Axel; it's about us too. I know what loyalty means to you, but I thought you'd prioritize us somehow."

He felt a lump form in his throat as he saw the pain in Maris's eyes. He knew she was justified, and the realization hit him like a swift kick to the ribs. He took a deep breath, trying to steady himself.

"You're right," he admitted, his voice heavy with remorse. "I was wrong to take my frustration out on you. This situation with Axel... it's tearin' me up, but I shouldn't have lashed out at you. This is just... I've always been the one to fix things for him, and it's exhaustin'."

Maris's expression softened slightly, but the hurt was still evident. "Well, we need to be facing this together. Not being on the same page will break us apart. You have to let me in." Maris stepped closer, her eyes searching his. "You don't have to carry this burden alone."

Colton felt a flicker of hope at Maris's words. He took her hands in his, feeling the warmth of her touch settled him. "I have no idea what I would do without you. I promise I'll keep you in the loop from here on out."

Maris squeezed his fingers gently. "That's all I ask."

They exchanged a subtle nod, an unspoken agreement settling between them. The room, though, still felt weighed down by the tension of uncertainty.

The silence was heavy, but Colton knew he had to break it. He took another deep breath, bracing himself for the next tough part of the conversation.

"Maris, there's somethin' else you ought to know," he said quietly, his voice steeped with regret.

She looked at him, her brows furrowing in concern. "What is it?"

"I don't have a lot of time to talk," he admitted, his heart aching. "I'm on the red eye tonight. I need to be back in Charleston as soon as possible."

A flicker of pain crossed Maris's face. "Tonight? Colton, that's so quick... Why didn't you tell me earlier?"

He swallowed hard. "I wanted to avoid makin' things harder for you. But unfortunately, the situation is urgent. I can't wait any longer."

Letting go of Colton's hands, she wrapped her arms around herself for comfort as she processed the news. "I just... I wish we had more time."

"I know. I wish we did, too. But we can manage this. No matter the distance, you'll always have me."

"How?"

"We'll call each other every day," Colton suggested, his voice earnest. "And we can text, keep each other updated on everything. I'll make time for video calls too, so I can still see that gorgeous face o' yours." He sounded like he was trying to convince himself as much as he was attempting to persuade her. "I'll sort this out quickly and be back before you know it."

Maris gave him a small smile, but it didn't reach her eyes. She stood on her tiptoes and kissed him, first on the cheek and then lightly on the lips, lingering in his space. "Take care, Colton."

The tenderness of her kiss was a bittersweet reminder of what he was leaving behind. He held her close for a moment, savoring the feeling of her in his arms.

"I will, Maris," he whispered, his voice thick with emotion.

She stepped back and gave him a brave smile. "Just come back to me."

"I promise," Colton repeated, his heart heavy with the weight of his commitment.

With one last look, she turned and stepped over the threshold, leaving him to prepare for whatever awaited him in Charleston. As the door closed behind her, he felt the finality of the moment settled in his chest like a stone. Breathing was becoming more difficult, and each inhale set his lungs aflame.

"I'll come back, Maris. I promise," he whispered again, this time into the void.

Colton's heavy heart nagged him as he packed his belongings in the hours that followed, a blur of hurried preparations. During the drive to the airport, he struggled to ignore the sinking feeling in his gut. As he began his journey back to Charleston, the city lights of Laguna Beach faded into the distance.

Every so often, while waiting at the gate, he checked his phone, hoping for a reassuring message from Maris or some sign that everything would be okay. But none came, and he feared that her disappointment with him for leaving ran deeper than she had let on.

The red-eye flight was long and restless. He tried to sleep, but his mind was a whirlwind of thoughts and worries about Axel, Maris, and the uncertainty that lay ahead.

Finally, the plane touched down in Charleston, and the familiar, humid air of the city greeted Colton. He felt a pang of nostalgia as he made his way through the terminal and out to the curb, where his dad was waiting in his mint-condition 1957 International Harvester S-110. The early morning light accentuated every curve and chrome detail, making the Harvester's red paint gleam as it did when it was first built. He couldn't help but smile as he approached the truck, memories of childhood rides flooding back.

"Hey, son! Didn't hear much from you while you were gone. How did things go? Your mother was worried," his dad said, his voice tinged with relief and undeniable curiosity.

Colton smiled as he set his bag down and embraced his father. "It went well, Dad. The new job was challenging, but I learned a lot. I missed you and Mom, though." He paused, contemplating his next words. "It's good to be home," he lied.

His dad nodded, patting him on the shoulder. "We missed you too, son. Better be gettin' back. Your mom's got your favorite, shrimp and grits, waitin'."

As they climbed into the truck, he felt a sense of belonging. The familiar rumble of the engine and the smell of the leather seats resurrected memories of simpler times.

When they pulled up the gravel drive to his parents' home, Colton's heart felt as though it would explode. The two-story white house with black shutters, hanging plants swaying in the breeze, and surrounded by giant oak trees, stood as a testament of simpler times. It hadn't changed in decades.

Axel's beat-up Range Rover in the drive was not a welcome sight and Axel, all six feet of him, casually leaned against the pillar of the wrap-around porch. Colton had half a mind to jump out of the truck and land a solid punch.

He wore faded black jeans, a black t-shirt, and a belt with a worn-out pair of Adidas Sambas. His hair, longer than Colton's, flipped out at the nape of his neck and the swoop of his widow's peak receded slightly. Axel had lost weight since Colton saw him last and shaved his beard, leaving only a mustache and some day-old stubble. The lines in his forehead deepened as he pressed his dark, thick brows together.

Axel looked surprisingly collected. How could he stand there so nonchalantly after the frustration he had caused?

Colton stepped out of the truck and Axel's earthy sage eyes met his, now clouded with loathing. Their dad gave him a reassuring pat on the shoulder before heading inside, leaving the two brothers alone on the porch.

"Colt, long time, no see," Axel greeted him, trying to sound blasé.

"Axel," Colton replied tersely, his fists clenching at his sides. "We need to talk."

Axel nodded, his expression faltering for a moment, before recovering. "Whatever do you mean, Colton? I'm just here to have a nice breakfast with my family," he said mockingly, before turning to go inside.

Colton felt a surge of exasperation but swallowed it down, following his brother into the house. His mind raced with thoughts of their strained history and the mess Axel had created. Entering the kitchen, the familiar scents of his mother's cooking filled the air. The comforting aromas brought him a fleeting sense of solace.

Their mother greeted them with a cluck and a smile, oblivious to the storm brewing beneath the surface. "Boys, sit down. Breakfast is almost ready."

Mama's boy that he was, Colton patted his mom gently on the back and gave her a quick smooch on the cheek before obeying her request. Taking a seat at the oval oak dining table set for four, he stared Axel down with obvious vehemence. He knew this wasn't the time to cause a scene, but rage simmered inside of him, begging to be released.

The others took their seats. Their parents' presence was intensely felt, mingling with the tension between the two men. A small cross-stitch hoop with the phrase "bless this nest" sneered at the semblance of an innocent family gathering. The clinking of cutlery and the soft hum of conversation filled the room, but Colton's focus remained on Axel.

"Here we go. Y'all dig in," their mother said, placing a steaming dish of shrimp and grits on the table.

Colton forced a smile, serving himself while his mind raced with questions. Axel seemed to sense the scrutiny, avoiding direct eye contact as he also helped himself to a generous portion.

"So, Axel, how have things been?" their father asked, breaking the awkward silence and apparently unaware of the real reason Colton was back in town.

Axel hesitated, glancing at Colton before responding. "Uh, things have been... challenging, but I'm managin'," he said, his voice lacking conviction.

Colton couldn't hold back any longer. "Managin'? Is that what you call it?" he blurted, his tone sharper than intended.

Their mother looked at her sons with thinly veiled irritation. "Colton, let's just enjoy breakfast, please."

"Sorry, mama," he muttered. But feeling a spike in his aggravation, he couldn't suppress his words any longer. "It's just… your son is a deadbeat!" he burst out. "This conspirin' pretender has no business bein' at our family breakfast. Let alone tryin' to pull the wool over your eyes and convince you he's managing," Colton continued, making quotations in the air.

Dabbing his mouth with a napkin, his father sat back in his chair and blinked. An extended moment passed before he spoke.

"Would someone please explain what in the Sam Hill is going on here?" he asked, confused and angry. The room fell silent, the suspense thickening as everyone's eyes darted from Colton to Axel. Colton took a deep breath, preparing to spill the story he had kept bottled up for too long already.

"Dad, Axel's been in trouble for a while now. Financial trouble. His incessant recklessness has finally caught up with him. Imagine that," he began. But before he could say anything else, Axel was by his side, hand on his arm, trying to drag him out of the room.

Axel's face flushed with anger and embarrassment. "Colton, this isn't the time or place," he muttered through gritted teeth.

"No, Axel. It *is* the time and place," Colton shot back. "Mom and Dad deserve to know what's goin' on. You called me to come here and save you, like I always do. Well, ya know what? This time, I'm not just goin' to bail you out and sweep it under the rug."

Their mother looked between her sons, worry etched on her face. "Axel, is this true?"

Axel sighed, raking his hand through his hair. "Yeah... I messed up. Made some bad decisions, and now I'm way over my head. It wasn't all just careless spending. I thought I could make some return on investments and stuff, but everything backfired. I'm only human, though, and I don't think I deserve to be nailed to the stake here."

"Oh you don't, do you?" Colton cut in. "Of course. But the sad thing is, Mom and Dad don't even know how many times we've played through this same scenario without them knowin'. You're forty-four years old, Axel. It's time to grow up."

Their father leaned forward, his expression stern. "Exactly what kind of trouble are we talkin' about, Axel?"

Axel shifted uncomfortably and studied the herringbone pattern on the parquet floor. "It's a lot, Dad. Debts from bad investments, some unpaid loans... a handful of those probably aren't even legit. Everything has spiraled out of control. I thought I could fix it on my own by my usual methods, but now... I can't. I'm in way over my head." Then, Axel raised his chin and eyeballed Colton smugly. "I only reached out to *you*," he continued, jabbing Colton in the ribs, "because, despite everything, you've always had a knack for fixin' things."

Except for the thing I couldn't fix, Colton brooded. *My wife's lack of devotion.*

Self-reproach began flowing through his bloodstream. He had ignored Axel's cries for help and had blown him off when he legitimately needed support. But how would he have known that this wasn't just a rouse for him to put more time and resources into a sinking ship?

"You should have told us, Axel. We're family. We could have helped before it got this bad." His mother's voice of reason broke through his depreciating thoughts.

"She's right, son. You should've been honest," his dad added.

Colton's anger ebbed slightly, listening to his parents rally around Axel even though he'd tried to deceive them. He didn't feel he had much choice but to show cautious support as well. He placed his hand on Axel's shoulder, feeling the friction between them lessen a fraction.

Shame was clear in Axel's posture. Colton's expression remained stoic, but he felt compassion slowly thawing the frost around his heart.

Over the next few days, the tornado of activity and mounting stress became Colton's new reality. He threw himself into helping Axel sort through the mess, dealing with creditors, and trying to stabilize the situation. His phone vibrated with messages and calls, but he barely had a moment to breathe, let alone respond.

Maris's texts served as a constant reminder of the distance between them. Each time his cellphone buzzed showing her name, a pang of guilt stabbed him. He wanted to reply, to reassure her he hadn't forgotten about her, but the words seemed inadequate.

Day 1:

Miss you. Hope everything's okay. Call me when you can.

Colton stared at the message, his fingers hovering over the screen, but a call from one of Axel's shady lenders pulled him away.

Day 2:

Thinking of you. Are you alright?

He typed a quick reply, but felt it sounded too dismissive. Hearing Axel shout for him from the other room, he deleted it and shoved the phone back into his pocket.

Day 3:

Colton, it's been days, and I'm really worried. Please just let me know if you're okay.

Her concern was almost too much to bear. He promised himself he'd call her later, but by the time he fell into bed each night, exhaustion overtook him, and the cycle began anew.

By the end of the week, he felt like he was running on fumes. Axel's situation was far from stabilizing. Every day, from sunup to sundown, he and Axel appeared to be trying to extinguish a dumpster fire with bottles of alcohol. The flames just continued growing, and the problems kept getting bigger.

Colton was having trouble finding the balance he once knew. He had tried hard to find normalcy after his divorce, and he discovered spontaneity with Maris. But with Axel involved, he'd only found misery. He knew this couldn't go on forever and that he needed to reach out to her, to hear her voice. But, that night, as he began to dial her, the words he groped for felt hollow and insufficient. A heavy sigh escaped his lips.

Tomorrow, Colton decided. *I'll make things right tomorrow.*

But tomorrow never came.

Within the Eye

Parking his car outside of Axel's disheveled house became a daily ritual. Each time, Colton took a few extra minutes to get out of the car and walk through the overgrown yard to the dilapidated cottage. The paint was peeling away from the wooden siding, and termite damage ran rampant. Sadly, the neglect and disrepair weren't confined to the outside of the home.

Entering the narrow foyer, Colton could see piles of unwashed laundry, scattered newspapers, empty pizza boxes, and beer bottles distributed throughout the living area. Axel owned very little furniture. There was a worn faux leather recliner, a weathered cotton sofa, and an antique dresser used as a makeshift TV stand. All of it had seen better days. The state of the front room alone echoed the condition of Axel's mind.

Axel emerged from the bedroom, looking as rummaged through as the house itself. His eyes were bleary, and his clothes hung slovenly from his body.

"Mornin', Colt," he mumbled, rubbing his eyes.

"We've got a lot to do," Colton replied, dispensing with pleasantries. He began picking up the craft beer remains and discarded papers, trying to create some kind of organization in the chaos.

Axel nodded, sinking into the old recliner with a heavy sigh. "I know, Colt. What I don't know is where to start."

"We'll start small. One step at a time. We'll tackle this giant stack of overdue bills first and see where we stand."

Axel rubbed his temples, looking around the disorderly room. "I appreciate you being here. I know I've made a mess of things. For years, I've been the brother you never wanted."

This caused Colton to stop in his tracks. "The brother I never wanted?" he repeated. "You really think so much of yourself that you'd say that?! I have more to do with my time than sit around wishin' my brother away. The world doesn't revolve around you, Axel."

Axel flinched at Colton's words. Disgrace, then annoyance crossed his face. "Never said it did, if you'd let me finish," he said sharply. "Just feels like I've been nothin' but a burden to you. I can't help but think you'd be better off without me."

Oh gosh, not a pity party this early in the day. Colton thought to himself. But he kept his facial expressions under control.

"Look, Axel, it's not about being better off without you. It's about getting through this and not repeating the same mistakes. This has to stop. You can't keep living like this," he said, spreading his arms wide. "And you can't keep expecting me to bail you out."

Axel's shoulders slumped, his defiance giving way to resignation. "You're right. I know you are. Living like this, constantly trying to dig myself out of a hole, is exhausting. But it's all I know. I'm not like you, Colt. Not smart or good with my hands. Not outgoing or six foot three and charming. I'm just a washed-up guy who lives rubbin' pennies together and hoping magic happens."

Colton felt a pang of sympathy, and then vexation. He knew Axel's self-deprecation was partly genuine, but it was also a convenient excuse to avoid taking responsibility.

"Axel, you're not giving yourself enough credit," Colton said, trying to maintain a balance between encouragement and tough love. "You have strengths—maybe you just don't see them right now. Stop making excuses and start taking action. Start by tackling one problem at a time."

They each took a deep breath. Colton shifted nervously on his feet, waiting for confirmation from Axel.

"I shouldn't have asked you to come. I don't want to keep dragging you down with me," he said finally, looking at the floor.

Colton crossed the room and stood in front of Axel. "Good," Colton replied, his tone softening. "Then let's start by sorting through these bills and making a plan. We need to get a handle on this before it spirals even further out of control," extending his hand to help Axel up.

The mountain of envelopes was large and unsteady, toppling onto the floor and exposing dozens of red final notice stamps. They spent the next few hours sorting through them and making calls to collectors. It seemed never-ending, but Colton knew if they were going to make any progress, they needed to stay focused. Beside him, Axel picked at his nail beds anxiously.

As the evening wore on, Colton's phone buzzed with yet another message from Maris. He glanced at it. The apology he owed her gnawed at him, but he knew he had to stay intent on Axel for now.

"Thanks for stickin' with me, Colt," Axel said quietly as they wrapped up for the day. "I know it's not easy."

Colton managed a small smile. "We'll get through this, Axel. One step at a time. But, listen…" the words were hard to say, but unavoidable. "You're goin' to need to sell some of your assets. Your tools would probably be a good place to start. We'll have to see. Maybe think about sellin' the Rover, too. Any little bit will help at this point."

Axel looked up, defeated. "Sell my tools? The Rover? I don't have much, Colt, but those are the few things I'd kinda like to keep around."

Colton remained firm, unapologetic. "I know it's tough, Axel. But you need to sacrifice to get out of this mess. Holdin' onto things won't help if you're drownin' in debt."

Axel sighed, his shoulders slumping further. "I don't like it, but… I'll try to figure up what I can get rid of, and we'll talk about it tomorrow, okay?" he urged, burned out.

"Yeah, okay," Colton agreed, and headed for home.

That night, as Colton lay in bed, he stared at his phone in the dark. All of Maris's unanswered messages haunted him from the eerie glow of the screen. The impact of the life he'd put on hold suddenly hit him. The love he had forced to wait. Colton cringed at the idea of putting Maris through this nightmare.

Rolling onto his side, he typed a reply, hoping it would be enough to reassure her.

As he hit send, fury and self-inflicted sorrow overcame him.
Colton knew he had to find a way to juggle it all more
responsibly, but for now, the storm within Axel's life demanded
his full attention.

October Night Skies

Thick clouds blanketed the city and obscured any view of the stars as Maris sat by the window. Her fingers repetitively traced the rim of her mug and the drizzling rain tapped against the glass. Each drop felt like a countdown, marking the days since she had last heard from Colton. The world outside seemed to mirror her internal turmoil—gray, bleak, and restless.

She tried to focus on her freelance research and the deadline she'd imposed upon herself for her self-published book release. She had even promoted it and posted teasers on her Instagram account. She reviewed each caption, emoji, and quote she used with extreme care before sending it into the metaverse. Now, she was waiting to hear from an illustrator with a proof of character art. It was so exciting to be manifesting her author's dreams. Yet, in the quiet moments, devoid of marketing strategies and collaboration requests, all she could dwell on was Colton.

She knew he was dealing with a lot, helping his brother out of a difficult situation, but the silence was becoming unbearable. She missed the sound of his voice, their late-night conversations, and how he made her feel safe and understood. Sometimes it was all she could do to keep her mind from drifting to a dark place and asking if perhaps he had forgotten about her. Or maybe he hadn't been as invested as she was. These ruminations returned like clockwork whenever she was at home alone, on nights such as tonight, looking out at the somber October sky.

Maris picked up her phone and went through her scheduled posts for the week ahead. There was one regarding a new fantasy novel that all the people she followed were talking about, and she joined in the conversation. The others were a mix of content about her writing process, her inspirational mood board, the exclusive playlist she had created for her story, and various other literature-related topics. It was hard work to advertise for herself but, without an agent or a publisher doing these things for her, she had to keep her head down and persist.

Determination fueled her as she crafted each post, handpicking images and words that would resonate with her audience. Her dreams of edging toward success as an author were within reach, and she was ready to seize every opportunity. Even as she worked, the feeling of loneliness lingered, but she channeled it into her creative pursuits.

Suddenly, a banner appeared at the top of her screen, signaling that she had received a text from Colton. After all the days she had waited for a reply, the unexpected message caused a frantic sensation to take over. She stared at the alert, hesitating to read it.

C'mon, Maris. It's just a text. Open it, she commanded herself, pressing the messaging icon.

Staring back at her, in a small gray speech bubble, were four sentences.
I'm so sorry, Mar. Things are tough here, and I'm swamped. I miss you and will call you as soon as I can. Please understand.

Please understand. It wasn't a question; it was a request.

She stared at the message, feeling relief and frustration. The briefness of his words left her longing for more. She desired to be there for him, to support him through this difficult time. And, selfishly, she wanted the encouragement to be reciprocated. But the distance and silence made it hard.

Taking a deep breath, she decided to focus on her dreams. She refused to let worry consume her. She closed her eyes for a moment, trying to steady her racing heart. She knew she wasn't able to manage Colton's situation, but she could manage her own.

With determination, she dived back into her work. She refined her social media posts, ensuring each one was perfect. The excitement of sharing her creative journey with her followers gave her a sense of purpose and fulfillment. She reviewed her book's promotional content, double-checking the details and planning future teasers. Her dedication to her dream kept her moving forward, even when her heart felt burdened.

Navigating the world of self-publishing was a process filled with both difficulties and rewards. Maris had learned to wear many hats—author, marketer, designer, and distributor. Each day presented new tasks: coordinating with editors, managing budgets, and reaching out to potential readers. The endeavor demanded perseverance and resourcefulness, often pushing her out of her comfort zone. Yet, the sense of ownership and artistic expression was unparalleled. Every decision was hers to make; each victory was a testament to her persistence and vision. She cherished the direct connection with her audience, valuing their feedback and support. The road was not without its bumps, but the ability to shape her story, from the first draft to the final publication, made the challenges worthwhile.

As the hours passed, she received an email notification. Her designer had sent the proofs of character art. Maris opened the attachment, her breath catching at the sight of the beautiful illustrations that brought her story to life. Each figure was depicted with such care and detail, perfectly capturing her vision. She was even more excited to share these concepts with the advanced copy readers she had lined up.

Although having her work reach her audience for the first time was anxiety inducing, she also felt proud of what she'd been able to do so far. A sense of accomplishment washed over her as she sent her feedback, expressing her sincere gratitude for the artist's effort. With each step she completed toward releasing this novel, Maris felt her confidence strengthen and blossom.

The idea of self-publishing had been daunting at first. But the exhilaration of creative freedom was empowering. From choosing the cover design to managing the marketing strategy, each decision became a thrilling journey of self-discovery.

Determined to keep the momentum going, she turned her attention to her next task. She opened her manuscript, scrolling through the chapters with a critical eye. She knew that every word, every sentence, had to be perfect. Her readers deserved the best she could offer, and she was committed to giving them just that.

As she worked, Maris found herself lost in the world she had created. The characters, the settings, the intricate plot twists— all of it reflected her passion and dedication. As the rain outside gradually eased, the steady rhythm yielding to calm stillness, the hours slipped by.

She looked out at the night sky. The gray clouds were parting, revealing glimpses of stars twinkling above. It was a reminder that even the darkest nights could give way to moments of light and clarity.

Maris picked up her phone to check for any new messages. Seeing none, she sent another message to Colton, offering him her unwavering support.

Hey, Colton. Just know that I'm thinking of you I know things are hard right now, but sometimes we need time and space to figure things out. Please take care of yourself.

The days turned into weeks, and October drifted toward its end. The once-gray skies gave way to crisp, clear nights, but Maris's heart remained clouded with uncertainty. Colton's messages were sporadic and brief, each one was full of apologies and reassurances. She appreciated the few words he could spare, but they left her longing for the deeper connection they once shared.

Maris found respite in her work, pouring her energy into her writing and promotional efforts. Her early readers gave overwhelmingly positive feedback, and she was shocked that they all finished the book so quickly. Though, despite her professional accomplishments, the personal void grew larger each day.

The hours she spent immersed in her creative world were both a refuge and a distraction. Yet, as fulfilling as her career was, Maris couldn't ignore the desire of a companion to share her triumphs and struggles with. She had hoped Colton would be someone with whom she could have it all. But the reality of their obviously conflicting priorities made her question if it was meant to be.

In need of comfort, Maris reached out to Liza. She and River had returned from their honeymoon a while ago, but the couple had been busy trying to sell River's condo and find a new place in Morro Bay. Maris missed their frequent hangouts and cherished the moments they stole away from their hectic schedules.

One chilly afternoon, she headed over for a visit with Liza, two lattes with an extra espresso shot in hand. The familiar sight of the apartment brought a deluge of nostalgia, along with a stabbing pain. She knocked on the door, and it wasn't long before Liza's cheerful face appeared, welcoming her inside.

"Maris! It's so good to see you!" Liza exclaimed, wrapping her friend in a tight hug. "Come on in. It feels like it's been forever."

She smiled, feeling the unease within her wane. "I brought us some lattes," she said, handing one to Liza. "Thought we could use the boost."

"You're a lifesaver," Liza replied with a grin, taking a sip of the warm coffee. "So, tell me everything! How's the book coming along? And how are you holding up?" she asked, settling onto the couch. She patted the cushion next to her, offering Maris to sit down.

Shedding her jacket and tossing it over the armchair, Maris crossed the room and conceded to Liza's request. She was grateful for the opportunity to share her bottled-up thoughts with her friend, but she hardly knew where to begin.

"The book is coming along great. The readers have all loved it, which was a huge relief. And the cover art is perfect. But... I'm still struggling with Colton. He's been so distant, and I know he's doing his best, but it's hard not to feel disconnected."

Liza nodded, her expression empathetic. "I can imagine. It's tough when you want to support someone, but you find yourself on the outside. Have you been able to talk to him at all?"

"Here and there," Maris admitted. "His messages are short and to the point. I know he's overwhelmed, but... I guess I just feel sort of abandoned. But part of me wonders if leaving me behind is what's best for him. Maybe what we had was fleeting infatuation and now, he's the one that got away."

Liza reached out and squeezed Maris's hand. "I'm sure he misses you, too. It's just a rough patch. But you're doing amazing things with your book, and that's something to be incredibly proud of. Sometimes all the other stuff has to work itself out."

Maris patted her friend's hand. "Thanks, Liza. How about you? How's everything with you and River?"

Liza beamed. "We're good! Busy, but good. Obviously, we're in the process of selling the apartment and looking for a place. It's been hectic, but exciting. I can't wait for you to see our new house once we find it."

Maris smiled widely. "I'm so happy for you guys. It sounds like things are coming together."

Liza nodded enthusiastically. "They are. It's a lot of work, but we're getting there. And I promise, once we're settled, we'll have you over for a proper housewarming. It'll be like old times."

The thought of a future gathering with her friends brought an aura of calm to Maris. She took a sip of her latte, savoring the gentleness and the familiarity of their conversation.

"It's a date," she said, settling into a fresh feeling of hope. "I've missed our hangouts. It's been too long since we've caught up like this."

They spent the rest of the afternoon exchanging tales and laughing together. Maris felt support in Liza's presence, a comforting reminder that she wasn't alone on the road ahead. Yet something still troubled her mind.

As they chatted, her thoughts occasionally drifted back to Colton. She couldn't shake the feeling that there was more she could do, that somehow, she should be able to bridge the distance between them. At the same time, she felt like she wasn't the only one who could make more of an effort to preserve what they had.

As they finished their lattes and Maris prepared to leave, Liza gave her a final, reassuring hug. "We're here for you, Mar. Reach out whenever you need to talk."

Maris hugged her back, grateful for the support. "Thanks, Liza. I really appreciate it."

As she drove home, the sky had darkened, and the streetlights cast a soft glow on the wet pavement. The conversation with Liza had provided some comfort, but the nagging feeling about Colton stayed with her. She replayed their chat in her mind, trying to find peace in Liza's reassurances.

Just as she turned onto her street, her phone buzzed with a new message. Maris's heart raced as she pulled into her driveway and parked the car. She grabbed her cellphone, hoping it was Colton.

She glanced at the screen and froze. It was him, but instead of a tender note, the context was urgent.

We need to talk. Call me as soon as you can.

The gravity of the message pressed down on her chest, feeling as heavy as a stone. Her mind raced with questions as she hurried inside. What could be wrong now?

Tempest

Colton stared down at the phone in his hand, waiting for an indication that Maris was texting back. Searching for those three little dots that would appear if she was responding was the only thing keeping him sane. He and Axel had just gotten off the phone with the lawyer, and the conversation hadn't ended positively. Reliving the call, his grip on the phone tightened.

"Mr. Vance?" the lawyer had begun. "I'm sorry to inform you, but you're facing serious legal charges." Then, "Colton, he'll need your assistance immediately."

Colton's mind raced as he replayed the details. Axel had always drawn trouble to himself, but this was different. This was serious. As he waited for Maris to call him back, the magnitude of it all closed in on him, making it hard to breathe.

Axel, already drowning in debt from years of bad investments and online gambling, was now facing charges of doing so playing cards for money illegally and tax evasion. The magnitude of the situation crashed over Colton, overwhelming him like a powerful wave. Not only did Axel's actions put him in legal jeopardy, but they also threatened to drag Colton deeper into a vortex of complications and emotional turmoil.

"Axel's failure to report the winnings—including from illegal games—has put him at risk of prison time," the lawyer had explained. "The authorities are cracking down hard, and we'll need to act quickly to reduce the damage."

Colton exhaled slowly, the weight of the revelation settled heavily on his shoulders. He realized he had no choice but to help Axel navigate the legal battle, despite the personal cost and his commitment to Maris. He told himself he must stay; that Axel couldn't face it all alone.

Dehydrated, he took a sip of water and steeled himself for what lied ahead. He found Axel sitting on the couch, staring blankly at the dark screen of the television. The room was dim and the air was heavy.

"Axel, I need to talk to you," Colton stated.

Axel looked up, dread and exasperation in his eyes. "What is it now, Colt?"

Colton took a seat beside him, choosing his words carefully. "You heard what the lawyer said. This isn't somethin' we can just ignore. It's goin' to take a lot of work to get through this."

Axel's face paled, and he sank back into the couch, his hands trembling. "How could I have let this happen?"

Colton sighed, running a hand through his hair. The lines in his face made deeper from his disquieting thoughts. He was only thirty-seven, but he felt years older under the constant strain of being the responsible brother.

Axel buried his face in his hands, his voice muffled by despair. "What am I goin' to do, Colt? I can't go to prison."

Colton's heart ached as he saw his older brother, usually so defiant and stubborn, now utterly defeated. He took a deep breath, determined to stay strong for Axel.

"We'll figure it out together. I know it's overwhelming, but I'm goin' to help you get through this. I don't have a plan yet, but we'll come up with somethin'."

Axel looked up, his eyes filled with fear and helplessness. "I've messed up so badly this time. I didn't think anyone would notice. And I was so desperate for money… I can't keep a job to save my life. I just needed to get back on my feet. I figured if

I could win a few hands, things would start lookin' up and I could worry about the rest later."

Colton squeezed his brother's shoulder, trying to convey a sense of reassurance. "We'll start by gettin' organized and working with the lawyer to understand exactly what we're dealin' with."

Axel's eyes welled up with tears. "I don't deserve your help but thank you."

Colton's shoulders sagged beneath his brother's reliance on him. When his phone buzzed and Maris's name flashed on the screen, he gave Axel a small nod, then stood and walked to the hallway to answer. His voice was tense with worry as he spoke.

"Maris, thanks for callin' back. I... I wanted to talk to you about Axel. He's in serious legal trouble and things are progressively gettin' worse."

As Colton began to explain the situation, the gravity of Axel's predicament became clear. Maris listened intently, offering her support and encouragement. Despite her bolstering, Colton's heart condemned him. He felt torn between his loyalty to his brother and his promise to Maris.

"Colton, you're doing the right thing by helping Axel," Maris said softly. "He needs you right now, and I get that. It's just...

this is a really hard situation. I don't know how it's all going to work out, but we'll take it one step at a time."

"I just... I don't want you to feel like I'm not there for you," Colton replied.

"I know you're trying to make it all alright," Maris replied gently. "That's what you always do. Axel is fortunate to have you."

"Thanks, Maris," Colton said, his voice softening. "I promise I'll do everything I can to make this work."

"I know you will," Maris expressed. "Just take care of yourself too, okay? Don't carry all the weight on your own."

Colton nodded, even though she couldn't see him. "I'll try, Mar," was all he could get out.

After they said their goodbyes, Colton returned to Axel, who was still seated on the couch, absently picking at the frayed edge of a cushion.

"Let's get started," Colton said, his voice resolute. "We need to gather all the documents and information the lawyer will need."

As they worked late into the night, he held onto the belief that they could weather this tempest together. He and Axel painstakingly organized the documents and information the lawyer had requested, their determination unwavering despite the mounting pressure.

The next morning Colton and Axel were seated in the lawyer's office, the atmosphere heavy with tension. The lawyer, a stern man with sharp features, methodically shuffled through the stack of papers they had provided. The room was silent, apart from the rustling of documents and the steady ticking of a wall clock.

"Thank you for coming in," the lawyer began, looking at both brothers over the top of his reading glasses. "I've reviewed the preliminary information, and I won't sugarcoat it—this situation is severe. Axel, the charges against you include multiple counts of illegal gambling and tax evasion. If convicted, you could be facing significant prison time."

Axel's face drained of color, and he gripped the edge of his chair, his knuckles white.

The lawyer, unfazed by Axel's reaction, continued, "It's crucial that we approach this methodically. We'll need to build a strong defense, and that means full transparency and cooperation. Colton, your support will be invaluable during this process."

Colton nodded, his resolve strengthening. "We'll do whatever it takes. Just tell us where to start."

The lawyer leaned forward, steepling his fingers. "First, we need to gather a complete and accurate picture of your financial situation, Axel. Every transaction, every document—nothing can be overlooked. We'll also need to prepare for potential plea negotiations, but that will depend on the evidence and how cooperative you are."

Axel swallowed hard, his voice low. "I'll do it. I'll provide whatever you need."

Colton glanced at Axel, who looked more vulnerable than ever. "We're in this together," Colton said quietly, offering his brother a reassuring nod.

The lawyer continued to outline the steps needed, the legal jargon blending with the urgency of the circumstances. Colton scribbled notes, his mind racing with strategies and contingencies. The road ahead was sure to be rough, but he was determined to fight for his brother and help him navigate this legal storm.

"…this will take a lot of time and effort," the lawyer concluded, his voice solemn. "But with full cooperation and a strong defense, we can navigate this."

As Colton and Axel exited the lawyer's office, the gravity of the situation bore down on them. Colton attempted to comfort his brother, yet his own mind was a whirlwind of doubts and questions. He knew they needed all the help they could get.

On the drive back, a memory flickered in Colton's mind— Camille, an acquaintance from high school who had gone on to become a paralegal. They hadn't been in touch for a while, but he remembered how wholeheartedly she threw herself into her work. Maybe she could help them understand more about the complex legal processes they were facing.

That evening, Colton found Camille's work number online. He called and left a message explaining the situation and asking if she could meet to discuss Axel's case. To his relief, Camille responded quickly, agreeing to meet the next day.

Wandering toward the bedroom, he found Axel face down on the bare mattress, wallowing in his despair. Axel didn't raise his head when he walked into the room.

"Axel, I've been thinking," Colton began. "There's someone who might be able to help us understand all this legal stuff. Her name is Camille; we went to high school together, and she's a paralegal now. She could explain the terminology and what to expect during different stages of your case."

At that, Axel looked up, his eyes still filled with anxiety. "Do you think she'd be willing to help? I don't want to drag more people into this mess."

Colton nodded affirmatively. "I already reached out to her, and she agreed to meet us tomorrow. We need all the help we can get, Axel. Mom and Dad can't handle this kind of stress—not with their health—and I told them I'd take care of it. So let me do that. Camille knows her stuff, and she'll help us figure out the next steps. Havin' someone who understands the legal system could make all the difference."

Axel sighed, fear evident on his face. "If you think it will help, then let's do it. I don't have many options at this point."

The next afternoon, Colton and Axel met Camille at a local delicatessen. As they walked in, the warm scent of freshly baked bread and roasted coffee filled the air. Camille was already seated at a booth near the back. She was exceedingly composed, but there was a subtle warmth in her smile when she saw Colton.

"Colton, thanks for calling. Axel, it's nice to meet you," Camille greeted them, standing up to shake their hands. "I'm sorry to hear about your situation, but I'm here to help in any way I can."

"Thank you for meetin' us, Camille," Colton replied, his tone earnest. "We're feelin' pretty lost right now and could really use your guidance."

Camille gestured for them to sit down. "Let's get started. I've brought some materials that might help clarify things for you." She pulled out a folder and spread its contents across the table, focusing her attention on the task at hand.

As Camille explained the legal terminology and what they should expect during the different stages of Axel's case, her professionalism shone through. However, there were fleeting moments when her gaze lingered on Colton, and she would occasionally brush her hair back in a way that seemed more than just a habit.

Camille's almond shaped eyes, a shade of hunter green, were full of passion about her profession. The burgundy suit jacket she wore made her caramel complexion glow, and the matching skirt showed off her long, smooth legs. Her wavy, dark hair parted naturally on the side and her plump, coral lips parted to reveal a gleaming smile as she chatted with the brothers.

Colton, absorbed in the information Camille was providing, remained oblivious to the subtle hints she was attracted to him.

"First, we need to ensure Axel is fully transparent with his lawyer—no details should be withheld, no matter how minor they may seem," Camille said, her tone serious. "Cooperation is key. I'll help you go through all the documents to make sure nothing is missed."

As they talked, there were moments when her hand seemed to rest on Colton's forearm longer than necessary and she offered him smiles of admiration whenever their eyes met.

"Here are some key terms you'll need to understand," Camille continued, pointing to a list she had prepared. "These will come up frequently during the legal process."

Colton leaned in, studying the list intently. "This is really helpful, Camille. Thank you for breakin' everything down for us."

Camille's smile widened. "It's my pleasure, Colton," she replied, lightly tracing the edge of her notebook with her fingertips. "I'll be here to support you both every step of the way. If you have any questions, don't hesitate to reach out."

By the time Colton and Axel left the deli, they both felt more prepared to face the legal challenges ahead. Axel couldn't help but chuckle as they stepped into the brisk air.

"Man, you're an idiot," he said, glancing sideways at his brother.

Colton frowned. "An idiot? Why?"

Axel raised an eyebrow, smirking. "Camille, dude. The way she kept touchin' your arm, flashin' those coy, toothy smiles. Pretty sure she wasn't doin' that for *my* benefit."

Colton shook his head with a huff of laughter. "Axel, stop. She's just bein' friendly—it's her job."

Axel snorted. "Friendly, huh? Sure. Guess I'll let you stay blind to it for now, but I'm callin' it—she's got her sights set on more than just helpin' with this case."

Colton rolled his eyes, but a flicker of uncertainty crossed his face. "We've got enough goin' on without you stirrin' the pot."

"Just sayin'," Axel added with a knowing grin. "She's got her eye on the prize, and it might just be you. But don't go makin' things messy with Maris, alright? That girl's good for you, and you know it."

Colton froze for a moment before shaking his head with a chuckle that didn't quite reach his eyes. "You're dreamin', Axel. And Maris…she's important to me. But we've got bigger problems to deal with right now."

Axel didn't push further, but a knowing grin still tugged at his lips. "If you say so. Just keep your head straight, alright?"

Over the next several weeks, the brothers worked tirelessly gathering bank statements, receipts, and every other document relevant to the case. While Axel had all but admitted he was guilty of the crime, Colton still felt protective of his brother.

Regardless of the outcome, he would try to put the past behind him.

Their days were filled with long hours spent talking with the lawyer, meticulously preparing Axel's defense. Camille's generous assistance was a source of reassurance. Evenings often stretched late into the night, with Colton and Axel huddled around the kitchen table, discussing strategies.

One evening, after a particularly grueling session with their lawyer, Colton and Axel sat down to review their progress. They needed to ensure every detail was accounted for. Camille had just left.

Axel sighed, rubbing his temples. "Colton, I've been thinkin'. Maybe we should consider settlin' out of court or makin' a plea deal. I don't know if I can handle a full trial. The risks, the stress—it's too much."

Colton looked at his brother, the truthfulness of Axel's words sinking in. "A plea deal might be our best option," he admitted, feeling the exhaustion in his bones. "It could lessen the fallout and give you a chance to move forward. But it's a big decision."

Axel nodded, his fingers twisting together. "I just want this to be over. A trial would drain me completely—I barely have the strength to gather these papers as it is. I haven't even made it into a courtroom yet!" He paused, taking a deep breath. "And honestly, Colton, the evidence against me is pretty strong."

As Axel got up, he mumbled a goodnight to Colton and told him to let himself out. It was obvious he wasn't coming back to finish the discussion, and it seemed like his mind was made up. Colton found himself alone in the shadowy room, reflecting on the past few months. It was now December, and the brisk air outside matched the heaviness in his heart. He thought about all the sacrifices he had made for Axel—the late nights, the constant worry, and most painfully, the strain on his relationship with Maris.

They had only talked a handful of times since Axel's legal troubles began. Their conversations had been brief and not particularly affectionate. Colton missed her deeply, but every time he thought about picking up the phone, guilt and exhaustion stopped him. What could he say that wouldn't feel like another empty promise? He told himself he'd call tomorrow, and then the next day, but time seemed to get carried away in the flood of all the havoc. And it left nothing but remnants of what might-have-been in its wake.

It wasn't just Axel's situation—it was Colton's inability to balance the turmoil. Every day brought new flames to smother, another piece of Axel's mess to clean up, and by the time the day was over, Colton felt too drained to be the man he promised Maris he'd be when he left. The realization gnawed at him, but rather than confront it, he buried himself deeper into the current situation. It was easier to tell himself there'd be time later than to admit he was failing her now.

Still, Maris lingered in his thoughts—a tether to something steady and meaningful, if only he'd reach for it. He wondered how long she'd wait for him to pull it together and whether he deserved her patience at all. But right now, Colton couldn't shake the feeling that if he didn't hold things together for his brother, the consequences would be unbearable. He told himself Maris would understand. But deep down, he worried that someday, she wouldn't.

His memory wouldn't relent. It overwhelmed him with images of the two of them enjoying the early autumn, California air and the way Maris seemed to glow in the sunlight; the way they would lose track of time, immersed in conversation, her laughter like a melody. He recalled the delicate scent of her perfume mingling with the salty sea breeze, and the feel of her soft hand clasped in his. He hadn't lied; he wanted to be there for her in every way he could. But what did those ways look like now?

Colton's phone buzzed, pulling him from his thoughts. He glanced at the screen, hoping for a message from Maris, but it was just a reminder for an upcoming meeting with the lawyer.

He sat forward, resting his elbows on his knees, and cradled his head in his hands. His feet rocked gently, heel to toe. He couldn't shake the feeling of guilt—guilt for neglecting Maris, for not being able to do more for Axel, and for the confusion that clouded their future. As his mind turned back to Maris, he wondered if they could ever find their way back to each other after all this.

He stood up, squared his shoulders, and prepared himself for the next day's challenges, holding onto the hope that brighter days were just around the corner, until his phone rang.

Colton saw the name on the caller ID and groaned. Mickey Fassbender, the lawyer, was waiting for him to answer. At that moment, Colton would've rather thrown his phone into oblivion, letting his frustration get the better of him. Instead, though, he tapped a green button on the screen to accept the call.

"Colton? Good, you're still awake. Look, I couldn't reach Axel on his cell, but I've got bad news. We've hit a major setback. New evidence against Axel has been uncovered. We need to regroup and come up with a new strategy ASAP."

Colton's heart sank. The impact of this new development felt like a crushing blow, compounding his already heavy burden. He listened as Mickey detailed the implications, feeling the hope he had clung to slipping away. When the call ended, Colton was left in the dimly lit room, staring at the swinging, solitary lightbulb hanging from the ceiling, in disbelief. The storm had just intensified, and the path ahead grew even more vague.

He suddenly couldn't push down the rising tide of despair any longer. There was no turning back now. He would have to dig even deeper, find more strength, and he didn't know where. He was barely at the workshop making new inventory or fulfilling orders, never got to talk to Maris and tell her how he thought they could heal each other if they got half a chance, and was always expected to play the hero. Colton had had enough.

With one swift movement and a powerful fist, he released the pent-up anger and anguish that plagued him. His balled-up hand made contact with the decayed wood of the paneled wall, and it gave way with a brittle crunch, sending a spray of dust and small debris into the air. The impact echoed slightly in the empty space beyond the wall, and Colton stood, staring into the hole he created. A hollow cavity that mirrored the one in his chest.

In the quiet that followed, his thoughts turned once more to the distance that had wedged between him and Maris, but he clung to the hope that they could still find a way forward. For now, he had to focus on the immediate battle, but he resolved to reach out to her soon, to mend the fraying threads of their relationship. He had to find a way to show her she was still a vital part of his life. How?

Echoes of Doubt

On a late December evening, in a stormy Carlsbad, Maris sat curled up in a blanket on her parents' couch. As the twinkle lights glowed softly outside, they cast a magical spell over the evening, making it look as though fairies were gracefully flitting around the house. Wind roared past, slightly rattling the windows. All was quiet as Maris read her newest purchase from Driftwood Shelves.

Her fingers traced the edges of the book, the familiar scent of paper and ink mingling with the subtle aroma of cinnamon from the candles her mother had lit. Despite the cozy surroundings, her mind was far from at ease. The words on the pages blurred as thoughts of Colton crept in, their unresolved tensions looming like a shadow over her heart.

She sighed, closing the book and setting it aside Memories of Colton flickered through her mind like scenes from an old film—the way his laughter lit up the room and the warmth of his embrace made her feel safe. She missed him more than words could express, but the distance between them felt impossible. The brief messages they exchanged lacked the depth and connection they once shared.

With each passing day, their two cities seemed to drift even farther apart. The east coast felt like another world, as unreachable as outer space. No matter how hard she tried, it never seemed like enough to break through the barrier that kept them apart. She was always grasping for a connection that felt unattainable.

Maris drew the blanket tighter around herself, craving its security; as if it could shield her from the world. The wind outside howled louder, as if echoing the turmoil in her heart. She took a deep breath, trying to steady her thoughts, but they remained unstable.

Her parents' house felt like a refuge from the storm inside her. The lights outside cast a soft glow, creating a stark contrast to the darkness she felt. She longed for the days when no distance seemed too great to span.

With a heavy heart, Maris stood up and walked to the window, pressing her palm against the cold glass. The stormy night mirrored her emotions, turbulent and unpredictable. Outside, the quiet hum of the season—marked by gatherings and moments meant for togetherness—only deepened her solitude.

She whispered a silent prayer, hoping that somehow, perhaps in the new year, things could be different.

She hadn't told her family about the impact Colton's absence was having on her. Instead, she tried to stay positive and use humor to cope with the bad days. If it was a particularly dismal day, she would climb under the covers and listen to Bon Iver on repeat and pretend she was, once again, under the night sky in his arms.

Tonight, as she slipped on her headphones and pressed play, the music felt more like a lament. Each note was a reminder of what she was missing. She watched the candles flicker until her eyes stung from not blinking. When she finally did, silent tears slid down her cheeks.

That night, Maris's parents had held a family gathering, a tradition they upheld every year to celebrate their wedding anniversary. Everyone would come from wherever they were to spend this special time with them. Just like they were kids again, the girls would sleep over, stay up late, and eat French toast for breakfast in the morning. This year, the house was filled with the same joy of familiar faces and the hum of conversation, but Maris felt a world apart.

Alex, her older sister, and her family weren't there this year because Alex had given birth to a baby boy just eight weeks before. They didn't want to travel, exposing the baby to germs. Despite this, the rest of the family gathered as usual, sharing in games and giggles.

Maris had tried to join in the festivities, but her heart wasn't in it. She forced a smile and laughed at the right moments, but her thoughts weren't in the present. The burden of it all was overwhelming, and she realized she could no longer keep it inside.

Now, blowing out the last candle, Maris retreated to her old bedroom. She sat on the edge of the bed, hugging her knees to her chest. Her mind continued to race. She closed her eyes, taking slow, deep breaths, and tried to quiet the torrent of thoughts swirling inside her.

Eventually, she slipped into a restless sleep, her dreams filled with fleeting images of happier times. When she awoke, the first light of dawn was breaking through the curtains. Regardless of the early hour, she heard hushed voices downstairs. Likely her parents were tinkering with the coffee machine and readying things for breakfast. Today, she would tell them everything.

Maris took a moment to gather herself before slipping out of bed. She pulled on a warm robe and quietly made her way downstairs, the familiar creak of the wooden steps under her feet providing a small measure of comfort.

In the kitchen, she found her parents bustling about, occupied with the morning's chores. They looked so in sync. Her mother was heating the griddle, and her father was setting the table. They both looked up as she entered, and they greeted her with wide smiles.

"Good morning, sweetie," her mother said. "Did you sleep well?"

Maris shrugged. "I slept okay, I guess." She hesitated for a moment before continuing, "Can we talk? There's something I need to tell you."

Her parents exchanged a concerned glance and nodded, turning off the stove and setting the tablecloth down. "Of course, Mar. Let's sit down," her father said, guiding her to the kitchen table.

Her mother, sensing her distress, sat down beside her. "Sweetheart, you've been so quiet since you got here. Is everything okay?"

Maris took a deep breath, her eyes welling up with tears. "It's Colton, Mom. We got so close in such a short time. It felt like we had this incredible connection. He was there for me when I was going through a tough time, always knowing the right thing to say to cheer me up. We'd stay up late talking about our dreams and fears, and it felt like I could tell him anything. But now, with everything that's happened, I'm scared it was just a fleeting, momentary thing."

"What do you mean everything that's happened? You told us he had to go back to Charleston but is there something more serious going on?" asked her dad.

Maris felt the weight of her emotions pressing down on her. She could sense her parents' concern and knew she needed to be honest. "It's more than just the distance, Dad. Colton has been dealing with some serious family issues. His brother, Axel, is facing legal trouble, and Colton feels responsible for helping him through it. He doesn't know when he'll be able to come back to Laguna Beach."

"Oh, Mar. I'm sorry, honey. It sounds like a difficult situation for both of you. How can we help?" her mother said.

Maris's voice trembled as she spoke, "I just miss him. Everything between us felt so…real. I mean, I seriously misjudged him when we first met and never imagined he would turn into someone I cared about so much. The things we did together and the conversations we had meant a lot to me. Once, he even surprised me with a midnight trip to the coast just to watch the sunrise, and he built me the most amazing bookshelf from driftwood. Now I wonder if what I thought we were both feeling was more just one-sided."

"Sometimes, love can be confusing, especially when you're faced with so many challenges. But what you shared with Colton sounds truly special," her mother said, her eyes full of empathy as she put her arm around Maris and rubbed her shoulder.

"Don't doubt the genuine moments you've had together," her dad added. His tone was gentle but convincing. "You're stronger than you give yourself credit for, Mar. If Colton means this much to you, don't be afraid to fight for what you want—but remember, love's a two-way street. You deserve someone willing to meet you halfway."

"Thanks, guys. It's just so hard to not know what the future holds. All the what-ifs really get to me sometimes. And barely getting any calls or texts from him is making me crazy. I feel like maybe it was foolish of me to trust my heart," Maris said.

Her mom drew her closer. "That's not foolish. It's brave. But don't let the uncertainty make you forget your own worth. If Colton's the right one, he'll see that and make the effort to meet you where you are. You deserve nothing less."

"Yeah, he'll see what he's missing if he doesn't come back!" Jemma blurted, coming out of her hiding place. She had been eavesdropping and now wanted to add her support. "If he truly cares about you, Mar, he'll come back. And if not, you're strong enough to move forward. I've aways envied that about you."

Maris's eyes widened and she gave her sister a small smile. "I guess. I have come a long way in the last few months, and I have to choose myself at some point. Regardless of whether Colton comes back, I should keep pursuing my dreams and believe in myself. I wish him the best with all my heart but I think I need to stop pining for him and wallowing in the fact that he's gone. It's easier said than done but, I've got to try."

Jemma, proud of her older sister's resolve, began to clap. Soon, their parents joined in, and Maris grinned at them with gratitude. After their applause was finished, she hugged each of them.

"Thank you all. I really needed that," Maris said, her voice filled with emotion. "I'm going to go upstairs and change before breakfast."

Once in her room, she took a moment to gather herself, feeling a renewed sense of determination. She slipped into a warm sweater and sat down on the bed. Beside her, her phone showed that she had a new mail message. As she looked closer, her heart began to race. It was from one of the advanced copy readers she had shared her story with. Anxious to see their feedback, she nervously clicked to open the message.

Dear Maris,

I just finished reading your novel, and I had to reach out to tell you how much I loved it. Your storytelling is captivating, and the characters are so richly developed. I couldn't put it down! I'm planning to post a full review on social media to recommend it to my followers. Your work deserves to be celebrated, and I'm excited to share it with others.

Thank you for sharing your incredible talent with the world!

Best regards, An Enthusiastic ARC Reader

Maris felt a surge of joy and validation as she read the kind words. Tears of happiness filled her eyes as she realized that her hard work and dedication were paying off. It was a reminder that her dreams were within reach, urging her to keep pushing forward. She would no longer be defined by doubts but by the strength she had within herself.

Embers of Independence

Scrolling through her preliminary edits to ensure that everything was perfect was making Maris go cross-eyed. She had been staring at the computer screen for hours and the strain was beginning to wear on her. But she was determined to get through this last chapter before the hour was up. Her beta readers had played a crucial role in helping her feel her story was good enough to continue with. Their faith in her had spurred her on.

Also, in the past couple of months, tons of feedback from her advanced copy readers had come in. Most were glowing reviews, but a few had some constructive criticism, and she wanted to make sure she had taken that into account.

February swept in on the heels of a long and arduous January. The start of the new year held beautiful possibilities for her career but Maris had to keep her head down and press on toward her goal of publication. She was hoping to release her novel in just a couple of months and there was much to be done.

She took a deep breath and stretched, feeling the muscles of her back spasm in response. A glance at the clock revealed she'd been working for almost six hours without a break. Despite the fatigue, a sense of accomplishment washed over her. Each word she perfected brought her closer to her destination.

Taking a moment to study the view outside the window, Maris allowed herself to reflect on how far she had come. From the early drafts filled with doubt to the more polished manuscript in front of her, this journey had been transformative. She had poured her heart and soul into this manuscript, and it was almost ready to be shared with the world.

She had some quotes from her favorite reviews printed and tacked on the corkboard above her desk. The first one she ever received was the highest on the board.

Maris, your book is incredible! The characters are so relatable, the plot kept me hooked. I can't wait to see it in stores!

At the bottom edge the most recent thoughts from a popular social media influencer.

Your story is an absolute gem, Maris! From the very first page, I was captivated. The vivid descriptions make you feel like you're actually there. I highly recommend this book!

She smiled at the encouraging words, feeling renewed.
Although she knew the road ahead would be challenging, she
was ready to face it. Long gone were the days of running from
critique or hiding from disapproval. Once hesitant and unsure,
she was now confident; a force to be reckoned with.

Her Instagram account now sat at 13,241 followers and she was
creating quite a buzz about her writing endeavors. As she
worked, she couldn't help but think of the journey that had led
her here. The late nights, the moments of doubt, the support of
her friends and family, and the countless hours of writing and
rewriting had all culminated in this moment. She thought of
Colton, whose encouragement inspired her to self-publish. His
confidence in her potential had given her courage. Though, the
image of his face that flashed in her mind brought an ache to
her heart.

They had last spoken on the phone in early January.

"Colton, she had said, her voice sharp. "This isn't working. I
know you're in really deep with Axel, but I can't be the only one
fighting for us."

Since then, there had been occasional texts—short, generic
messages like 'Hope you're doing okay' or 'Sorry, been busy.' A
few times, they'd almost talked, but something always got in the

way—a missed call, a text replied to hours later, the weight of their own silence growing too heavy to uphold.

Often, when Colton reached out, she debated her reply for fear that hello would lead to another goodbye.

Maris scrolled through their last text exchange, reading Colton's one-word replies that felt more like placeholders than conversation. Was this just him being overwhelmed, or had she mistaken their connection entirely? The thought sat heavy in her chest, a growing knot of suspicion she couldn't untangle.

She leaned back and closed her eyes for a moment. Writing was her anchor, grounding her through the frenzied emotions. She took one more cleansing breath and turned her attention back to her manuscript. But, as she blinked her eyes open, she saw a desktop notification from her email account. New mail from a publishing house! With much trepidation, she opened the message.

Dear Maris,

I hope this email finds you well. My name is Cecily Harper and I am a senior editor at Whispering Pines Press in Portland, Oregon. I recently came across early reviews of your book and was impressed by the feedback. Your storytelling and the depth of your characters have captivated readers, and we believe your work has immense potential.

We would love to discuss the possibility of picking up your story for publishing. Please let us know if you are interested in exploring this opportunity further. We are eager to work with you and help bring your book to a wider audience.

Regards, Cecily Harper

Maris was in disbelief as she read the email. This unexpected development was a testament to her hard work and dedication. She knew that this was a defining moment in her journey, and she was ready to embrace it with open arms. This is what she had always dreamed of!

Her fingers trembled, her heart pounding with nervous energy. She carefully composed her response.

Dear Cecily,

Thank you so much for your kind words and for considering my book for publication. I am thrilled and honored by the opportunity to work with Whispering Pines Press. I would love to discuss this further and discover the possibilities.

Looking forward to hearing from you soon.

Best, Maris Oakwood

With a deep inhale, she hit the send button and spun around in her chair, the thrill of release taking over.

She felt good about what this publisher was offering—a chance for her writing to be accessible to more people. For Maris, it wasn't about a paycheck. It was about the difference her words might make to anyone out there looking for love or striving to get to know themselves. With a few more keystrokes, she finished the initial round of edits and closed her laptop.

Deciding she needed some fresh air, she grabbed her coat and headed out to convince Chrissy to grab an afternoon snack and catch up. Plus, she couldn't wait to share the publishing news with someone. Chrissy had finally taken on an assistant, and she could hopefully be persuaded to delegate some tasks to him while they went out.

The crisp February air felt refreshing as Maris made her way from the car into Chrissy's bookstore. Upon arriving, she spotted Chrissy at the counter, deep in conversation with her new hire, Leo. Chrissy looked up, her expression softening.

"Maris! It's so good to see you. What brings you in today?" she asked.

"Hey, Chrissy! I was hoping we could grab a bite and catch up. I have some news to share." Maris could barely contain her excitement.

Chrissy's eyes sparkled with curiosity. "News? I'm intrigued! Let me just wrap up here and we can head out."

She turned to check a clipboard hanging by the counter, quickly scribbling a note.

"Leo, can you handle things for a bit?"

The young man gave a hesitant nod, which Chrissy didn't seem to notice—or chose not to comment on.

"Let's go," she said, linking her arm through Maris's as they headed to Salty Sands Café down the street.

Settling in, Maris realized she hadn't been there in an eternity and her thoughts flickered to Colton, uninvited. The last time she was here was before they'd met. But, within an instant, Chrissy interrupted her reflection.

"Okay, spill," Chrissy said, leaning forward with keen interest. "What's the big news?"

Maris's face lit up. "I got an email from a publisher. Whispering Pines Press wants to pick up my book for publishing!"

Chrissy's eyes widened in delight, and she gasped, clapping her hands together. "Oh my gosh, Maris, that's amazing! I'm so proud of you!" Her excitement spilled over in a delighted laugh. "As soon as your book is available for order, I'm getting a bunch of copies for the bookshop and hosting a signing event for you. It's going to be epic!"

"Thank you so much, Chrissy. It's all so surreal! I couldn't have imagined, in my wildest dreams, that this would happen."

"Anything for my favorite author!" Chrissy said with a wink. "So, what's next on your agenda? Wait! So... are you going to tell Colton? About the book?"

Maris hesitated, fidgeted with the corner of her napkin. "I don't know," she admitted. "We haven't really talked much since… well, since everything started with Axel."

Chrissy's smile faded into a look of concern. "Maris, what's going on with you two? You've been quiet about him lately."

Maris sighed, her emotions bubbling up. "It's complicated. I feel like... I'm always the one reaching out. And when he does text or call, it's just about Axel, or what's going on with the case. It's never about us. And honestly? I'm tired of feeling like I'm the only one trying to hold things together."

Chrissy studied her for a moment, her lips pressing together as she nodded gently. "Mar, I don't blame you for feeling that way. But don't hold all that in. You deserve to be heard—and he deserves to know what you're feeling."

"Well," Maris began, "I don't think I'm going to bother him with it right now. I'm leaving tomorrow to visit Alex and her family in Chicago. They had the new baby five months ago already, and I'm really excited to meet him. Plus, I'll be attending a writer's festival while I'm there. It's usually held in the spring, but, right now, there is a special winter session. It will be a busy trip, but I can't wait."

Chrissy clucked disapprovingly, a hint of concern in her eyes. "Maris, you wouldn't be bothering him. This is huge news, and he should know how amazing you're doing."

A small smile played on Maris' lips. "Yeah, maybe someday I'll tell him. For now, I'm just focusing on my writing and taking things one step at a time."

Chrissy nodded. "Well, if you ever need to talk about it, you know I'm here for you. Now, tell me more about this writer's festival in Chicago."

Maris's eyes lit up with excitement. "It's going to be amazing! There will be panels, workshops, and lots of opportunities to network with other writers and professionals. I'm hoping to learn a lot and maybe even get some inspiration for my next project."

"That sounds like a fantastic opportunity," Chrissy said. "And visiting Alex and her new baby will be so special. You have so much to look forward to, Mar. I'm so proud of you. You're doing incredible things."

The two friends chatted and laughed, savoring their afternoon together. But as Maris headed home, she contemplated what Chrissy had suggested—that Colton should know about the publishing offer. She wasn't planning on telling him but now she weighed the options. Maybe their relationship wasn't meant to last. Maybe it was better off this way. But, what if not?

Parking outside her house, she retrieved her phone from her purse and opened a new text message. Assigning it to be sent to Colton, she typed. A few sentences in, she reread what she'd written. It sounded formal, cold, and like she was addressing a stranger.

What's the point? He probably doesn't care anymore. I'm on my own now, she thought. And, one by one, she deleted the words. Decisively, she tucked her phone back into her purse and headed inside.

There were a few more hours for her to finish last-minute packing and prepare for the flight to Chicago in the morning. Maris went through her checklist, ensuring she had everything she needed. Clothes, toiletries, her laptop, and all the materials for the writer's festival were carefully packed into her suitcase. This trip was an important step in making progress as a writer, and she was determined to make the most of it.

Before fastening her bag, she reached into the suitcase and took out a small velvet pouch. Inside was the yellow pearl she had found on Victoria Beach back in September, right after her interview with Colton. She held it gently in her palm, the smooth surface catching the light. As she admired the pearl, she couldn't help but reflect on the deep emotions she had experienced since that day—the joy, the growing connection with Colton, and the misgivings following his departure.

With a lingering glance at the pearl, Maris returned it carefully to the pouch and tucked it back into the suitcase. She zipped the bag and set it at the foot of the bed. After changing into her pajamas, she climbed under the blankets, her mind buzzing with thoughts of the festival and her upcoming visit with Alex and her family. She forced herself to take slow, calming breaths, and soon the excitement faded into the background as sleep finally overtook her.

Morning came early, announced by the sound of Maris's alarm clock. She stretched and yawned, feeling a surge of readiness for the day ahead. After a quick shower and a hearty breakfast, she double-checked her bag one last time. Everything was in order.

As she headed out the door, suitcase in tow, her phone buzzed with an incoming call. She glanced at the screen and her heart skipped a beat. It was Colton. She hesitated for a moment before answering.

"Hello?" Maris said, surprised.

"Hey, Maris," Colton's voice came across the line, sounding a bit wobbly. "I know it's been a while, but I need to talk to you."

"Colton? I… I'm on my way out right now. What's going on?"

Crossroads

He had rehearsed what he wanted to say a hundred times, but now that the moment was here, words seemed to escape him. He took a deep breath and dialed Maris's number. The phone rang once, twice, and then her voice filled the line.

"Hello?" Maris said.

"Hey, Maris," Colton's voice came through, sounding a bit wobbly. "I know it's been a while, but I need to talk to you."

"Colton? I… I'm on my way out right now. What's going on?"

He hesitated, glancing at the envelope in the passenger seat next to him. Inside was a letter he had written, baring his heart. But he hadn't had the courage to send it. Unsure if she wanted to hear his feelings about the distance between them, and how desperately he wished to rekindle what they had.

"I don't want to keep you," he began. "I just… wanted to let you know that you've been on my mind. I realize I haven't been as good at keepin' in touch as I wanted to be… as much as I should've been. But Axel is on a precipice. He could go to jail, Mar."

"What? What do you mean?" Maris asked with urgency.

"He's in massive debt and bein' taken to court for illegal gamblin' and tax evasion. I'm so frustrated and at a loss for any solution. I feel like I'm failin' him. But I also feel like I've failed *you*. I couldn't just leave him to handle it alone but, it's overwhelming and I hate that it's kept us apart this long," Colton confessed.

"Colton, you should've told me all this before now. I don't want to say it's too little, too late, but you just disappeared," Maris said, an ache in her voice.

Colton's voice, too, was thick with emotion. "I know, Mar. I know I've messed up. I thought I could handle everything on my own, but it's been keepin' me awake at night. Axel's my brother, but in tryin' to help him I didn't just push you away—I completely abandoned everything that mattered to you. Your accomplishments, your dreams... I should've been there to celebrate with you, to lift you up. But I wasn't. I let you down, and I hate that I made you feel like you were on your own. I never wanted that."

There was a long silence on the line, and Colton hoped his words sounded sincere. He regretted leaving the way he did, but he hadn't seen any other options at the time. Hearing Maris's breathing on the other side of the phone call made his heartbeat go wild. She was so close, yet so far.

"I should have opened up to you. I want to make things right, Maris. I care about you so much, and I don't want to lose what we have," he added, when she didn't reply.

Her voice came out low and strained, carrying the heft of her exhaustion. "Colton, I appreciate your honesty. Truly. But I can't just pick up where we left off. Even the idea of it… it's a lot to take in. I need to focus on myself right now. I'm sorry."

He felt as if the wind had been knocked out of him; suddenly gasping for his next breath. Colton closed his eyes. The magnitude of her words settled over him like a heavy fog. He understood, even if it hurt more than he could express. He hadn't proved to be the person he promised her he would be.

"I understand," he said, his voice shaky. And I respect your need to focus on yourself. I just wanted you to know how I feel. I don't expect anything from you, but I hope... I hope eventually you can give me a chance to make it right."

There was another pause. He could almost feel Maris processing his words. "Thanks, Colton," she finally said, her voice soft. "I appreciate that. We'll see where things go, okay?"

"Okay," he agreed, trying to mask his emotions. "Take care of yourself, Maris. I'll be here if you need anything."

"You too," she replied. "Goodbye, Colton."

"Goodbye, Maris," he replied, and the call ended.

Well, I guess that's that, Colton thought. *I screwed it up and now I'm nothing to her.*

He sat in the silence of his truck, staring out at the rain-soaked world beyond the windshield. The envelope on the passenger seat was like an anvil tied to his heart. All the unspoken thoughts and unresolved feelings were dragging him down. He yearned to express his affections to Maris, yet none of his words seemed enough to prove his commitment. His actions had already overshadowed what he said.

For now, he would focus on doing what he could for Axel and bettering himself. If not for Maris, then for his own sake. He started the engine and drove away, the rain tapping a steady rhythm on the roof.

Colton gripped the steering wheel tightly, the muscles in his forearms straining. Every mile he covered felt like he was further away from the possibility of making things right with Maris. But he knew he couldn't afford to dwell on his mistakes. Axel still needed him. He turned the truck onto the highway, heading toward Axel's place. He wasn't sure what he could do to help anymore, but he was determined to try.

The drive gave him a chance to reflect on his actions and the impact they had on the people he cared about. He had always been the one to shoulder the burdens, to attempt to fix everything himself. But maybe it was time to learn that he didn't have to do it alone. Maybe it was time to trust others and let them in.

As Colton navigated the familiar roads, he was submerged in memories of his time with Maris. He could still hear her soft giggle, see her smile, and feel the tenderness of her touch. He gritted his teeth, determination hardening his resolve. He knew that if he wanted to be the man Maris deserved, he had to be more reliable and transparent.

Colton also knew he should respect Maris's boundaries. She had said she had to focus on herself. But hanging up the phone and walking away seemed like he was letting her go too easily. What if her journey didn't lead back to him? What if he needed to put himself in her path again to really be sure things were over? Would he ever be able to find peace if he didn't show his position wasn't going to change? That he would be waiting for her until the end of time?

Arriving at Axel's place, he slammed the gearshift into park, the truck jerking to a halt with a lurch that matched the knot in his chest. His grip was still tight on the wheel as he stared at the small house, now even more weathered and worn down than before.

Axel opened the door as Colton approached, his eyes tired.

"Hey, Axel," Colton said, forcing a reassuring smile.

Axel led Colton into the living room, where piles of discarded paperwork littered the floor. He slumped down on the couch and looked up at Colton. His eyes were filled with willpower.

"Colt, if takin' this plea deal means doing time, then so be it. I've made mistakes, and it's time I faced the consequences. I've thought long and hard about it. Fightin' it this long has only prolonging the inevitable, and it's not fair to you or anyone else. I'm just hopin' that dealin' with it this way will give me a chance to start fresh when it's all over."

Colton nodded, understanding that nothing he could say would change Axel's mind.

"Camille will be here any minute and I think it's time I thank her for her help so far and be done with it," Axel stated.

Colton felt a surge of emotions—sadness, anger, but also a strange sense of relief. "Are you sure about this?"

Axel sighed, his shoulders drooping further. "Yeah, I'm sure. I can't keep pretending that everything will magically work out. I need to face this head on."

Colton sat down next to his brother; the truth sinking in.

"Alright, Axel. If this is what you want... I'm here to support you."

"No," Axel replied. "I'm well aware of the toll this is takin' on you, Colton. You've sacrificed a lot and probably lost your chance at happiness because of me."

Colton's eyes widened with surprise. "What do you mean?"

"C'mon, man. You've been walkin' around here moping for weeks. I know a lovesick fool when I see one. And Maris deserves better."

Colton looked away, rubbing the back of his neck. "Maybe, but it's complicated," he muttered.

Axel shook his head. "Complicated, huh? That sounds like you're tryin' to dodge the real issue. Spit it out, Colt."

"Maris and I… we had somethin' special, but I messed it up. I thought I could handle everything on my own and I kept her at arm's length. Dude, Maris is real, and smart, kind, and the sort of gorgeous I don't deserve. She lights up the room and makes you feel like anything's possible. Now, it's over. She's gone."

Axel leaned forward, his expression softening. "Dude, you can't blame yourself for everything. You're human, and humans make mistakes. But if she means that much to you, you can't give up without a fight."

Colton shrugged. "I don't know. She said she needs to do her own thing right now. If I try to rush and fix things too soon, I might just make it worse."

"It's never too soon to do the right thing. Trust me, I've learned that the hard way. You should go get her, Colt. Make things right before you run out of time," Axel advised.

Colton managed a small smile, feeling a glimmer of hope amidst the turmoil. "Thanks, Axel. Quite the wise man."

Axel placed a reassuring hand on Colton's shoulder. "Alright, let's get this plea deal sorted out. If I'm goin' to jail, I'm goin' on my terms," he said with an awkward chuckle.

Just as they finished collecting the paperwork, there was a knock at the door. Colton went to answer it, finding Camille standing on the porch.

"Camille, thanks for coming," Colton said, stepping aside to let her in.

She walked into the living room, her eyes scanning the mess of papers.

"So, I came to go over the last bit of info from the lawyer, Axel. I want to make sure you understand everything," she said.

"I've thought a lot about it, Camille. I know it might not be exactly what we were all hopin' for. But it's time to stop runnin'. I'm goin' to talk to Mickey and go with whatever plea deal he thinks is most fair."

She nodded. "If that's what you think is best. Although I have to admit I'm surprised."

As they discussed, Camille seemed to edge closer to Colton, her demeanor becoming more affectionate. She slid her hand up to his shoulder, her touch purposeful and unyielding

"Colton, I know this has been hard on you too," Camille said softly, her voice laced with concern. "You don't have to go through this alone. I'm here for you." She moved even closer, her hand now resting on his shoulder. "I mean it, Colton. We could get through this together."

Colton shifted uncomfortably. "Camille, I appreciate your support, but I think it's best if we keep things professional. I need to focus on helpin' Axel, and I have some things of my own goin' on." He gently but firmly removed her hand, taking a step back.

Camille's expression faltered, disappointment flashing in her eyes. "I get it," she said quietly. "I'll give you two some space."

"Thank you for everything you've done. We wouldn't have gotten this far without you," Colton replied, trying to soften the rejection.

With a nod, Camille gathered her things and left. Once she was gone, Colton sat down and took a deep breath, feeling relief and determination. He turned to Axel and said, "Let's finish this up, and then I'll book my flight to see Maris."

Axel nodded, a hint of a smile on his face. "Attaboy, Colt."

Reunions

As the plane touched down at O'Hare International Airport, Maris felt a flutter of excitement in her chest. The writer's festival was just around the corner, and she was eager to immerse herself in the literary world. But making her way through the bustling terminal, her thoughts shifted to the family reunion awaiting her.

Stepping off of the escalator, Maris spotted Alex waving enthusiastically, a wide smile on her face. Alex's new baby was nestled in a carrier on her chest, and her two nieces, Thalia and Maisey, were beside her, bouncing with joy.

"Maris!" Alex called out.

Maris's heart swelled with joy as she hurried over, enveloping Alex in a tight hug. "It's so good to see you!" she exclaimed.

Alex laughed and her eyes sparkled. "We've missed you so much! Meet your nephew, Otto! Isn't he adorable?"

The baby gazed up at Maris with big, green eyes identical to Alex's. "He's perfect, Sis. I'm so happy to be here."

"Come on, the girls are dying to get home and show you the pictures they drew," Alex said, taking Maris's hand.

Maris turned to Thalia and Maisey, who were beaming up at her. "I can't wait to see them," she commented, ruffling their hair. "You two must've known my refrigerator looks lonely."

As they walked to the car, the steady rhythm of their steps seemed to anchor her. The city buzzed with energy, but in this moment, surrounded by family, she felt a deep feeling of peace.

Arriving at Alex's cozy home, Maris was met by the delicious aroma of homemade soup simmering on the stove, tended to by Alex's husband. She settled onto the couch, holding Otto for the first time, marveling at the tiny fingers and toes. Smiling down at him, she listened to his soft baby sounds and gushed over his gummy grin.

As she sat in the living room, cradling baby Otto, Maris thought about the whirlwind of the past few months but, in this moment, everything felt right.

Thalia and Maisey ran into the room, clutching colorful drawings in their hands. "Aunt Mar, look what I made for you!"

Thalia exclaimed, holding up a picture of a sunny beach with a bright yellow sun.

Maris's eyes lit up. "These are wonderful! You two are such talented artists," she praised. "I can't wait to put them up."

As the evening wore on, Alex and Maris caught up on each other's lives, reminisced about their childhood, and marveled at how much had changed over the years. Alex's husband, Cillian, joined them, adding his own witty anecdotes and making everyone laugh.

Soon, Maris yawned. Tired from her journey and sapped of energy by the anticipation of tomorrow; the first day of the writer's festival. She wanted to make sure she got enough rest before she spent the entire time rubbing shoulders with published authors and she clung to the belief that this experience would open doors for her. Already she had a leg up with the offer from Whispering Pines Press.

Standing up to go to bed, she said goodnight to Cillian and kissed each of the girls, asleep on the couch, on the forehead. Alex, rocking Otto in the recliner, motioned her closer and whispered.

"So, before the trip's over, you have to tell me what happened with you and that Colton guy."

"There's nothing to tell," Maris whispered back, though her eyes betrayed her pain. She forced a smile as tears unexpectedly sprung up. "Time for bed," she added, rubbing Alex's shoulder lightly.

Maris woke up early the next morning, the soft light of dawn sneaking through the curtains. Today marked the beginning of the writer's festival, and she was eager to dive into the world of creativity and inspiration. Too nervous to eat, she gulped down a cup of coffee, gathered her materials, and set off to the festival venue.

Alex had offered to drive her, but Maris preferred to explore and observe on her way into the city from their quaint Blue Island home. The white craftsman-style house, built in 1915, underwent complete renovation, down to new windows and a new air conditioning unit. Cillian didn't take shortcuts and didn't abridge budgets. It resulted in a modern and comfortable space, perfect for raising the kids.

The ride through Chicago was invigorating, and Maris felt a sense of excitement building within her. Skyscrapers and monuments flashed by as she sat in the back seat of her Uber. She looked out the window with growing impatience. Upon arriving at the lively venue, she saw writers and literary enthusiasts gathered to celebrate their shared passion.

Maris registered at the front desk and was given a badge and a welcome packet.

"Welcome to the festival!" the volunteer said with a warm smile. "We have an impressive lineup of events and panels today. Enjoy!"

With her badge proudly displayed, Maris stepped into the main hall. The atmosphere was electric, filled with the buzz of conversations and the energy of creative minds at work. She walked through the booths, observing the variety of books, posters, and displays. The smell of fresh paper and ink was intoxicating, a reminder of why she loved the world of literature.

She listened to multiple panels and participated in workshops throughout the day, diligently taking notes. She listened intently as established authors spoke about their experiences, offering insights and advice that resonated deeply with her. During a break, she found herself at a refreshments station, chatting with a group who were just as enthusiastic about the festival as she was. They exchanged business cards and ideas. She was elated meeting people who shared her obsession with writing.

"I've seen early reviews for your book online, Maris. It sounds fantastic! I can't wait to read it," one of them had said.

That's so cool! Maris thought. *Word about my book is actually traveling!*

As the sun set, she felt a sense of accomplishment. The first day of the festival had exceeded her expectations, and she was proud of herself for effectively making connections throughout the sessions. Despite aching feet and a desire to take off her shoes, she found herself highly motivated.

Just as she was about to leave, she heard a familiar voice calling her name. "Maris? Is that you?"

She froze mid-turn, her expression shifting to one of stunned disbelief. "Oliver? Oliver Cronan?"

Oliver, an old classmate from her college days, stood before her with a charming smile. He had always been the life of the party, and it seemed like time had only made him more charismatic. "It's been ages! How have you been?" he asked, pulling her into a friendly hug.

"I've been good, thanks! How about you?" Maris replied, feeling overwhelmed with nostalgia.

"I'm doing great. I actually just published my first novel," Oliver said, his grey eyes shining with pride. "I never would have guessed we'd run into each other at a writer's festival."

Maris laughed. "What are the odds? Congratulations on your novel! I really want to hear more about it."

They spent the next few minutes reminiscing about old times and discussing their writing journeys. Oliver was as pleasant as ever, and Maris genuinely enjoyed their conversation.

As the festival wound down, he handed her a business card. "Let's not lose touch again. I'd love to catch up properly sometime. Here's my number."

Surprised, Maris gave a crooked smile as she took the card. "I'd like that. Here's mine as well," she said, after a long search through her disheveled purse.

"Great," Oliver replied, tucking the card into his pocket. "I'll give you a call soon. Take care, Maris."

"You too, Oliver," Maris returned, feeling warmth in her chest.

As Maris made her way back to Alex's home, she couldn't help but think about her unexpected meeting with Oliver. She felt a mix of emotions—an uplifting spark striking in her heart. When she arrived, it was already dark, and the house glowed cozily with evening lights.

Alex greeted her at the door, a curious look in her eyes. "How was your day?" she asked, ushering Maris inside.

"It was incredible," Maris replied, a smile spreading across her face. "I met so many amazing people, and you'll never guess who I ran into—Oliver Cronan, from college!"

"Oliver? Wow, that must have been a surprise!" Alex said, her eyes widened in interest. "Did you guys catch up?"

Maris nodded. "Yeah, we exchanged numbers. He's doing great, just published his first novel. It was really nice to see a familiar face."

As they settled into the living room, Maris couldn't shake thoughts of Colton from her mind. The encounter with Oliver had stirred up old memories, but it also made her reflect on her unresolved feelings for Colton. Alex seemed to sense her internal conflict.

"Maris, can we talk for a minute?" Alex asked gently, gesturing toward the seat beside her.

Maris sat down, sensing that her sister wanted to have a serious conversation. "Sure, what's on your mind?"

Alex took a beat before speaking. "I've noticed that you've been a bit off, even before you got here. Especially when it comes to Colton. Do you want to talk about it?"

The words tumbled out before Maris could stop them.

"It's just... it's all so confusing, Alex. Colton and I had something I thought was irreplaceable, something so rare it felt untouchable. But then he pulled away. Now, he wants another chance, but I don't know if I can trust him again. I don't want to get hurt."

Alex nodded, her expression compassionate. "I understand. It's hard to open up again when you've been let down. But sometimes, people deserve another shot. Do you still have feelings for him?"

Maris hesitated, then nodded. "Yes, I do. But I'm scared. What if he lets me down again?"

"If you believe that he genuinely wants to make things right, maybe it's worth giving him that chance. No one's perfect. But I understand you want to protect your heart too. You have to do what's best for you. Just remember, trust takes time to be built. You and Colton didn't even really get a fair shot before he had to leave."

"I just don't know what to do," Maris confessed.

She sat quietly, processing her sister's advice. Just as she was about to speak, her phone buzzed. She glanced at the screen and saw an unknown number flashing.

"Yes? This is Maris," she answered.

"Hey, Maris," a man's voice replied with a hint of excitement. "This is Oliver. I know I said I would call soon, but I even surprised myself by doing it *this* soon. I just couldn't wait."

Maris chuckled softly. "It's nice to hear from you. What's up?"

"I was wondering if you'd be interested in having dinner with me tomorrow night," Oliver said, his voice sincere. "I'd really like to make up for lost time. And... if I'm being honest, I always had a bit of a crush on you back in college."

Maris's cheeks reddened instantly at his confession. She glanced over at Alex, who was watching with an encouraging smile, and then turned her attention back to the phone call. Her mind raced with thoughts and emotions.

She remembered the easy friendship she had shared with Oliver during their college days. He had always been charming and kind, someone she could count on for a good laugh or a comforting word. With his tousled dark hair and twinkling eyes, Oliver had an effortless way of making everyone around him feel at ease. His enthusiasm for life was contagious, whether they were embarking on a spontaneous road trip or simply sharing late-night conversations about their life after graduation.

Oliver was the guy who would bring her coffee just the way she liked it, without her having to ask. He had a knack for sensing when she needed a break from studying and would whisk her away for a walk by the lake or a movie night. Their bond had been special, built on mutual respect and a shared sense of adventure.

But now, things were different. She wasn't nineteen anymore, and her heart had been through its share of highs and lows.

The recent confusion around Colton loomed large in her mind. Could she really consider opening up to someone new when her feelings for Colton were still so unsure? And what if giving Oliver a chance meant missing out on something that could be salvaged with Colton?

But then again, Oliver's sincerity and warmth seemed genuine, even over the phone. The idea of catching up and seeing where things might lead was both tempting and chilling. She knew she had to make a decision. Did she cling to the past with Colton, or did she dare to explore a new possibility with Oliver?

"Maris?" Oliver's voice broke through her pondering, a note of concern in his tone. "Are you still there?"

Her heart pounded in her chest as she wrestled with her choices. She opened her mouth to respond, but the words caught in her throat. She glanced at Alex once more, seeking silent reassurance.

"Yes, sorry. I..."

Maris's fingers trembled as she tightened her grip on the phone. Her heart pounded in her chest, each beat echoing the tumult of emotions swirling inside her. A bead of sweat trickled down her temple, mingling with the warmth of her flushed cheeks. She took a deep breath, feeling the gravity of her decision settle upon her.

Under Pressure

Colton stared out the airplane window, his mind racing as the city lights below blurred into streaks of gold and white. He had gotten a flight as soon as possible from Charleston to Los Angeles as regret engulfed him from the inside out. The way Maris had hung up the phone as if it were a last goodbye haunted him. He couldn't shake the thought that if he didn't act now, he might lose his chance forever.

Colton clenched his fists, feeling the turbulence of the flight mirrored in his own restless emotions. He thought about the misunderstandings, the harsh words, and the conflict between them in the beginning. But then his thoughts shifted to the way they had learned to trust each other, the moments of vulnerability they shared. He remembered the late-night conversations that developed their closeness, the supportive gestures that eased their fears, and the unwavering belief they had in each other's potential. Now, with every mile that brought him closer to Maris, he felt a renewed determination to mend what was broken. To fight for something he realized he couldn't afford to lose.

The flight attendants moved down the aisle, offering drinks and snacks, but Colton couldn't focus on anything other than his mission: to find Maris and show her he was willing to do whatever it took to gain her trust.

The plane touched down at LAX, and he wasted no time. He rushed through the terminal, grabbed his rental car, and drove directly to Maris's house. His pulse thundered in his ears as he lifted his fist and rapped against the door, the sound sharp and demanding in the quiet air. But there was no answer. He peered through the windows, but the place looked as lonely as he felt.

Undeterred, Colton drove to River and Liza's apartment, hoping they might know where Maris was. He banged on their door, but again, there was no response. Frustration gnawed at him as he realized they were likely out for the day. He pulled out his cellphone to try River, but the call went straight to voicemail.

Not willing to give up, Colton headed to Malachi's Beach Brew, hoping she would be there writing an article or working on her manuscript. He pushed through the door, scanning the room for any sign of her. Spotting Malachi behind the counter, he approached him with urgency.

"Hey, Malachi," Colton said, trying to keep his voice steady. "Have you seen Maris around?"

Malachi shook his head without looking up. "No, I haven't seen her in a while. She hasn't been here lately."

Colton's shoulders sagged with disappointment. He thanked Malachi and turned to leave, noting the growing fear inside of him he might not find her. Thinking of one other place she could be, he decided to search for Chrissy—starting with Driftwood Shelves, where Maris often browsed for new reads.

As he approached the store, Colton's eyes scanned the street, hoping for a miracle. Just as he was about to enter the bookstore, he spotted Chrissy stepping out, holding a stack of books. His heart leaped with hope as he hurried over to her.

"Chrissy," he called out, relief in his voice. "Have you seen Maris? I've been looking for her everywhere."

Chrissy took a step back, visibly startled at the sight of him. "Colton? What are you doing here? Maris is in Chicago. She left yesterday."

"Chicago?" Colton said. He looked stumped.

"Yeah," Chrissy replied. She seemed exasperated, but Colton hoped he looked pitiful enough that she would divulge more.

"She went to a writer's festival there. There was a special winter session," she explained. "Plus, she wanted to visit her sister and the new baby."

"Oh...," he managed. The gears were turning in his mind. Chicago was where he needed to be. "Chrissy?" he continued. "Does Maris hate me?"

Chrissy peered up at him with compassion. It was obvious he was miserable. With his bomber jacket unzipped, he hunched his shoulders against the wind. The cold air was blowing his dark curls to the side and his nose was growing red. Hands shoved into his pockets, he looked like an insecure young boy.

"Colton," Chrissy said, her tone gentle. "I don't think Maris hates you. She's just... confused and hurt. She's had a lot to process."

"I need to talk to her, Chrissy. I flubbed up and I have to make it up to her."

"Then go to Chicago," Chrissy encouraged. "Tell her how you feel. Show her you're serious. But only if you mean it."

Colton nodded, gratitude in his eyes. He thanked Chrissy for the advice and left. He was already planning his next steps. As he drove back to the airport, he couldn't help but feel urgency and hope. This was his chance! He booked the earliest flight to

Chicago, his determination stronger than ever to show Maris how much she meant to him.

The hours leading to takeoff were a blur. The memory of their last conversation played on a loop in his head, each replay fueling his resolve. By the time the plane touched down in Chicago, he was both mentally and physically exhausted. He had spent a large sum of money on flights and now needed to find a hotel.

He quickly checked online for a nearby place to stay and went to drop off his luggage as they readied his room. Exhaustion tugged at him, but the anticipation of seeing Maris again made it hard to be still. After a quick meal at a restaurant close by, Colton returned to his hotel, but sleep was elusive. He spent the night tossing and turning, his mind racing with thoughts of what he would say to her.

Is she even going to give me the time of day? he wondered. *I'm not sure I deserve a clean slate with her.*

As dawn broke, Colton sprang out of bed, adrenaline kicking in. He showered and dressed, grabbing a coffee to-go as he headed straight to the festival venue. The cold Chicago air bit at his face, but it only sharpened his focus. He navigated the busy streets, his thoughts solely on finding Maris.

The convention center atmosphere was electric with movement and chatter. Writers, publishers, and readers filled the halls, making it feel like the search for her would be impossible. Booths lined the aisles, and he dodged groups of people, his eyes scanning the crowd for her unforgettable face—the face he'd dreamt of every night since they parted.

Just as he rounded a corner, he collided with someone, sending their armful of belongings flying. Papers, books, and pens scattered across the floor. Colton knelt to help pick them up, his jaw clenched, frustration pounding through him. As he gathered the items, his hand brushed against another, and he looked up to see Maris, startled and unsure.

"Colton?" she said curiously.

"Maris," he breathed, feeling a rush of relief and nerves. Before he could say more, he noticed a man standing beside her, watching them with a curious expression.

The man cleared his throat, breaking the tension. "Is everything okay here?"

Colton stood up, holding out the papers he had gathered. "I'm sorry. I didn't mean to bump into you both."

Maris took the papers, her gaze still locked on Colton. "It's... it's fine. What are you doing here?"

He swallowed hard, glancing briefly at the mysterious man beside Maris before focusing on her. "I came to find you. I didn't feel right lettin' things end the way they did. Please, can we go somewhere and talk?"

Maris's companion then stepped back, giving them a wider berth. "I'll catch up with you later, Maris," he said.

Maris nodded, her eyes never leaving Colton's. "Okay, Oliver. I'll see you later."

Oliver politely stepped away, though his inquisitive glance lingered a moment longer. As he disappeared into the crowd, Colton felt gratitude wash over him.

"Maris," he said again, his voice softer now that they were alone. "I know this is totally unexpected, but I had to see you. I need to explain."

"Colton, I told you I needed to focus on myself. Why did you come all this way? How did you even know I was here?" Her face was guarded.

"Chrissy told me when I went to Laguna to find you. I messed up, Mar. I know I hurt you, and I've regretted it every single day. I couldn't stand the thought of moving on without trying to make things right. I'm a fool."

Maris's gaze softened slightly, but she remained silent, waiting for him to continue.

"I came here because I need you to know how much you mean to me," Colton went on. "I made mistakes, and I'm sorry. I was lookin' down all the wrong roads to find what I thought was goin' to fulfill me, and then you came along." His eyes were earnest, and he spoke with conviction.

"I've been so confused, Colton. I really don't know what to think about all this," Maris replied.

"I know that what I'm asking isn't simple. But I also know that all these months you've been tryin' to act tough and convince me you're fine. It was a lie. I know you, Mar. And I'd walk through fire for you," Colton answered.

Maris blushed, glancing around at the exhibition. Oliver stood nearby, pretending not to observe the exchange.

"You can't just show up here, Colt, and expect that I'll just get lost in your eyes and forget everything that's happened," Maris stated.

Colton took a deep breath, his eyes never leaving Maris's. "I don't expect you to forget, Mar. I've got a lot to make up for. But I'm here because we're right for each other. I don't think you can say that you haven't thought about a moment just like this. We both know I've been an idiot. But I think each of us also knows that we belong together. I'm willin' to do whatever it takes."

Maris looked torn, her gaze flickering between him and the surrounding crowd. "Colton, I need time clear my head before I make any decisions. It means a lot that you came all this way, but I'm just not in a space where I can deal with this right now."

"I'm not goin' anywhere, sweetheart."

Maris nodded, a smile playing at the edges of her mouth. "I figured…," she said, rolling her eyes. "Why don't we meet up for a drink after the session?"

A wave of relief came over Colton, though he tried to maintain his composure. "I'd like that. Thanks."

They agreed on a time and place to meet later, and Maris returned to her session. Colton watched her walk away, knowing this was just the beginning of the journey to reconciliation. The hours until their meeting felt like an eternity. He wandered the convention center, trying to keep his mind occupied. He bought a ticket, browsed through booths, and listened to a few panel discussions, but his thoughts always went back to Maris. Eventually he left to sight see, regardless of the frigid temperatures, hoping it would prove to be a distraction.

He arrived at the designated bar later that evening. It was a cozy spot with dim lighting and a relaxed atmosphere. Colton found a velvet sofa in the back and waited, his nerves buzzing with suspense and dread. When Maris walked in, his heart skipped a beat. She looked beautiful in a fitted, off-the-shoulder cerulean sweater. Dark skinny jeans elongated her silhouette, and her ankle boots made her at least two inches taller than her normal five feet seven inches. Looking around, she spotted him and made her way over.

"Hi," she said, sliding into the seat across from him.

"Hi," Colton replied, smiling. "I'm glad you came."

"Me too," Maris replied.

They ordered their drinks and settled into a conversation. The initial stiffness faded as they talked about their experiences since they last saw each other. Colton listened intently as Maris shared her thoughts and feelings, and he spoke honestly about the realizations he had come to.

Finally, Colton's curiosity got the better of him. "Is somethin' goin' on with you and that Oliver guy? Does that have anything to do with why you're hesitatin'?"

Maris looked taken aback by Colton's question. She paused for a moment, then sighed and looked down at her drink. "Oliver and

I are just friends. He asked me to dinner and confessed that, when we were in college together, he had a crush on me. But I turned down the invitation and told him I was flattered but not interested. If I'm being honest, I said no because I couldn't stop thinking about you. And I figured that meant something important."

Colton felt a surge of hope at Maris's words. "Thanks for that. It means more than you know."

"So many times, I wanted to see you come running back to me and say all the things I was longing to hear. But I also knew that Axel needed you and I didn't want to make you resent me for holding you to a promise you made me after we only spent a small amount of time together," Maris confessed.

Colton's heart ached as he realized just how greatly she had been struggling. "Resent you? Mar, I've been so focused on tryin' to fix things with Axel that I didn't see the hurt I was causin' you in the process. And, by the way, you're all I ever wanted."

"I just didn't know how to make you see what I needed. It felt like you were putting everyone else first, and I was just... there," Maris admitted.

Colton leaned forward, his fingers lightly brushing hers before settling on the edge of the table, a silent plea in his eyes.

"I promise you, I'm here now, and I see you. I got into hero mode when I went back home and, while I'm glad it led to Axel and I hashin' out our issues, I never meant to make you feel abandoned. I just felt like maybe my words weren't enough and they were all I had to offer."

Maris gently placed her hand over his, her eyes softening as she listened to him. "I just needed to know that I mattered to you too, that I wasn't just an afterthought."

"You were never an afterthought, Maris. And I will never make you feel that way again."

Maris looked down at their hands, taking a deep breath. "Colt, I told you I wanted to take some time…"

"I know you did. And maybe we'd be fine stayin' apart. But look me in the eyes and tell me one good reason why we would do that?"

"I can't," she said, then paused for a beat. "I want to try to see if we can make this work. I've really missed you. But if it's not gonna be authentic, us against the world, reach for the stars stuff, I don't want it. There are two things I want. You and us."

Colton's heart swelled with hope at Maris's words. "I've missed you too, Mar. More than you can imagine. Every day we were apart, it felt like I was missin' my right arm. I swear to you, darlin', I'm all yours."

She reached into her bag and pulled out a small velvet pouch. Slowly, she opened it and took out the pearl within, holding it gently in her fingers. "I carry this with me to remind myself of the beauty that can come from something unexpected," she explained. "It's a symbol of hope and transformation. I want you to have it."

Maris pressed it into Colton's palm, her touch lingering. Colton looked down at the pearl, feeling its significance. He closed his hand around it, his eyes meeting Maris's.

"Thank you, Mar. This is amazing," he said.

They sat in silence for a moment, absorbing the impact of their conversation. It felt like a new beginning, a chance to build something stronger together. By the time they left the bar and stepped outside, the frosty night air greeted them, but the warmth of their mutual understanding kept the chill at bay. Snowflakes fell gently, transforming the street into a wonderland. Walking side by side, they each silently promised to care for the fragile connection they had just renewed.

Afterglow

By the time Colton made sure that Maris arrived safely back at Alex's and had gotten back to his hotel, it was late, and fatigue was wearing on him. The jet lag after two long days of travel, the stress of seeing Maris and trying to convince her of his devotion, and all the money he'd blown through in a short time were hitting all at once. Sleep, however, evaded him.

Regardless of whether he lay on his back or his side, stared at the ceiling or closed his eyes, he couldn't rid himself of the feeling that despite his reconciliation with Maris, something still stood between them. He couldn't blame her for being hesitant to rekindle their romance after what he'd put her through. Though he had no words to express his relief that she had turned down advances from Oliver.

When he'd seen them together in the hall during their run-in at the festival, a pang of jealousy had struck. The thought of his girl with someone else, sharing the same jokes, the same dreams… it made him uncharacteristically possessive. Something he knew he had no right to be. Not after his months of absence. Still, as much as he respected that Maris was a grown woman and could make her own choices, he wanted to be one of them. He wanted to be the someone she couldn't live without. The first one she thought of in the morning and the last one late at night.

As unwelcome visions of Oliver sweeping Maris off her feet circled in Colton's mind, his phone buzzed on the nightstand. He glanced at the screen and saw Maris's name, picking up without hesitation.

"Hey, Mar," he said softly, trying not to sound too eager. "Everything okay" His voice, although low, echoed in the sparsely furnished room.

"Hi," Maris responded. Her voice was quiet and tinged with drowsiness. "I couldn't sleep so I thought I'd call. I hope I didn't wake you."

"No, no. It's okay. I couldn't sleep either. What's goin' on?"

"My mind won't shut off," she yawned. "No matter how badly my body wants to rest. I just keep going in circles, thinking about us."

"Oh yeah?"

"Yeah. I mean, I'm glad you're here and all. It's just… you have always been good at making things sound simple. And nothing about us has been simple from the beginning. Chaotic, maybe. A whirlwind. But not simple."

"I guess, I have to admit it's been a little bit of a goat rodeo." His tone betrayed his shame.

She laughed softly into the receiver, her voice carrying a blend of exhaustion and quiet amusement. It was a sound he hadn't realized just how much he missed. They say you never know what you've got until it's gone, and the lack of her giggles of delight had taught him that there was no sound more welcome to his ears than her happiness. He was desperate to please her, yearning for her approval.

"I've missed that sound," he murmured. He could almost picture the way her eyes would crinkle at the corners, a small smile on her lips.

"It's been hard without you," she said, interrupting his thoughts.

Her comment touched his bones.

"I won't say I know how you feel, because I don't. I let you down. But I am sorry for all the times I wasn't there when you needed me to be."

"Of all the beaches, in all the towns, why'd you have to walk onto mine?" she asked.

"Because in every version of reality, I end up with you," he said firmly.

"I want to believe that," she confessed.

"Then believe it, darlin'. Because you and I are made of the same things. Salt, sweat, and tears have made us and we remake each other."

Maris felt a lump form in her throat, touched by the raw honesty in Colton's words. When she didn't respond, he continued.

"I look at you, Mar, and I see everything that terrifies me and makes me whole. You are tangled around my heart, and it's my favorite feelin'."

"I'm so glad I called to hear your voice," she admitted.

He felt a surge of emotions at her words. "I'm glad you did too. Talkin' to you makes everything feel a little easier."

"Mm hmm." She yawned again.

"You'd better go to bed, sweetheart. I don't want to have to put you over my shoulder on the way to the airport tomorrow."

"Okay," Maris whispered, amused. "Goodnight, Colton."

"Goodnight, Mar," he replied, his breathing slowing, steadying as he spoke.

He ended the call, his heart lighter. No doubt she was on the other side of the city, lying back on her pillow, the same way he was now. Though she was likely drifting off to sleep while his brain was alive, dreaming of her although he was wide awake.

He thought back to the first time he'd heard mention of Maris from Eve Vasquez. The first person to ever bring her up in conversation, besides River. The whole idea had been not to fall in love with her. She was going to be stuck up and snarky. A power-hungry reporter, just looking for her next big break.

Oh, how the mighty have fallen, Colton mused, chuckling to himself.

She'd turned out to be nothing like the woman he'd pictured, and his Trojan horse attack strategy hadn't fazed her. The rest had been out of their control. A longing glance here, a stolen kiss there. Maris was right; their love had been a slow burn that erupted into a whirlwind once they finally came together. And then, Colton ghosted. His pulse on life vanished, through no fault but his own.

His mind drifted to the moments they had shared during drinks. The way her eyes sparkled with hope and hesitation, the sound of her voice filling the room. It was a stark reminder of everything he stood to lose if he didn't get his act together. But he was determined to prove that he was worth her trust and love.

Turning onto his side, exhaustion began to take over. His journey to redemption was just beginning. But Maris had opened her heart to him again, and that was more than enough to keep him going.

Together We Rise

Maris and Colton stood on the front porch of Alex's home, bags packed and ready to go. Alex, Cillian, and their two daughters gathered to see them off, with little Otto sleeping in his mother's arms. Bittersweet emotions filled the air.

Alex wrapped Maris in a tight, one-armed hug, her eyes welling up with tears. "Promise you'll visit again soon," she whispered.

Maris nodded, her own eyes misting. "I promise. Thank you for everything, Alex. Best big sister ever."

Alex turned to Colton, and they squeezed each other briefly.

"Nice to finally meet you, Colton. Take care of my sister," she said, playfully punching his shoulder.

He smiled. "You can count on it."

Cillian clapped Colton on the back, a wide grin on his face. "And don't be strangers," he added.

Thalia and Maisy, the energetic twin girls, bounced around excitedly. Thalia tugged on Colton's sleeve; her eyes were wide with curiosity. "Are you really leaving, Uncle Colton?"

Maisy chimed in; her voice was full of innocence. "Will you come back soon?"

Everyone laughed nervously at the girls' endearing questions. Colton knelt at their level, a gentle smile on his face. "Yes, we're leaving, but we'll come back to visit. I promise."

Maris crouched beside him, bopping them on the nose affectionately. "You two take care of your mom and dad, okay? And Otto, too."

The twins nodded enthusiastically, their eyes shining with trust and admiration. "Okay, Aunt Maris!"

They exchanged final hugs and goodbyes, and Maris felt a deep thankfulness for the support and love they had received from Alex and her family. They loaded their bags into the car and climbed in, waving one last time as they drove away.

The journey back to Laguna Beach was filled with a comfortable silence, both lost in their thoughts. As they traveled, the landscape changed, eventually leading them back to the familiar coastal town. Waves crashing on the distant shore grew louder, a welcome sound as they returned.

Stepping out of the car, Maris inhaled deeply, savoring the fresh air that felt like a much-needed reprieve from the stuffiness of the airplane. The scent of pine trees and ocean salt filled her senses, bringing a sense of home. Together with Colton, she walked toward a bench overlooking the waves.

As they sat side by side, she reached into her bag and pulled out her phone, checking her email out of habit. Her heart skipped a beat when she saw a message from Cecily Harper, the editor she had been eagerly awaiting a response from.

She opened and scanned the email, her mind blown with each word.

"Cecily just replied about my manuscript. I forwarded the story to her when I was at Alex's, and she's already finished it! She loves it and thinks it has great potential. She wants to set up a meeting to discuss the details and talk about the next steps!"

"That's fantastic! I'm so proud of you," Colton said, pulling her into his embrace.

Maris settled against his chest and looked out at the water.

"Thank you, Colton. I couldn't have done it without you. Your encouragement to go down the path of finishing the book and the nudge to consider self-publishing got me here. I wouldn't have had the courage on my own."

"Sure, you would've," he replied. "You're a strong, determined woman, Mar. You could accomplish anything, and I believe that." He looked down at her and contemplated his next words. "I just wish I could stay longer to help you with everything."

"I know you would if you could. We'll make it work, even if it means juggling a few things."

Maris was caught between quiet satisfaction and the weight of unspoken thoughts.

"You know, it's funny how things work out. Just the other day, Liza mentioned that she and River finally found a house in Morro Bay. They're planning to move soon and will put their apartment up for sale. I'm happy for them. They've been searching for a while."

"Mm hmm. I remember him mentioning that to me. I wonder how much they're asking for the place. Probably a lot, considering that view," Colton mused.

Maris nodded, her mind drifting to the stunning panorama from River's apartment. "It is incredible. I'm sure they'll get a good price for it."

Colton's thoughts spun. "You know, I've been thinking… California has its perks," he said with a grin. "Maybe it's time I relocated my workshop."

Maris snapped to attention. "You'd really consider moving here?"

"Absolutely. I mean, I'd miss my family and I'm not sure what will happen with Axel yet. But it seems like everyone is movin' forward with their life and I don't want to be stagnant anymore."

"I love that idea. This could be a new adventure," Maris said.

Colton tapped a finger against his lips, his eyes distant with thought. "I'll talk to River and see if we can work something out. I have a small amount of savings."

Later that evening, Colton reached out to River to discuss the condo. River, thrilled at the idea of selling to a friend, offered to meet Colton the next day to discuss details.

The following morning Maris woke, eager to see Liza and to get more information. She couldn't believe that Colton was considering moving his life to be nearer to her, and the thought made her jittery.

Providence Oasis Resort was among the more upscale dining options in Laguna Beach and a fitting place to have a farewell brunch with their friends. Seated in a mauve leather booth, River and Liza sipped mimosas, looking like quite a newlywed couple.

The décor was light and airy with a mix of rich, feminine hues complimented by bright white and neutral tones. The main dining room was centered on a four-and-a-half-foot fireplace. Adjacent to that was an intimate bar area with an innovative cocktail list.

"Hey, it's great to see you both!" River greeted them. An easy energy radiated from him.

Liza leaned in with glee. "It's been a minute, Colton! We're so excited to catch up."

Maris and Colton slid into the booth, exchanging hugs with their friends. Contentment filled the air, palpable and friendly.

After ordering their meal and filling each other in on recent events, River turned to Colton with seriousness. "So, let's talk about the apartment. We're happy you're interested. It's a great place, and I think it would be perfect for you."

Colton nodded. "I'm definitely intrigued, River. It's a beautiful place, and it would mean a lot to me to have a home base here while I figure out movin' my workshop."

Liza smiled. "It'll be awesome having you out here. We're offering the place at a friend's price, and we can discuss any adjustments you might need."

River handed Colton a folder with all the details, including photos and a suggested cost. Colton took it, feeling a sense of possibility. "Thanks. I'll look over this and get back to you soon. I really appreciate the offer."

"Now, there is the matter of BioHaven, Colt. Are you still plannin' on movin' forward with that? I'm still interested in being a part of it. And with you comin' out here, it could be a real opportunity for us."

Colton nodded thoughtfully. "I've been thinkin' a lot about BioHaven lately, and I still want to continue with it. But I've come to the conclusion that it needs to be less about makin' money and more about educatin' people on sustainability. We need to focus on creating a lasting impact. With everything that's happened the last few months, I guess I just feel like the business part of it comes in second."

River's drummed his fingers lightly on the table. "I completely agree. Education and awareness are the priority. If we can inspire people to live more sustainably, that's worth more than any profit. But how exactly do we do that?"

Maris felt a sudden spark of inspiration, her eyes shining. "Would you guys consider adding another partner?" she asked.

"I would, but I don't know anyone else, off the top of my head, who wants to join in. Do you know someone?" Colton replied.

"Me, silly!" she responded, giggling. "What if BioHaven was a nonprofit? We could offer workshops on sustainable living, renewable energy, and conservation. Plus, we could integrate creative writing retreats I can oversee. It could be a space for people to learn and create."

Colton nodded eagerly. "That's an incredible idea, Mar! It would bring a whole new dimension to BioHaven."

River nodded in agreement. "I love it. It's the perfect way to combine our passions and make a meaningful difference. Maris, we'd be thrilled to partner with you."

"This is amazing!" she squealed, and planted a kiss on Colton's cheek. "What if we keep the name BioHaven and just add something to it that advertises exactly what it is? An environmental learning center."

Liza spoke up, echoing the mood of the others. "BioHaven Environmental Learning Center. It has a nice ring to it. You could even invite guest speakers and experts to share their knowledge."

River leaned back in his seat, his eyes gleaming with enthusiasm. "We could also partner with local schools and community organizations to reach a wider audience. Imagine kids learnin' about sustainability and then writin' stories inspired by what they've learned."

"You could even teach a sketching class, Colton! Your sketchbook is full of ideas to build on," Maris suggested enthusiastically.

Colton's mind was spinning. "And we can create hands-on experiences. People can take part in building eco-friendly structures, plantin' community gardens, and exploring renewable energy solutions."

As they continued to chat, their vision took shape. They discussed potential funding sources, outreach programs, and finding the perfect place to house their moving parts.

They felt a renewed sense of purpose by the time they left the café. Maris walked along the beach, hand in hand with Colton, feeling weightless. Though he seemed to have something on his mind, beyond elation about their new plan for BioHaven.

He knitted his brows together and squeezed her hand firmly, deep in thought. Maris worried about the growing silence. She attempted to chat about the sights on the beach and the and the beauty of the ocean, but Colton remained unusually broody.

Finally, she stopped walking and turned to face him, concern etched on her features. "Colton, what's on your mind? You've been awfully quiet."

He sighed, his gaze drifting to the horizon. "I'm just thinkin' about everything. The move, BioHaven, Axel… It's a lot to take in."

Maris nodded. She couldn't argue with his concerns. "I get it, Colton. It's a big transition, and there are a lot of unknowns. But we'll figure it out. We've got a great plan for BioHaven, and we'll find a way to balance what matters most."

She paused, studying his face. Even his own mention of Axel had seemed to cast a deeper shadow over him. Maris knew how much his brother meant to him—how things were just now improving after years of a rocky relationship. She wondered if Axel's influence could cause Colton to reconsider the move. The thought sent a flicker of fear through her. What if he decided to stay behind, to keep closer to Axel and the familiarity of the life he knew so well?

He wrapped his arms around Maris, and she settled into the safety of his embrace.

Colton's voice broke through her thoughts. "I've been the only one really there for Axel. He doesn't have a lot of friends. Leavin' him behind sort of feels like I'm deserting him."

Maris paused, choosing her words carefully. "I know how important supporting Axel is to you. Maybe we can have video calls or something. Anything to make sure you don't feel like you're slipping too far away."

Colton's hold on her tightened. "I'm just worried, you know? What if I'm not strong enough to handle all of this? What if I mess things up again?"

She pulled back to look up at him, her eyes filled with empathy. "The journey is just beginning. Of all people, I know about doubts and fears. But you helped me rise up and face mine. Now, look. I'm going to publish a novel!"

Colton looked down at her. His marked by emotion. "I just don't want to let anyone down, Mar. I want to be strong."

"You are strong, Colton. You've already shown that by everything you've done to get to this point. Doing your best is all anyone can ask for. I think I should've been more sensitive to that before. I'm sorry," she replied.

He gently cupped her face, his touch soft and reassuring. "You don't have to apologize. Your belief in me keeps me goin'. And we're learnin' together."

Maris smiled, feeling affection and reassurance. "And we'll keep learning together. We'll face the challenges, and we'll celebrate the victories, no matter how small."

Colton's eyes softened, and he leaned in to kiss her gently. "You're right, Mar. "We've got a lot of work ahead of us, but I think we can do it."

"I know we can," she said.

With the sun setting behind them, painting the ocean in shades of amber and gold, they continued their walk along the shore, arm in arm. By the time they reached the end of the beach, the sky was a canvas of deep blues and purples, dotted with the first stars of the evening.

Maris looked up at the sparkling constellations, a sense of wonder filling her heart. She remembered the nights she spent gazing at the night sky as a child, making wishes and dreaming of a bright future. Tonight, she felt that same wonder and promise.

"Look, Colton," she whispered, pointing to a falling star. "Do you see that one?"

He followed her line of sight and nodded, a smile playing on his lips. "Yeah, I see it. What are you thinking?"

Maris closed her eyes for a moment, making a silent wish. After a brief pause, she opened her eyes again and looked at him, deep fondness stirring within her. She nestled her head against his shoulder, and together they looked heavenward until the sky turned deep black and the breeze became too cool.

As the night air wrapped around them, they headed back towards the parking lot, their hearts full.

Beacons of Change

The next month was filled with things to do. Colton was busy! Attempting to juggle the logistics of a move, a new business, and maintaining support for Axel while he awaited sentencing. March had begun with a flourish of activity and there was no sign of it slowing.

Each day was a balancing act of coordinating with moving companies, securing the apartment, and laying the groundwork for BioHaven. Despite the chaos, Colton found comfort in the moments he spent planning collaborations, workshops, and envisioning the positive impact they could make.

Amidst the surge of demands, Axel's situation remained a constant concern for Colton. Axel's lawyer, Mickey, was working diligently to ensure that Axel received a fair deal. Mickey had gathered a few character references and presented evidence of Axel's commitment to turning his life around. He had also tried to show Axel's remorse for his actions. The rest would be in the hands of the powers that be.

"Mickey seems optimistic about the case," Colton said one evening as he updated Maris on the latest developments. "He's confident that the judge will take Axel's efforts into account."

She nodded thoughtfully. "That's good to hear. It's important that the judge sees his progress and the support he has."

Colton crossed his arms loosely. "I just hope it's enough. Axel deserves an opportunity to turn things around. He's been workin' so hard to make things right."

"Things have changed so quickly. Our lives are always in motion. I can't promise that Axel's situation is going to have the outcome you want. But I can guarantee that, even if it doesn't, the rough patch is temporary," Maris replied.

Colton looked into Maris's eyes, touched deeply by her support and care.

"You're right, Mar. No matter what happens, this rocky stretch won't last forever, but you are forever to me. You're my anchor. You keep me grounded. And you're the strength I didn't know I had. Just because I seem to carry burdens well doesn't mean I don't feel their weight. But you help me bear up underneath them."

Maris felt a surge of emotion at Colton's words. "You do the same for me. You make the sun shine brighter and my world more vibrant. And you gave me the courage to chase my dreams."

Colton smiled, pulling her closer. "Aw, shucks," he said, feigning embarrassment. Then, his expression straightened, and he spoke with seriousness. "Mar, I just want to take care of your heart and make you happy. And that's all I'm gonna want for the rest of my life."

At this, Maris hugged him tighter. "Colt, those are some serious commitments. Not that long ago we wanted to kill each other," she said, hoping he wouldn't regret his words.

"I know better now… that in the chaos of life, you're my happy place. Even when you sass mouthed me the night we met, it didn't drive me away. It only intrigued me more. And maybe you deserve somebody better than me, darlin'. But I'm just not okay with losing you."

Maris opened her mouth to respond, but the sound of her phone ringing interrupted the moment. "It's Whispering Pines Press," she told Colton as she answered.

Colton nodded, giving her an encouraging smile.

"Hi Maris, it's Cecily from Whispering Pines Press. I wanted to touch base on your novel. We've reviewed the latest draft, and we're really excited about it! However, we'll need to work fast to get the final draft polished and ready for publication. Can you partner with the editor to ensure we meet our deadline by the beginning of April?"

Maris felt a rush of adrenaline. "Of course, Cecily. I'll do everything I can to make sure it's perfect."

"Great! I'll have the editor reach out to you with the specifics. Thanks, Maris, and congratulations again. This is an exciting time."

"Thank you, Cecily. I appreciate it."

She hung up and her emotions were plainly visible as she turned to Colton, caught between joy and anxiety.

 "They love the latest draft! But I need to get the final version to them by the beginning of April."

"You should be jumpin' up and down, Mar! That's great news! Why do you look like you're goin' to puke?"

Maris took a deep breath, trying to steady herself. "I'm thrilled, really. But the timeline is so tight. There's so much to finalize, and I want everything to be perfect. What if I can't get it done in time?"

"You've got this. One step at a time. Just give it your all and it'll be amazing. I know it," Colton reassured her.

As Maris turned her attention to her manuscript, Colton couldn't help but feel a ripple of doubt. He had been reassuring Maris, but his own worries were simmering just beneath the surface. Eve had been pressuring him to have sketches ready for the tech startup's new product line, and the deadlines were looming.

Colton sighed and put his hands behind his head. "Speakin' of pressure. Eve's been on my case about those sketches for the tech startup. She needs them done soon, but with everything goin' on, I don't know how to get it all accomplished."

"I know you feel like you're being pulled in a million different directions," Maris began. "But try to carve out some time. Especially since this is a huge client for you."

Colton felt the oppressiveness of the responsibility. He let his arms drop and his shoulders slumped forward. "You're right. This job is a big opportunity, and I need to give it my best shot. But findin' the time feels impossible."

"Oh, c'mon. With everything you've already gone through in the last six months, you can do this. We'll tackle it together," she pledged.

The rest of the month flew by while Colton and Maris were consumed in the bustle of completing their tasks. Late at night, after the day's chaos had settled, they would sit together at the dining table, surrounded by papers and sketches, cups of coffee in hand.

Maris would pore over her manuscript, making edits and adjustments. Colton, ever uplifting, offered fresh perspectives and ideas. And Maris would jot down notes, grateful for his input.

On other nights, Colton focused on his sketches for the tech startup. Maris, always organized and prepared, helped him plan out his project. Colton would nod, smiling at her, appreciating her encouragement.

Together, they worked through their individual challenges. Their late-night sessions were filled with creativity, inspiration, and shared determination. The dining table became their collaborative workspace, a place where ideas flowed freely, and reassurance was always on hand. And, at the end of the evening, when Colton would say goodnight, he left lighter than when he came. More determined than ever to bring his visions to life.

By the end of March, they had made significant progress. Maris submitted her final draft, and Colton's sketches were ready for review. They reveled in their achievements with a quiet dinner, a tangible pride lingering in the air..

"We did it," Maris said, her eyes reflecting relief. "All the hard work, late nights... it was worth it."

Colton nodded, his grin matching hers. "Absolutely. This is just the beginning," he remarked, pouring them each a glass of special reserve bourbon to celebrate.

But the next morning his heart sank. That day, among his usual email messages, was one from the grant committee regarding the application he had submitted for BioHaven. Upon opening it, he read:

Dear Mr. Vance,

Thank you for your interest in the California Community Schools Partnership Program: Implementation Grant and for submitting your application on behalf of BioHaven Sustainable Education Center. We appreciate the time and effort you have invested in this project.

After careful consideration, we regret to inform you that we are unable to provide funding for your project at this time. We received an overwhelming number of applications, and, while your proposal was strong, we had to make difficult decisions based on our current funding priorities.

We encourage you to continue your important work and consider applying again in the future.

Regards,

Lewis Greene

California Department of Education

"Who needs you anyway?" Colton mumbled to himself. The rejection felt like a blow, especially after all the effort and hope they had put into the application. He jammed his phone into his pocket and stomped over to the coffee maker.

He and Maris were supposed to spend the day together since they both had a small amount of free time in between commitments. But now he didn't feel like doing anything. The grant was going to make an enormous difference in how much they could offer the community. Without it, he would have to scale back his ideas and try to think of all new ways to operate.

Maris noticed his change in demeanor and looked up from her laptop. "What's wrong, Colt?"

"We didn't get the grant for BioHaven. I really thought we had a chance," he said, as he punched the buttons on the machine.

"I'm sorry," Maris replied. Her tone was empathetic. "I know that you really wanted it, but we'll find another way. BioHaven will happen. We just need to be resourceful."

Colton dropped into a chair, an unruly curl falling onto his forehead. "But how? Without the grant, we won't be able to offer near as much."

Maris pondered for a moment. "What about crowdfunding? We could set up a campaign to raise the funds we need. There are so many platforms out there where people can contribute to causes they believe in. Why not ours?"

"Okay, let's do it. We'll share our story, our goals, and the impact we want to make. Somethin' that really resonates with folks. Maybe even offer some incentives for backers."

Maris smiled, her excitement contagious. "We should let River know. Between the three of us we can definitely create something worthy of people's support."

With a new plan in place, they spent the rest of the morning coming up with ideas for their crowdfunding campaign. They looped in River with a video call, outlined their story, planned out the content they would need, and set a timeline for launching the initiative.

By the end of the day, Colton had forgotten all about the rejection email and was focused on where he could channel his energy. Perhaps they were taking a detour to get there, but he knew they would reach their destination.

Physically preparing to raise money, though, proved to be more work than any of them had anticipated.

Colton, Maris, and River worked tirelessly to create compelling content that would resonate with potential backers. They filmed heartfelt videos explaining the mission of BioHaven, showcasing their passion for sustainability and education.

Maris wrote captivating descriptions and updates for the campaign page, drawing on her skills as a writer to tell their story in a way that would inspire others.

"We need to show why BioHaven matters and how their support can impact everyone in the area," she said, typing furiously on her laptop.

Colton sketched out designs for the rewards they would offer to backers, from eco-friendly merchandise to exclusive workshops and tours of BioHaven.

"Everyone loves tangible rewards," he explained. "It gives them somethin' to look forward to and feel connected to."

River handled the technical side of things, setting up the crowdfunding page and making sure everything ran smoothly.

"We need to make it as easy as possible for people to contribute," he said, checking the site for any potential issues.

As they worked, they grew more energized and optimistic, believing they could make BioHaven a reality. Their joint determination was lighting the way to a brighter future.

Finally, launch day arrived. With nervous hearts, they hit the "publish" button and watched as their campaign went live. They shared it across social media, reached out to friends and family, and did everything they could to spread the word.

In the days that followed, the support poured in. Donations came from all corners, from people who believed in their vision and wanted to be a part of it. The trio watched the numbers climb beyond expectations. Each contribution, no matter how small, felt like a vote of confidence in their project. The messages and encouragement from those who donated fueled their determination. Before long, they reached their first milestone.

As the days turned into weeks, the campaign continued to thrive. They held virtual Q&A sessions, hosted live updates, and shared behind-the-scenes glimpses of their progress. The momentum built steadily, and their vision for BioHaven became clearer with each passing day.

Colton knew, though, that they would need to do something big, something memorable when it came time to launch their project. He wanted to capture the imagination of everyone involved. A myriad of ideas swirled in his mind.

That's when he got the call…

Guiding Lights

Colton's mind was a whirlwind of thoughts and ideas as he mulled over the possibilities for BioHaven's grand launch. He was determined to make it unforgettable. But before he could settle on a plan, the sharp trill of his phone broke his train of thought.

"Hey, Axel. How's it goin'?" he said anxiously.

"Colton," Axel's voice was steady, but Colton could sense the underlying disappointment. "I wanted to let you know the judge's decision came in. I got a $250,000 fine, but no jail time."

His body relaxed. "That's... that's great news, Axel. No jail time means you can just focus on rebuildin' your life."

"Yeah, but $250,000 is a huge amount. It's goin' to take me a long time to pay off," Axel said, his voice tinged with worry.

Colton's mind raced. He was relieved that Axel wouldn't be going to jail, but he couldn't ignore the daunting fine. "Don't worry, Axel. For now, you should celebrate!"

Axel let out a small laugh, yet it was clear he still felt the weight of the fine.

"I suppose you're right," he said. Though Colton was unconvinced, he meant it.

He leaned against the door frame and gazed outside. "One step at a time. We'll come up with somethin'," he replied, trying to project confidence.

"Thanks, Colton. Hey, listen, there are some things I've got to go over with Mickey. But I'll call you later, okay?"

"Yeah, man. And thanks for lettin' me know."

After hanging up, he lingered in silence, lost in thought. The reality of the fine quickly overshadowed the relief of Axel avoiding jail time. He knew Axel needed a support system, but he also couldn't afford to lose momentum on BioHaven.

There were beads of sweat on his forehead, and a small stream trickling down his back. The onset of a panic attack gripped him, tightening his chest and clouding his thoughts. It wouldn't take long before he felt helpless to make it all work. Could he leave BioHaven to Maris and River while he flew off to save the day? Would Axel be able to fight his own battles and leave Colton to his plans? Axel was in so much debt already. Surely this fine would bury him.

Colton knew he needed to share this information with River and Maris. Maybe they would have some idea of what he should do. They were supposed to meet for dinner to discuss finding a venue to function as their office and workshop facility, while River was in town. Perhaps then would be a good time to bring it up.

As the hour of the meeting drew nearer, Colton felt an overwhelming urge to retreat and escape the compounding stress of the moment. Obligation was pressing down on him, and the fear of making the wrong decision gnawed at his mind. But he knew running away wasn't an option.

He was an honest man and had never made it a habit of deceiving people, especially those closest to him. His resolve to open up to Maris and River remained steadfast. They weren't only the woman he'd envisioned for himself and his best friend. They were his business partners, and they deserved to know when his head wasn't in the game.

Walking into the restaurant, Colton was woozy. And, as the hostess led him to the table where River was already waiting, he felt a wave of nausea. If he backed out of the learning center now, he would be disappointing two people who meant the world to him and look like a hypocrite to River.

He had once told Maris that it was easy to run away from problems, harder to face them head-on. But that didn't mean it wasn't worth trying.

Silently, he sat down and glanced at the menu before him, refusing to make eye contact with his friend. River's expression was serious as he waited for Colton to speak, but there was nothing except the sound of piano music coming from the lounge area.

After a few minutes, Colton collected himself, ready to announce his dilemma. But before he could say anything, Maris appeared, leaning against the table and out of breath.

"Woah! What's goin' on with you?" Colton asked.

"Jemma… Hendrix…engaged," she replied, gasping for air.

"What?! Hendrix and Jemma are engaged?" Colton inquired, unsure how he should react to the news.

Jemma and Maris had rekindled their connection and sisterly affection for each other. They talked and texted regularly again, and Hendrix had landed a lucrative job. But his proposing was a big deal. Almost too much to fathom. Colton considered how long it had been since he witnessed Maris and Jemma facing off at Driftwood Shelves. Nine months had already gone by and now he wondered if he and Maris should be moving more quickly to secure their future.

"Yes!" Maris cried. She pulled her cellphone from her purse and thrust a photo of Jemma with a modest sparkly diamond ring on her left hand and Hendrix kissing her temple.

Colton blinked in surprise, staring at the picture Maris showed him. "Wow, that's... amazing. I didn't see that comin'."

Maris beamed. "Ya know, I'm so glad I didn't let that stuff about Hendrix come between me and Jemma. I would've hated to lose my little sister just because of some old grudge," she said, plopping down next to Colton. "And now there's going to be a wedding! My mom and Alex are over the moon. The group chat has been going off nonstop."

Colton forced a smile, trying to share in the joy, but he was still preoccupied with Axel and the impact his situation could have on BioHaven's future. He knew he couldn't keep this to himself any longer.

"Y'all, there's somethin' I need to tell you," Colton said, gathering his resolve. "Axel called earlier. He got a $250,000 fine, but no jail time."

River's smile faded, replaced with concern. "That's a lot. How are you feelin' about it?"

Colton took a deep breath. "Relieved that he won't be goin' to jail, but the fine is overwhelming. I'm worried I might need to put BioHaven on hold to help him. I don't want to let you both down."

"Do you think that delaying BioHaven and all your hard work is what Axel would want you to do?" Maris asked.

He thought about this carefully. Axel had said he didn't want to drag Colton into any more of his messes and had apologized profusely for putting him in the position of having to be a savior figure in their family. Plus, their parents were willing to at least be there for moral support.

"He probably wouldn't," Colton admitted. "It just eats at me that he's up to his eyeballs in a situation I can't fix. I'm the fixer. It's always been my job. It irked me for the longest time, but now I'm so used to it that I feel helpless when I stand by and watch things happen. The thing is, Axel did commit a crime and there is only so much energy I can throw at it before I realize it's not goin' away."

"Colt, I get that you're used to finding the solutions, but sometimes, being supportive means recognizin' that you can't solve it all on your own. Axel knows that, and he doesn't expect you to sacrifice everything for him," River expressed.

Maris nodded in agreement; her eyes filled with empathy.

"Thanks, guys. I really appreciate your understandin'. Maybe you're right," he shrugged.

"We're a team, Colt," Maris added. And that was that.

Throughout dinner, they discussed ways they could all pitch in to help Axel, where they might be able to incorporate rehabilitating those that could use a fresh start with BioHaven, and if there was a suitable building space to house their operation. Starting the organization from Maris's dining room, especially when River came down from Morro Bay, was increasingly difficult.

Just as dessert was being served, River cleared his throat and tapped a knife against the edge of his glass.

"Well, Liza wanted to be here and tell you both in person, but she's not well and didn't feel up to the trip. But you two, besides our parents, will be the first to know that Liza is pregnant," River announced.

Colton looked at Maris, who seemed like she might faint. Her face was pale and her mouth hung open as if she had forgotten how to breathe. Though she quickly gathered herself, smiling as she found her voice.

"That's incredible news, River! Congratulations to you and Liza," Maris said, her tone filled with genuine happiness. Colton squeezed her thigh under the table.

"Congrats!" he echoed.

River beamed and his eyes sparkled. "Thanks. We're thrilled, but also a bit nervous. It's a big change."

Maris nodded in agreement. "Absolutely. But if you need anything, we're only a couple hours down the road. I can't wait to give Liza a good lashing for not telling me last time I called!" she giggled.

As they finished their meal, the conversation took on a lighter tone. River's news had brought a fresh energy to their discussion. And, on the heels of Jemma's engagement announcement, it seemed like everyone was embarking on exciting new chapters in their story and the future held endless possibilities for each of them.

As they wrapped up the evening, Maris and Colton exchanged a knowing glance, silently acknowledging that their journey together, both in their personal and professional lives, was just beginning.

Stepping into the night air, Colton noticed a fleeting shadow of unease on Maris's face.

"Hey, are you okay?" he asked, brushing a stray lock of hair from her face.

Maris forced a smile, but Colton could see the turmoil in her eyes.

"Yeah, I'm fine. It's just... I guess I'm feeling a bit overwhelmed with everything going on."

"Everything that's goin' on?" Colton raised an eyebrow. "What's really botherin' you? Because sayin' 'everything' is takin' the easy way out."

She leaned into his arm. "I guess I'm a little jealous," she admitted, her voice low. "All the big announcements tonight. Jemma's engaged, Liza's having a baby... It feels like everyone around us is moving forward with their lives, and here we are, still figuring things out."

Colton frowned, realizing the depth of her discontent.

"I mean, I'm happy for them. But sometimes I wonder if we're moving too slowly. If I'm missing out on something. Or if I'm supposed to be at this point in my life," she confessed.

Colton's heart ached seeing her so envious and doubtful.

"You're not missin' out on anything, Mar. Our journey is our own. Comparing yourself, or our relationship, to everybody else is only going to make you unhappy with what you have," he stated. "I wouldn't trade what we've got for the world. And, if you want somethin' different or there are things we need to work out, then let's talk about them. Because you're stuck with me."

Maris chuckled softly, a small smile breaking through her worry.

"You're right. It's just hard sometimes, especially when it feels like everyone else is moving forward so quickly."

"Look, Mar. I might not be down on one knee, but I am goin' to try my darndest to make everyday life into somethin' extraordinary for ya." Colton kissed her forehead. "I love you," he said. "And I love what we've got goin'."

It was the first time he'd ever said those words to her, and they seemed to change everything between them.

Maris's breath caught in her throat, and she gazed up at Colton. His declaration steadied her and stirred her all at once. "I love you too," she purred.

"Love looks pretty great on you," he mused. A smile ghosted across his lips.

He rested his forehead against hers and for a few minutes they stood embracing the familiarity of each other and the promise

that lay in their confession. Then, with their hearts laid bare,
they walked to the car hand in hand. They had each other, and
that was more than enough.

Full Circle

"A hundred and fifty thousand dollars?!" Maris was beside herself.

River, punching numbers into his calculator, was tied in on a video call with her as they began the initial planning of their BioHaven launch party. The only issue was they still didn't have a venue. After months of rejections and roadblocks, finding out they had raised more than enough money to get their mission off the ground was the best news. But making crucial decisions about location and logistics in a short time was going to prove difficult.

"Colton's gonna freak! This is amazing!" Maris added.

River grinned, his excitement palpable even through the screen.

"I know! This gives us so much more flexibility. We can finally get things moving and give BioHaven the launch it deserves."

Maris nodded, her mind already racing with possibilities.

"I'll start making calls about event spaces right away. There has to be a place that can accommodate us on short notice. We just need to be creative. I'll add outdoor spaces to my list of options, too. Just in case."

As they wrapped up their call, Maris felt empowered. They had come so far, and with this new influx of funds, their opportunities had widely expanded.

The warm wet days of July had slipped in amongst the pursuit of their goals. Maris, Colton, and River were deeply involved in planning, driven by their excitement and tireless work. Every spare moment was spent refining the details to ensure BioHaven's launch would be nothing short of spectacular.

Maris sat at her desk, her phone glued to her ear as she made call after call, inquiring about event spaces. She scribbled notes in her planner, listing potential venues and their availability. Glad to have something to preoccupy her time aside from her freelance work. Waiting on her book to go through editorial review and further revision seemed to take forever, and she was worried she would go stir crazy without another activity to spend time on.

Colton had been obsessed with finding vendors and the best deals on decorations and entertainment. He was determined to ensure every detail was impeccable, reflecting the essence of BioHaven's mission.

River, always the tech-savvy one, worked on creating promotional materials and updating their website with the latest news. He also planned to reach out to local media, eager to spread the word and generate buzz. This launch was more than just an event; it was the culmination of their hard work, dedication, and shared vision for a better future.

Unfortunately, no matter how many calls she made, Maris couldn't find an available place for them to hold a large grand opening on the date they needed. They planned on having a ribbon cutting in three weeks. But, without a home for their project, how could they advertise?

She rubbed her temples, her lips pressed into a line as she glanced at the long list of potential venues. Each one crossed out.

"We're running out of options," she muttered to herself. "We need a miracle."

She wracked her brain to shake loose any ideas she hadn't already taken advantage of. But nothing came to her. Just as she was about to give up for the day, her phone chimed with a new message notification. Grateful for the distraction, she opened her inbox and saw a message from Cecily Harper.

This was it. The email she had been waiting for since spring. She trembled with delight.

Realizing she hadn't heard anything from Colton for most of the day, Maris decided to call him and share this amazing news.

They would usually check in with each other regularly but, even if he was busy, this was worth interrupting for.

Picking up her phone, she dialed his number.

"Hey, Maris! What's up?" Colton's voice sounded cheerful, which put her at ease.

"Colton! I just got an email from Cecily," she said, her excitement bubbling over. "They're sending an extended contract tomorrow! They want the first right of refusal for my future work!"

"That is huge! Congrats!"

"Thanks! I can't wait to see where this goes. I have a thousand more ideas for novels in my head and now that I have the possibility of someone being interested in publishing them… I'm just in shock," she replied.

"Speaking of shock… I need you to meet me somewhere. It'll knock your socks off."

"Okay… Where is it? Does it have anything to do with why I haven't heard from you much today?" she asked.

"Guess you'll have to wait and see. I'm textin' you the address," Colton said. "Just head there and I'll be waitin' for ya."

"Okay, I'll see you soon," Maris said.

Shortly after, a message with the address popped up on her phone.

6572 Innovation Drive

Irvine, California

With butterflies in her stomach, she grabbed her things and headed out, eager to see what Colton had planned.

When she arrived at the location, she saw him standing outside of a large, low office building with a mysterious smile on his face.

"What's this all about?" Maris asked, her curiosity getting the best of her.

"You'll see," Colton said, leading her inside. "I think you're goin' to love it."

Curious, Maris allowed him to lead her around the corner and into a business suite labeled '500'. The sight that greeted her as they crossed the threshold stole her breath away.

There was no furniture or décor, but the empty rooms before her were stunning. The floor was made up of dark porcelain tiles, adorned with a retro starburst pattern. The glassed in conference space had one wall completely paneled with cork. A small kitchen area with a bar top island had beautiful travertine countertops and a frosted glass backsplash. At the far end of the suite was a large section with rich mahogany floors and it was flooded with light.

"Are you thinking what I'm thinking?" Maris whispered, her eyes wide with awe.

Colton nodded enthusiastically. "This could be the new home for BioHaven," he said, his voice filled with expectation. "It's perfect, isn't it?"

Maris took another look around. She could see the possibilities unfolding before her eyes. "It's more than perfect," she replied, her voice quivering. "It's everything we've been looking for."

"I knew you'd see it too. I've been in talks with the property manager, and they're willin' to work with us. With the funds we've raised, we are in good shape to lease the place. And it's only twenty minutes from Laguna."

Maris felt a rush of adrenaline as the reality sank in. As they walked through the rooms, discussing their vision for each area, she marveled at Colton's passion. Agreeing to send the listing details to River, she sensed that the potential of the space mirrored the possibility she saw in her growing partnership with Colton, more than just professionally.

"This is going to be amazing," Maris said, her voice brimming with hopeful energy. "I can already picture the classrooms, the workshops, and the community events we'll host here. It's the perfect environment."

They spent the next hour exploring the suite, making notes and brainstorming ideas for the layout and design. She could feel the energy and potential in the air. Maris only hoped River could take a virtual tour of the property and that they would be able to work out the leasing contract in time for BioHaven's opening.

In the following days, with River's approval, they worked to finalize the agreement and prepare for the big day. They set up displays, organized the schedule, and brought in furnishings. Colorful couches covered in organic cotton and mango wood tables were strewn throughout the space. Every detail was meticulously planned, from the layout to the sustainable design elements that reflected BioHaven's mission.

July twenty-fifth snuck up and tapped them on the shoulder. The day had arrived to show Southern California what they had in store. And the community came out in spades to support the environmental learning center. They could hardly believe the turnout.

The morning light danced across the venue, brightening every corner as Maris, Colton, and River made final preparations. Liza, with her growing baby bump, stationed herself by the door with welcome favors. Guests arrived, their faces filled with curiosity and awe.

Maris was overcome with emotion as she saw families, students, and local news crews arriving. She guided them through the beautifully decorated space, explaining their vision and mission for BioHaven. It was a cozy, inviting atmosphere, while the sustainable design elements underscored their commitment to environmental responsibility.

Colton mingled with the guests, recounting the milestones and challenges they had faced to bring BioHaven to life. He could see the spark of interest in their eyes as they learned about the various programs and initiatives that were planned. While River was busy capturing moments on camera and live streaming the event on social media, Liza greeted each guest with a smile and a small token of appreciation.

As the day progressed, the energy in the air was obvious. People gathered to take part in mock workshops and discussions about sustainability and protecting natural resources.

The ribbon-cutting ceremony was a resounding success, with local media capturing the moment and spreading the word about BioHaven's grand opening. Colton stepped up to the microphone, addressing the crowd with heartfelt gratitude.

Maris beamed as she got out her phone to record the occasion.

"Thank you all for being here today and supportin' our vision. BioHaven is more than just a learning center. It's a community effort to create a sustainable future for all of us. We couldn't have done it without each one of you," Colton began, his voice sincere.

He paused, letting his words sink in. The crowd watched him intently, captivated by the resonance of his words.

"Today marks the beginning of a journey we've all been dreaming of. BioHaven is a place where ideas flourish, where learnin' and sustainability go hand in hand, and where our community can come together to make a real difference," he continued. "None of this would have been possible without the unwaverin' support of you who believed in our vision."

She glanced around at the sea of faces, seeing the smiles and nods of agreement. This was the moment they had all been working towards.

As Colton wrapped up his speech and invited River and Maris onto the stage with him, the crowd erupted in applause. His eyes shone with appreciation and joy.

After some time, the cheering subsided and the three of them stepped away. Colton noticed a quiet corner away from the commotion and gently guided Maris toward it. They found themselves in a small alcove, bathed in soft sunlight streaming through a nearby window. The noise of the crowd faded into the background, leaving them in a bubble of calm.

Maris wrapped her arms around his neck and leaned into him, feeling intoxicated with happiness and the earthy scent of him. Colton held her close, the intimacy of their embrace making the world outside seem distant. He gently ran his fingers through her hair, savoring the quiet moment amidst the whirlwind of activity.

"This is surreal," she said softly.

Colton smiled and dug into his pocket. "There's something I wanted to show you," he said, pulling out the small, yellow pearl she had given him back in the winter. He held it gently in his hand, the light catching its soft sheen. "Remember this? It's been with me every step of the way, just like you."

She reached out to touch it. "I remember. The day I found that was the day we called our truce, ya know? Who knew a promise like that would lead to all this?" she said, smiling.

"All I know is, together, we're stronger," Colton replied. He kissed the top of her head. "It's only going to get better from here."

As the event wound down, Maris felt her phone buzz in her pocket. She glanced at the screen and saw an email from Cecily. Her heart skipped a beat as she opened it.

Subject: About Your Manuscript

Hi Maris,

I wanted to share some fantastic news. Whispering Pines Press believes your manuscript has the potential to reach a wide audience and make a significant impact. Let's discuss the next steps regarding how we can maximize promoting this opportunity.

Looking forward to chatting soon!

Best, Cecily

She looked up at Colton, who was deep in conversation with a guest. She knew she needed to share this news with him, but the timing would have to be just right. A subtle smile lingered as she pocketed her phone. The air was thick with unimaginable prospects.

Epilogue

Maris stood in the welcoming atmosphere of Driftwood Shelves, waiting to begin. Twelve months had passed since the grand opening of BioHaven. Yet today, she experienced the same excitement she'd felt then. Her heart pounded as she looked around the quaint store, thoughtfully decorated in the theme of her novel. The book launch party of her dreams. Chrissy had done everything she could. "Uncharted" was on track to be a best-seller and all of her family, friends, and even those who supported BioHaven were gathering to celebrate this milestone.

Colton stood beside her, his hand resting on the small of her back, a proud smile on his face.

"Darlin', it's gonna be great," he whispered in her ear.

She drew in a steady breath. "I know, it's just... I can't believe this is really happening," she replied, looking into Colton's reassuring eyes.

Colton gave her a gentle squeeze. "You deserve every bit of it, Mar. You've worked so hard for this moment."

As she looked around, she spotted familiar faces. Liza and River holding their baby girl, Poppy. Alex and Cillian with their growing girls and Otto, almost two years old. Jemma and Hendrix, the picture-perfect newlyweds, basking in happiness. Her parents, beaming with pride, gave a small wave from the nook where they sat. Even Colton's mom and dad had flown out for the occasion. There were also BioHaven members who had become like family, and some new acquaintances who had been drawn to her work. The turnout was overwhelming, and she felt a flood of gratitude rush over her.

Then she looked down at her left hand. Her engagement ring glinting in the fluorescent lights. The simple yet elegantly cut diamond was a constant reminder of Colton's love and the life they were building together. It was a promise of the adventures to come, the challenges they would face side by side, and the dreams they would continue to chase.

Chrissy came around with a handheld microphone.

"Ready to do this?" she asked, catching Maris's eye with a reassuring look.

Maris nodded and took the mic from her. Colton gave her an encouraging wink and planted a kiss on her cheek, leaving her in the middle of the room. All eyes were on her.

"Thank you all for being here tonight," she began, her voice steady but filled with emotion. "This has been an incredible journey, and it means so much to me that you care enough about me and the words I penned to show up for me in this way. I never thought my little manuscript would turn into an actual book, though it was always my dream."

She paused, glancing at Colton, River, and Liza, her soul filled with love.

"This novel is a piece of my heart," Maris continued, her voice growing more confident. "It's a story of hope, resilience, and the beauty of human connection. I trust it will resonate with you as much as it did with me while writing it."

The crowd clapped and her dad stood up, whistling loudly. She took a moment to let their appreciation sink in, a grin spread across her face.

"But tonight is not just a celebration of what has been achieved," Maris hurriedly added, her voice steadying further. "It's also a look towards the future. This is just the beginning. I have more stories to tell, more characters to breathe life into, and more hearts to touch. I am incredibly excited about what lies ahead and to continue sharing this journey with all of you."

Stepping aside, Colton folded her into his warm embrace.

"I'm so proud of you," he said.

"Thank you," she replied, her voice choked with emotion. "And thank you for showing me that the challenges of the past can show us the road to our future."

They rejoined their family and friends. Maris signed copies of her book, each signature a testament to her hard work and dedication. The room hummed with lively chatter and bursts of laughter, the store alive with the spirit of celebration. Suddenly, the sound of the door opening drew everyone's attention.

"Sorry I'm late!" Axel called out, a wide smile on his face as he came in.

"Axel!" Maris exclaimed, her eyes alight with happiness. She quickly put down the book she was signing and rushed over to hug him.

"You didn't think I'd miss this, did you?" Axel said, laughing as he embraced her.

Colton strode over and exchanged a hug and greeting with Axel. His arrival making the event even more special.

As the celebration continued, Maris felt a profound sense of fulfillment. Surrounded by the people she loved, she knew she was exactly where she was meant to be. She stood close to Colton, letting their shoulders touch, feeling utterly whole

Peering beyond the party, she could see the moonlit ocean and thought of the path ahead, filled with endless potential for great things. Her future promised new adventures and challenges, but, as she felt Colton put his arm around her, she knew that together, they could face anything.

Later, as they cleaned up, Colton noticed a copy of Maris's book on a nearby table and picked it up. He gently opened the cover, and his eyes fell on the dedication page. Reading the words to himself, his eyes fill with tears.

To Colton, my rock and my inspiration. Thank you for believing in me, for standing by my side through each challenge, and for helping me turn my dreams into reality. This book is for you. I fall in love with you again, every single day.

Acknowledgements

Dear Readers,

Writing a book is really hard. Like, really hard. Like, harder than I ever imagined. And I loved every second of it! How long until we do this all again?

First and foremost, I have to thank my husband, Jon, who cheered me on the entire time and constantly told me how proud he was of me. He still doesn't understand what a trope is, but I forgive him. Almost 14 years into doing life together, and I wouldn't trade it.

And I can't move on without mentioning my kids here. They've tried to be so understanding of "mom's writing time". I love each of you endlessly.

To my best friend, Kate. You're the real MVP. Always on standby for my late night texts; to celebrate the wins and empathize with the losses. I don't know what I'd do without you.

To my betas, especially Madelaine, who gave me so much constructive feedback that really helped mold the clay of this story into something recognizable. Thank you for falling in love with Colton from the get-go & for knowing this debut was special.

To my mama, for always commenting on my posts and hyping me to strangers even though you don't like reading. The ultimate champion.

Mrs. McKitrick, you might never read this but, our 7th grade English class was what started this whole journey. Endlessly grateful for the Power of the Pen & the effort you put forth to help me cultivate my passion.

To author Sharon Creech, your book *Bloomability* was my preteen favorite and made me feel seen. Helped me become empowered. You aided me in believing I could do hard things.

Kate Love Simpson Library, in McConnelsville, Ohio—you literally helped raise me. And, my favorite librarian, Miss Laura—thank you for letting me spend my time volunteering to organize books and VHS tapes. You rock!

A big thanks to Corrine Dalton, for letting me bounce ideas off of you and for trusting me with your own. I hope we can always support each other. I love you!

Annie Winston, you indie author QUEEN! Your sweet messages along the way, especially when I was dealing with

doubt or uncertainty, were a lifeline. You have no idea! Thank
you x a million.

And, finally, thank you to the shadows of my younger years,
and the obstacles I've had to overcome. Experience is a
teacher—whether good or bad may lie in hindsight.

This one is from one small-town girl to all the rest. Spoiler alert:
the tides always turn.

MARIS & COLTON'S
TAGLIATELLE FOR TWO

4 oz tagliatelle

1/2 tbsp olive oil

3-4 fresh basil leaves

1 clove minced garlic

1/8 tbsp red chili flakes

1 cup canned crushed tomatoes

2 oz fresh mozzarella

Parmesan cheese for serving

Heat olive oil in a large pan over medium heat add garlic and a pinch of chilli flakes if using and cook for 1 minute, then add half of your basil and tomatoes, bring to a boil, then turn the heat down and let it simmer for 10 minutes.

Toss with al dente tagliatelle pasta, stir in large torn pieces of mozzarella and basil leaves. Take off the heat as soon as mozzarella melts and turns stringy. Serve immediately topped with a bit of freshly grated Parmesan.

Quintana McConnell is an author dedicated to crafting wholesome, slow-burn romances that resonate deeply with readers, delivered with emotional authenticity and devoid of explicit material.

A self-proclaimed mood reader and avid traveler, she draws inspiration from life's journeys—whether on a scenic hiking trail or enjoying new foods. Quintana values building genuine connections with her readers, often sharing her personal insights and inspirations along her writing journey via social media.

Her passion for storytelling lies in creating a space where readers can find solace, inspiration, and love.